THE DIVINE KEY AWAKENS

JAMES E WISHER

SAND HILL PUBLISHING

Edited by: Janie Linn Dullard
Cover art by: B-Ro
ISBN: 978-1-68520-007-7
092520211.0

CHAPTER 1

Shara's forehead wrinkled as she tried to force the ether to appear before her. Her teacher, the shadow sorcerer Daktari, had explained the process several times each day for the last week. He'd showed markable patience with her.

At least she thought so. Every day they met in the small, out-of-the-way room that had been converted to serve as a classroom for the two of them. Not that much conversion had been needed. The empty room used to serve as extra storage, so after a good cleaning, the servants brought a table, two chairs, and a slate board. She felt like a little girl going to meet her tutor. Not that her old teacher had been anywhere near as intimidating as her current one.

She smiled when she remembered the glances the servants darted at the sorcerer. They looked like they feared being turned into a frog or blasted to ash any second. It wasn't really funny. Not long ago, she might have looked at him the same way. Since they started working together, she'd had a chance to get to know the man and found him calm, even-tempered, and generous with his explanations. Amazing the difference losing a demon in the back of your mind could make.

"You're not focusing." Daktari's voice still held the same chill it always did. Maybe that was just the way he naturally spoke. Still, it would be nice if he managed something a little friendlier.

She looked up at her mentor. He wore his usual dark-purple robe trimmed in black. His dark eyes met hers and she shivered. Despite knowing he'd changed his ways, Shara still felt the darkness in him whenever she met that gaze. She would have sworn that they flashed with an internal light once in a while. She debated asking him about it, but in the end chose discretion.

"I'm sorry, but it's hard to concentrate for long periods when nothing's happening."

"It's been ten minutes."

She winced. "It felt like longer. What am I doing wrong?"

"Aside from not concentrating for more than five minutes at a time, I'm not certain. Some apprentices connect with the ether more quickly than others."

"I suppose you mastered this basic stuff just like that." She snapped her fingers.

"On the contrary, I needed nearly a month and even then, it was only during a sensory deprivation exercise that I finally connected." He stroked his chin. "Hmmm. Maybe that's what we need, some way to cut you off from all the distractions. Though the biggest one seems to be your own wandering mind."

"Hey! It's been a rough few months, no thanks to you. I've got a lot on my mind."

"Such as?"

"I…Well, mostly I was thinking it was kind of funny how all the servants shy away from you like you were a demon yourself even though you seem okay." Heaven's mercy that sounded pitiful.

"I see. As long as it's only the truly important thoughts intruding on your study time. Perhaps I should bring you to my home. It's not as comfortable as the palace, but there are fewer distractions."

"No! No, I'll do better."

Her heart raced at the prospect of returning to that cold, dark cavern. Thoughts of the horrible slimy presence infiltrating her body filled her until she feared the panic would drive her mad. A few deep breaths calmed both her mind and her heart. No matter what, she wouldn't go back there.

"No offense, but I have a lot of lousy memories of your cave. I'm sure I'd be more upset there than here. Maybe if you walked me through the process again?"

He took a long, deep breath and let it hiss out. "Very well. The ether is a chaotic energy field visible only to those with the ability to use it. Wizards, sorcerers, call them what you like. Others can wield its power in other ways, but only these special individuals can control it directly."

"Is it possible I don't have the gift?" Shara asked, interrupting his speech. She'd heard it enough times that she could have given it herself.

"Perhaps, but we would be foolish to assume so based on a single week of practice. While we lack the time a more traditional apprenticeship would have, I think we can safely give it another week. After that, we will explore other options."

"Let's explore them now. I'm sick of trying to see something that I know is there only because you tell me."

He ran a hand over his bald head. "As you wish. Given your unique circumstances, perhaps an alternate approach will yield better results. I can always conjure a sensory deprivation field later."

She shivered at the way he said it. Like it would be a punishment should she fail at this new method. That was probably all in her head of course.

Daktari walked over to the door and pointed at the handle. "I've locked the door. There are no magical protections, just the physical lock. Come here and open it. Pay special attention to anything you feel as you do so."

Shara stood and crossed the room. She reached for the handle and stopped halfway to it. "What should I expect?"

"I have no idea. The Divine Key is a rare, nearly unique phenomenon. I couldn't find a thing about it in my library and the information hidden in the Temple of Soom, while useful, focused more on how you use it to open and close portals. We're just groping along in the dark trying to figure it out."

That wasn't terribly helpful. She grasped the handle and turned. It opened easily and she felt nothing.

"Did you need something, Princess?" asked the servant stationed outside to attend her and spy for her father.

"No, thank you. We're just experimenting." She closed the door again and turned to Daktari. "It opened easily and I felt nothing."

He nodded, seeming deep in thought.

"Anything you want to share?" she asked.

"I watched what happened. The reason I think you felt nothing is that opening a simple lock like the one in the door uses such a minute fragment of the power flowing through you that it doesn't create a ripple in the ether. If I hadn't been watching that spot at the exact right moment, I wouldn't have noticed it either."

"So..."

"So, we need to make the test a bit more difficult. Since I have no idea how the key will react to magical barriers, I hesitated to test it, but our choices seem a bit limited."

He pointed at the door again and this time a glow formed around the handle, an ugly, purplish glow that reminded her of a bruise.

When the light faded, he said, "I've locked the door and sealed it with a barrier of shadow magic. It's far from the strongest ward I can create, but it should be enough to draw some kind of reaction from the key. Don't worry, I didn't include any traps or curses. Even if you fail to open it, there's no danger."

"Great, how thoughtful of you." She shot him a glare, but if either it or her sarcasm bothered him, Daktari gave no indication. Who was she kidding? He'd probably been glared at by demons; she didn't exactly compare in the intimidation department.

Whatever. Putting it out of her mind, she reached for the handle again. A faint vibration ran through her palm when it got close to the bronze handle.

That was different. The ether remained invisible to her, but at least she felt something.

Wiggling her fingers, she kept going. She grasped the handle and turned.

There was no flash of light or crack of thunder. Instead, the door simply opened exactly as it had before. The servant remained silent and she shut it again.

Shara turned to find Daktari smiling with seemingly honest satisfaction. "What?"

"I saw how it worked. I feel confident that I at least understand the process. With that I should be able to teach you how to use the magic even if you can't see the ether."

She let out a long breath of relief. Finally, progress.

CHAPTER 2

Robert had never visited a port that serviced pirates and from the smell, he never wanted to again. The ship still had an hour of sailing at least before they reached Black Rat Cove, but even at this distance the town's stench reached him in all its nauseating glory, like a mix of vomit and rotting corpses.

He peered through the spyglass, but found no reassurance. Most of the buildings near the water appeared built from the hulls of wrecked ships. The locals had cut window holes in them along with doors, but otherwise they still looked like hulls. The docks themselves weren't much more encouraging. He feared putting a foot through the planks when they disembarked. If the water had anything in common with the architecture, they might be better off drinking their own piss.

The one thing he actually wanted to look rotten, the pirates' ships, appeared well cared for, their dark hulls freshly patched and sealed with tar. And even the smallest, a sloop barely a third the size of *The Grateful Journey*, sported a ballista in the prow.

Most places did their absolute best to find and hang pirates and brigands as quickly as possible. A perfectly sensible policy, though he'd resented it during his brief time as a bandit. This place resembled Reaper's Crossing in that it welcomed everyone, though any honest ship would have to be desperate indeed to try their luck.

That described their own circumstances perfectly. He put the spyglass away and turned to study the crew. Everyone wore steel conspicuously on their belts, though they looked more fearful than fearsome. Blade more than made up for that. She swaggered around, looking every inch the pirate queen in her white top and tight black leather pants. Her hair blew in the wind where it had escaped its pony tail.

He grinned. She could probably find a better fight here than in the Tao arena. Overhead, a roughly made black flag with a crude skull sewed on it snapped in the wind. They'd done everything in their power to pass for pirates, but their lack of siege weapons combined with the men generally having all their limbs and teeth kind of undercut the effort.

Oh well, desperate times and desperate measures and all that.

Blade spotted him watching and jogged up to join him on the foredeck. "Are you sure this is a good idea?"

Robert shook his head. "Not at all, but dying of thirst is a worse idea. If this place is all about business, we should be fine. We're looking to buy supplies from these people. If they murdered everyone that showed up, the town wouldn't last very long. The plan is, we tie up, and a small shore party heads into town to buy casks of water while the others guard the ship. We're out of here in half a day, tops. And if anyone's stupid enough to try and follow us, I suspect our scaly protector will make quick work of them."

Blade kissed him. "I love your optimism, Bobby, but when was the last time anything went the way we planned?"

"I don't recall, but that only means we're due. How are the guys managing with their swordsmanship lessons?"

"They all know which end of the sword to hold and some of them can even swing it with a reasonable chance of hitting their opponent rather than their own legs. They are eager to learn, which helps a little. Still, if it comes to a fight, I'd just as soon they stayed out of my way rather than tried to help."

"I suspect they feel the same way. For the shore party, I'm thinking you and me, plus six guys to carry the supplies."

She nodded. "That works. Are we going to do any sniffing around or strictly business?"

"Unless you hear something in passing, strictly business. You-know-who is in a big rush and I fear I agree with him. Whatever else happens, I think we don't want to be late."

"What the hell is wrong with the world when *we* have any sort of say in whether or not it survives?"

Robert shrugged. He'd been asking himself that question since they left Dagon's Chosen behind. He wanted to be a simple businessman, make some gold, see the world. That seemed like little enough to ask. Yet here they were, sailing off to find a dragon with the threat of a demon attack hanging over their heads.

"Robert?" Thompson's voice carried easily from his place by the helm.

"Sorry, darling, duty calls."

He left Blade for the considerably less attractive company of Thompson, his second-in-command. The brawny north-erner handled the helm with practiced ease and there were no threatening ships in the area, so Robert couldn't imagine what he wanted.

"There seems to be no harbor patrol," Thompson said. "Where do you want us to tie up?"

Robert considered the empty berths for a moment then shrugged. "I don't think it matters. Just pick one as far from the other ships as you can get."

"I'd like a spot on the other side of the world from them."

Robert couldn't fault him for the sentiment. Merchants and pirates mixed like oil and water. Everyone needed to remember that they weren't merchants right now, they were pirates. As long as they didn't act like a target, they wouldn't get targeted.

Hopefully.

With pirates you never knew. He'd heard plenty of stories about pirates that attacked and looted their own kind, usually after a successful raid left the victors weakened and rich. As strategies went, it made a lot of sense. Not only would someone that attacked pirates not face the noose in a real port, they might be treated as heroes. Of course, should they run into a fit and eager pirate crew, Robert shuddered to think what might happen.

They reached the docks a little over an hour later and the crew quickly secured *The Journey*. How they were going to get turned around and back out to sea was another matter. Hopefully one of the half dozen or so pirate ships tied up further down the dock would leave and reveal the process.

"All secure!" one of the crewmen shouted.

Robert, Blade, and the rest of the crew gathered on deck. Robert explained the plan, ending with, "Thompson, you'll keep an eye on the ship. If any of the pirates leave, make a note of how they manage it. I don't want to ask Master Serpent for help unless we have no other option."

"I second that, sir," Thompson said.

"Next I need six volunteers for shore duty. This is not going to be a fun shore leave. I have it on good authority that anyone that comes back drunk will be eaten." That announcement brought a flurry of nervous looks, but the men were somewhat used to the sea serpent that was serving as their protector, so no one panicked. "Finally—"

"Bobby, someone's coming."

Robert and Blade walked to the ship's rail. A small group of men dressed in ragged, filthy noblemen's outfits strode down the pier toward their ship. The fellow that led the procession wore a black top hat with a skull and crossbones patch on the front. His white waistcoat and trousers might have been nice once, but now bore a layer of grime. From the dark tone of his skin, Robert guessed he might have come from the vicinity of Tao.

Top Hat's companions had pale skin, blond hair, and carried a mix of swords and axes that would have looked more at home in the hands of northern raiders. The long leather jackets they wore looked heavy enough to serve as armor and had to be hot as hell.

The welcoming committee stopped at the end of the pier and Top Hat looked up at them with a smile that revealed a gold tooth front and center.

"Welcome, my new friends," Top Hat said. "So good to see fresh faces in Black Rat Cove. Would you be so kind as to lower your gangplank so we can speak face to face?"

Robert nodded to the guys and soon enough the gangplank thunked into place and Top Hat scampered up along with his guards. Blade stayed a step behind Robert and the rest of the sailors kept their distance.

"That's much better. My name is Jerrod, your humble host." Jerrod swept off his top hat and bowed revealing a huge bald spot on the top of his head.

"Robert Longridge, good to meet you." When Jerrod

straightened, he offered his hand which received an enthusiastic shake. "So is there a fee or anything to tie up?"

"Not at all. All ships are welcome to tie up free of charge. However, when you're ready to leave, there is a fee to use our tug. A very modest ounce of gold. There are also a few things you need to know about our peaceful little burg."

One of the guards chuckled at that, drawing a glare from Jerrod. "Sorry, boss."

"As I was saying, the rules for visitors are few but rigorously enforced. I hesitate to use the term 'laws' as many of our guests are uncomfortable with the concept."

Robert well understood that sentiment. "We appreciate you taking the time to inform us. My crew strives to stay on the right side of the powers that be wherever we go."

"Hah! Very good, sir, very good. You are a breath of fresh air compared to the savages I often have to deal with. Now, to the rules. First and foremost, all fighting is prohibited. If you have a problem with someone, solve it on the high seas, not in my town."

Robert nodded. If no one dared to draw steel, it would make his task much simpler. "Anything else?"

"Only one. All sales are final. If you get gypped, ripped off, or otherwise screwed over, it's not my problem. And if you think of demanding satisfaction on your own, see rule number one."

"Sounds simple enough. While I have no intention of breaking your rules, may I ask what the penalty is for breaking them?"

"We sink your ship. Anyone without a ship isn't a guest and therefore an open target. Most end up a slave in a pirate hold by the end of the first day. So, now that you know the rules, is there anything I can do to make your stay more enjoyable? We just received a load of fresh slaves for the whorehouses, so I recommend you get there quickly as they don't stay fresh for long."

Robert suppressed a grimace. "Tempting as that sounds, we're on a bit of a schedule. If you could point us toward a shop that sells water, we'll buy what we need, pay your exit fee, and be on our way."

"You're in luck as there are several provisioners right on the boardwalk. Also, if you're short of funds, you can fill your own casks at one of the free springs deeper in the island's interior. Though it's a shame you'll miss the many amusements Black Rat Cove has to offer, I understand a schedule all too well." Jerrod clapped the arm of the blond man on his right. "I'll leave Sven here on watch nearby. As soon as you're ready to depart, let him know and he'll fetch me at once."

Robert held out his hand again and they shook. "We appreciate your hospitality."

"That is my job, sir. And let me say that it has been a pleasure chatting with a civilized man for a change. Enjoy your shopping."

Jerrod and his guards took their leave. When they reached the end of the pier, Sven sat on a hacked-off timber, a blank, disinterested look on his face.

"Was it me or was that guy a little off?" Blade asked.

Robert shrugged. "Given some of the characters we've dealt with over the years, I don't think he's so bad. Still, the sooner we get out of here, the better. Pick the shore team. I need to go below and collect a gem to pay for the water and our exit fee."

Robert really hoped he could get a fair price for one of the emeralds, but at this point he'd take almost anything if it got them back to sea.

⋅—✦⋅

"I think I hate this place," Blade muttered as the shore party wound its way through the market.

Robert certainly couldn't argue with the sentiment. The deeper they went into Black Rat Cove, the worse the sights and smells became. So far they'd passed a pair of slavers, a tent run by the cult of Golmol offering to let you watch performance torture, and a whorehouse displaying the most ill-used whores he'd ever seen. One of them showed more bruise than smooth skin. The stench of waste, cheap ale, and vomit lay over everything like a wet blanket.

"I think we should go back to the ship, collect our empty casks, and fill them at the spring Jerrod mentioned." Robert grimaced in distaste. "The more I see of this place, the less I want to drink anything they might sell."

Somewhere to their right came a meaty smack followed by a woman's scream. The sailors all looked left and right, their hands never far from the hilts of their swords. They were all peace bound since Robert didn't trust them not to panic and draw steel when they shouldn't.

Small groups of the roughest-looking men Robert had ever seen wandered the streets in groups of two or three, their scarred chests bare. Many of them gave Blade appreciative looks, but so far no one had been stupid enough to try anything.

"I don't mind trying the springs," Blade said. "But don't we still need to find a fence?"

"Yeah. I haven't seen anything too likely though, have you?"

She shook her head. "Why don't we try further inland? This seems to be some kind of pleasure district."

For lunatics with a warped sense of pleasure maybe. Robert turned and soon they left the worst of the noise and crowds behind. The town didn't go that deep into the island. In fact, the buildings only ran three deep followed by a gap of maybe twenty yards, then jungle. Absolutely savage, exactly as Jerrod said.

After a few minutes of searching, he spotted a shop built out of wood and stone. It was the most solid structure he'd seen so far. Even better, on the sign outside someone had carved a scale, the symbol for a money changer.

"Thank heaven." Robert went right over, tried the handle, and found it locked. He knocked. "Hello?"

The door swung open, nearly knocking him on his ass. A huge man in dark leather and sporting a beard running halfway down his chest glared at him with pale, bloodshot eyes. "Watch where you're going."

And with that comment he stalked off toward the dock.

Robert shook his head. "Charming fellow."

"He's a pirate," Blade said. "What do you expect?"

"You've got me there."

"Can I help you?"

Robert turned to find a tiny man, maybe five feet tall and so thin he'd have to stand up twice to make a shadow, blocking the doorway. He wore a plain white tunic—actual, freshly laundered white—and equally clean gray pants. On the tip of his long nose perched a pair of wire-rimmed spectacles.

"Are you a money changer?" Robert asked.

"Yes, as the sign indicates."

"Do you deal in gems as well?"

"Certainly, but why don't we speak inside? Your men can wait out here, but please, bring the lovely lady. I see so much ugliness here, a splash of beauty is welcome."

"I like this one, Bobby," Blade said.

Robert would like him too, as long as he gave them a fair price for the emerald he'd brought.

The inside of the money changer's shop held little that

hinted at its purpose. No doubt the valuables were kept out of sight and locked behind a heavily warded steel door. Instead, the front room resembled a noble's drawing room. Four chairs sat around a square table. A pair of end tables held carafes of wine and pewter goblets. All in all, the place seemed too nice for Black Rat Cove.

"Please sit." The money changer took his own advice and when Robert and Blade had joined him continued. "My name is Archibald. How may I help you?"

Time to put his cards, or in this case his emerald, on the table. "We need gold to pay the exit fee and to purchase water, assuming any of it is actually drinkable."

Robert placed the gem on the table between them. The green stone twinkled in the lamplight. He'd chosen the smallest one in the pouch, though it still measured nearly an inch across. It had to be worth enough to buy a modest house. If Robert got a third of its true value he'd be thrilled.

"Exquisite. May I?"

At Robert's nod, Archibald picked up the emerald and pulled a small magnifier out of his pocket. With the device stuck into his eye socket, he held the stone up to the nearest light.

"Extremely high quality. I can't find a single crack. This may be the finest sample ever brought into my shop." He put the lens away and replaced the emerald on the table. "I'll level with you. I can't pay what this is worth; I simply lack the funds."

"Your honesty is as refreshing as it is rare," Robert said. "However, we're in a bind and this is the only thing we have to trade. What's your best offer?"

Archibald tapped his pointed nose a few times then said, "I can do two pounds of gold and three small diamonds of lesser quality. In addition, I'll write you a letter of introduction to the best outfitter in town. He collects his water from the spring and his casks are clean. We tend to refer each other clients as he may be the only person in this miserable town I trust."

"Why do you trust him?" Blade asked.

"We were slaves to the same owner, a now-deceased pirate captain. I handled all the ship's bookkeeping and Sean served as assistant quartermaster. We were released when our former owner saw death approaching and realized his soul didn't have a happy future waiting for it. Though how he imagined freeing two grubby slaves would offer redemption I can't imagine. Anyway, we worked together to build our respective businesses and we still send referrals from time to time."

Fascinating as Robert found Archibald's life story, he had no interest in fooling around any longer than he had to.

"We accept your offer," Robert said. "Our own business is pressing, so if you don't mind…"

"Of course, forgive me." Archibald stood. "I so seldom find interesting people to speak with I fear I got carried away. I'll fetch your payment from the safe in the back."

When Archibald had moved out of sight Blade asked, "How bad a deal did we make?"

"If we get what we need and off this island in one piece, I'll consider the emerald a bargain. But if we were somewhere civilized, I'd expect that gem to bring at least four times his offer."

"Ouch. Lucky we have a bunch of them."

Robert nodded, pleased that Blade kept her voice down.

There were some noises from the back room then Archibald emerged with a small wooden box. "Here we are."

He set it on the table and slid the lid open. Inside sat two large pouches, one small pouch, a folded parchment, and on top of all that, a gold disk stamped with a set of scales.

Robert picked out the top coin and sent it dancing across his knuckles. "Why is this coin separate?"

"That's exactly one ounce of gold and marked with my symbol. Jerrod knows it's the right amount for payment and won't give you any trouble. I trade quite a few of them."

Robert grinned and pocketed the coin. He took a large pouch for himself and handed the other to Blade. A quick glance into the small pouch confirmed a trio of cloudy diamonds. The stones were almost an insult given the value of the emerald, but he'd take what he could get. Finally, he tucked the letter into his pocket.

"The emerald's all yours. Pleasure doing business with you." Robert shook hands with Archibald.

A moment later the door burst in. The bearded man from earlier, now armed with an alarmingly large double-bitted axe, stood in the doorway. Robert could barely make out a couple more men, equally armed but slightly smaller, behind him.

"Can't you take no for an answer, Lawton?" Archibald asked.

"No, and neither can Captain Crow. He wants you back on the ship and I'm to bring you one way or the other."

"Do you really want to get crossways with Jerrod? I'm paid up on my protection money. You try and drag me out of here and he'll send *The Glaive* straight to the bottom."

"Ha!" Lawton took another step into the room. "Jerrod talks a good game, but if he messes with my ship, the captain will come and burn this shithole town to the ground. And Jerrod knows it. He don't even charge me to leave anymore."

"Gentlemen," Robert said. "Whatever your differences, they're no concern of ours. If you'll excuse us."

"You two aren't going anywhere." Lawton's men had the doorway completely blocked and they had axes of their own to make sure everyone understood. "The woman will fetch a great price, and I can probably get a few silvers for you too."

Robert winced. So much for getting out of here peacefully. "Don't say I didn't try and warn you."

Blade's sword cleared its sheath and slashed.

Lawton impressed him by blocking, though the silver-steel sword took a notch out of his axe.

The fight began in earnest and he backed well away.

"Shouldn't you help her?" Archibald asked.

"I am, by staying out of the way. There isn't a back way out of here, is there?"

"I fear not. Jerrod assured me that as long as I paid, I would be safe. It seems his promises weren't worth much."

In Robert's experience, a promise only held until it became inconvenient.

A particularly loud clash of steel saw Lawton's axe shatter into so much scrap.

Blade would have had him, but his flunkies rushed in to help.

They lacked their master's skill and one died in the first pass, his head going one way and his body the other.

Lawton fled and the survivor quickly followed.

"I'll be back!" Lawton shouted over his shoulder. "And next time I'll bring my whole crew!"

Blade flicked the blood off her sword and sheathed it. She didn't even look out of breath.

"You okay?" Robert knew the answer, but still had to ask.

"Fine, but I think we need to get out of here. If that asshole comes back with thirty or forty guys, even I won't be able to fight them all off."

"I like that plan." Robert clapped Archibald on the shoulder. "Best of luck to you."

"Wait, please. If I can't count on Jerrod's protection, I need to escape. Returning to *The Murderer's Nest* is a fate worse than death. Take me with you and you can have your emerald back."

"No, sorry. You seem like a nice guy, but we've got problems of our own."

Robert started for the door, but Archibald couldn't take a hint and followed along. "You don't understand. You defied Lawton, he'll never let it go. He'll hunt you to the end of the world if he has to. You're in just as much trouble even if you leave me behind. And I know things. I memorized all the old captain's maps and charts when he wasn't paying attention."

"We have to go, Bobby."

"I know." Robert ground his teeth. "Fine, you can come. Doesn't look like you eat that much and maybe you can get us a deal with your outfitter friend."

"Heaven bless you." Archibald sprinted into the back room and emerged only seconds later with a satchel over his shoulder. "Follow me. Sean's place is near the docks. If we hurry, maybe we can collect the water and make it back to your ship before Lawton catches up."

Blade snorted and Robert agreed. The way things had been going, they'd be lucky to reach the ship without the town burning down around their ears.

CHAPTER 3

Abin should have been delighted. He, along with the surviving members of the team dispatched to retrieve Prince Nord's head, were within sight of the desert. Another week or so would bring them back to Sultan's Oasis. Leaving the jungle behind ranked up there among the happiest moments of his life. If he never had to visit the hot, humid, insect-infested hole again, it would suit him perfectly.

Of course, now he had worse problems to worry about than a few itchy bug bites. They'd found the prince's head, only someone or something—Abin assumed the goblin lacked the skill—had attached it to a suit of magical armor. And the power that armor possessed...

He shuddered. The black flames that roared over their heads had turned his stomach in a way even demonic corruption never had. They felt wrong but he didn't know how to describe the feeling, not that it mattered. And now Nord intended to return to the capital and settle things with the sultan once and for all. Even if the entire army tried to face him down, Abin doubted they could stop Nord as he was now.

"Is he still back there?" Sergeant Harl asked, jolting Abin out of his thoughts.

Abin glanced at the ether behind them and found it warped and twisted, just like the wounds from the goblin's claws only on a bigger scale. His best guess put Nord a day behind them. He no longer seemed to need rest and every time Abin's group stopped, he gained. Only Nord's lack of speed kept the mounted squad ahead of him.

That and Abin figured Nord wanted them to reach the city first so they could inform Vilos of his approach. The idea of his brother's fear seemed to please Nord more than anything. Clearly his time without a body did nothing to improve his personality. You'd think he might want to find somewhere quiet to relax, but no, right back to causing trouble. Likely only death would put an end to Nord. Assuming anyone could kill him now.

"He's there," Abin said.

"Why didn't the crazy bastard just roast us and be done with it?" Harl asked. The former explorer had dark ridges under his eyes, pale skin, and a uniform reduced to rags, dirty ones. He looked like a castaway recently returned from a desert island.

"I suspect he wants us to be his heralds, telling everyone we meet that he's coming so they'll run in terror. The prince is not a good man, never was, but now he's more like a demon than a human. Whatever vestige of humanity remained within him stayed behind in the black pit. At least that's what I think."

"What are we going to do about it?"

Abin wished he had a good answer. He planned to tell Vilos and the princess to flee as far and as fast as possible. He doubted anywhere was truly safe, but hopefully they'd have a chance to delay the inevitable.

"We ride, and we report. Once the sultan knows all the

facts, he'll decide our course. With any luck, that course will lead to us all surviving."

"You don't sound too confident," Harl said.

"Are you, after what we saw?"

Only silence answered.

· —✧

A mane, high priestess of the Queen of Coins, sat bolt upright in her feather bed. She gasped for air like a fish out of water, lungs burning and head spinning. Her thin shift clung to her sweat-drenched body despite the chill of her bedroom. In her ten years as high priestess, she'd never had a vision from her patron. As long as she kept the temple coffers full and the kingdom's commerce flowing as it should, the archangel seemed content to remain silent.

She'd laughed privately at Saladin and his visions. It must have been horrible to serve such a demanding master.

Well, she couldn't laugh now. Something dark and horrible approached the city. Something wrong. And her patron expected Amane to confront it. The archangel made it clear that no failure would be accepted, better if she died in the attempt.

Amane finally swallowed the lump in her throat. She understood contracts and trade, not combat. A message would have to go to Ibreem at the temple of Branik. The high priest of the King of Swords would know what to do. From what she understood, all the high priests were getting the same vision.

She climbed out of bed and changed from her sweat-soaked shift into her formal white robes before topping it all off with a necklace of gold coins. Outside her bedroom door, a servant dressed in a plain white shift waited in case she needed something.

Amane turned to the girl. "Fetch a messenger. I need to send a note to the temple of Branik."

"Yes, Priestess." The servant, actually an initiate just beginning her training in the temple, bobbed a curtsy and hurried away.

Quick to obey, she liked that in her servants. No surprise since the Queen of Coins liked the same thing. The archangel expected Amane to jump every bit as quickly as she expected that girl to jump. Amane's task, however, wouldn't be as simple as running for a messenger.

Far too quickly the girl returned with one of the temple youths. The boy looked about ten, dressed only in shorts and sandals.

"I have a message," the boy said.

She frowned. "From who?"

"The high priestess of the Mistress of Healing. She's had a vision of something horrible and wishes to consult with you and the other high priests."

A clatter of steps kept her from answering. Another boy rounded the corner at a sprint and nearly collided with the group. "I have a message."

"From who?" she asked again.

"The temple of Branik. The high priest has had a vision."

She raised a hand to stop him. It seemed the Queen of Coins had lost a step on her fellows. Had she been the last to wake? Impossible to know and irrelevant. But they couldn't have messengers running around all over the place. Chaos would only help their enemy.

"Send replies to all the temples. Tell them I intend to make my way immediately to Branik's temple and I suggest they meet me there. Go now." She clapped once and the boys sprinted back the way they'd come.

"Will you go alone, Mistress?" the servant asked.

"It's only two blocks, I think I'll be safe enough in the temple district. Besides, should anyone be so foolish as to trouble me, the Queen protects her own. Tidy up my room. I'll likely be weary when I return and wish to rest."

The servant slipped into her chamber and Amane set out for the front gate. Ordinarily she'd take a procession of servants and guards whenever she left the temple, but today she had neither the time nor the inclination to bother. Hopefully Ibreem would have more information about both the danger and some way to deal with it. You'd have thought an archangel delivering a vision would put in more details.

Not that she would ever criticize. Amane drew a circle over her heart.

One thing about traveling at night, she found the air cool on her flushed skin and the streets empty. Perhaps she should spend more time out after sunset. No, most business happened during the day so her divine mission would continue to require her to act while the sun filled the sky.

When she reached the outer gates of Branik's temple, a pair of burly guards bowed to her and opened the door without question. Ibreem must have expected everyone to come to him. Not unreasonable under the circumstances and she appreciated that he didn't waste her time with a petty power play. The temples were in a difficult position in the High Kingdom after Saladin's failure to kill the princess left them with an extremely angry sultan on their hands.

She crossed the empty courtyard and another set of guards let her into the temple proper. The design resembled a fortress and the first room she entered held little in the way of comforts. Ibreem stood in the center of the room, dressed in gilded leather armor, a curved sword belted at his waist. His dark skin looked nearly as hard as the armor. Hours of training under the sun had left it baked and cracked. None of the gear was for show despite its fine design. She'd seen him fight and held no doubt that he could defeat nearly any opponent in the High Kingdom.

Beside Ibreem stood a figure in black robes, his face hidden by a deep cowl. She stared for a moment then her eyes went wide. "What's he doing here?"

"The Reaper spoke to me," the assassins' guild master said. "The darkness approaching can't be defeated by either the archangels' temples or the demon lords'. If we are to survive—if our world is to survive—we have no choice but to face it together."

Work with a priest of the Reaper? Such a thing had never happened, at least not that she knew about. The archangels and demon lords hated each other. What threat could compel them to combine forces? Amane didn't really want to know.

Over the next hour the other high priests arrived, including the heads of the temples of Golmol and Abaddon. Did only three of the nine demon lords have faiths in Sultan's Oasis or did the others not deem the threat so serious?

Again, she had no idea. Unlike the Reaper's Guild, the others kept a low profile. They offered nothing but pain and destruction and none of it for hire.

When no one else arrived after ten minutes Ibreem said, "You have all heard from your patrons. A dark force is approaching Sultan's Oasis, a servant of The Void more powerful than any we've ever faced. Only by combining our strength will we have a chance."

The Void? Amane had never heard of it. Granted, she spent little enough time in the archive, but surely her patron would have told her directly of such a thing. She glanced around the gathering and found several of the other high priests wearing looks as confused as hers. That the followers of the demon lords appeared to understand exactly what they faced annoyed her no end.

"What is The Void and what does it want here?" asked Soraya, high priestess of the Mistress of Healing.

Her question drew a chuckle from the many-times-pierced and tattooed priest of Golmol the Torturer. Amane bristled at the insult, but Soraya ignored him and kept her gaze on Ibreem. Amane considered herself quite graceful, but she always felt slow and awkward next to the tiny Soraya. Rumor had it that she worked as a dancing girl before receiving the call to serve and Amane well believed it. She seemed to glide rather than walk wherever she went.

"The Void is a cosmic entity, on par with The Creator and The Destroyer. It's been trapped just beneath our reality since the universe was formed. It wants to be free so it can destroy everything and return our reality to endless darkness."

"I believe the lady was asking more specifically what The Void's agent wants here," the assassin said. "My master believes it wants the princess, or more specifically the power she has inherited."

"Then Saladin was right?" Amane blurted out before she could think better of it. When everyone looked at her she added, "Should we have helped kill the girl?"

"No," Ibreem said. "Branik has commanded that no harm come to her. Even as we speak, Shara is learning to use her new abilities. Should she succeed, we will have a chance to free our world of The Void's influence forever."

"Only death is forever," the assassin said. "But for thousands of years certainly. The Reaper agrees that the risk is worth it."

"Do we have a plan?" Abaddon's priest asked.

"That is what we are here to work out," Ibreem said. "And we need to work quickly as The Void's agent will reach Sultan's Oasis in days."

CHAPTER 4

Robert followed Archibald through the narrow, twisting streets of Black Rat Cove with Blade bringing up the rear. The rest of the shore party should be back to the ship by now. According to Archibald, his friend made deliveries to docked ships via a dory. That would be ideal, assuming they avoided their hunters.

The dirt streets sent up puffs of dust as they moved quickly down back alleys nearly too narrow for Robert's shoulders. Maybe Lawton would follow and get stuck. Not that he could get so lucky.

They emerged onto the main street and Archibald looked both ways in a way that made Robert wonder if he actually knew where they emerged. He quickly turned left, partially alleviating Robert's concerns.

"How much further?" Blade asked.

"Not very. I can see his shop from here." Archibald pointed at a sturdy-looking building made of actual lumber rather than a repurposed hull. The shop had its own private dock and a black-hulled dory had been tied to the pier.

"Still no sign of Lawton. Any chance your friend will let us ride back to our ship when he makes the delivery?"

"Shouldn't be a problem." Archibald skidded to a stop. "That, on the other hand, is a rather large problem."

The large problem turned out to be an armor-clad man emerging from the shop's front door armed with a bastard sword. He looked a bit like the thugs that protected Jerrod only bigger. How come no one ever sent small, weak fellows after them?

Robert grabbed Archibald and twisted him around, so he was hidden by Robert's back. The little man had too distinctive of a silhouette. Anyone seeing it would instantly recognize him.

"Who is that?" Blade asked as they walked back the way they'd come.

"Gunner. He's Lawton's right-hand man. He must have known I'd come to see Sean before I left." Archibald looked like he'd like to pull his hair out if he had any.

"Is there somewhere else we can get our water?" Robert asked.

"Nowhere I'd trust not to poison us," Archibald said.

"Then we'll just have to get rid of Gunner." Blade pulled a dagger from her boot and palmed it, so her forearm hid most of its length. "We'll go with that trick we used on the ranger north of Reaper's Crossing. You remember?"

Robert nodded and pulled his own dagger, this one weighted for throwing. He didn't have fond memories of that fight with that ranger, but Blade's plan made sense under the circumstances.

"Excuse me," Archibald said. "I have no idea what you're talking about."

They reached a little alley out of sight of the shop. Blade grabbed Archibald and pressed him into the gap. "You don't need to understand. Just stay here and keep quiet. We'll be back for you when it's safe."

"And if you don't come back?"

Blade shrugged. "Then good luck with Lawton."

Archibald's eyes nearly bugged out of his head.

Robert grinned and squeezed his shoulder. "Relax. We do this sort of thing all the time. Honestly, I'd like to do it a bit less, but the point is we know our business. Stay here and keep calm. Everything will be fine."

"Right, good luck then."

Robert nodded then he and Blade headed back toward the outfitter's shop.

"You know, we haven't tried this trick since the rangers," Blade said. "Maybe you shouldn't have gotten his hopes so high."

"Maybe, but even if it doesn't work, I'm sure you can still take this idiot the old-fashioned way, it'll just be messier and attract a lot more attention. Hopefully since it's self-defense, Jerrod won't sink our ship as punishment."

"Do you think the serpent would let him?"

"Probably not, but we don't know what sort of magic Jerrod has. After everything we've seen, I don't want to assume anything."

Robert split off and angled across the street while Blade continued directly toward the outfitters. Gunner spotted her approaching and tensed. Lawton must have given him a description of Blade. That meant he'd recognize Robert if he got too close. Maybe the ranger trick wouldn't work after all. It totally depended on surprise. On the other hand, Blade's skill might be enough to pull off the trick anyway.

"Hey! Woman!" Gunner shouted as Blade drew closer. "My captain would like to have words with you."

"Your captain is a pig." Blade drew her sword. "And the only words I have for him are 'go to hell.' You can run along and tell him now, or you can tell him when he joins you there."

Half the people, the ones that looked like locals rather than pirates, went running in every direction. The rest, mostly big, scarred men, grinned at each other and started betting.

Yep, so much for surprise. Looked like they'd be doing it the hard way after all. Robert restrained himself from betting his pouch of gold on Blade and focused on the matter at hand.

Gunner raised his sword and tensed, either too stupid or overconfident to run away.

Blade darted in, sword leading.

Gunner batted it aside and countered with a head-high slash.

The swing whistled over her head.

Before he could recover, Blade lashed out at knee level.

Gunner leapt the slash by an inch and tried to bisect her with an overhead slash.

While everyone was busy watching the fight, Robert eased his way around to the outfitter's shop. He peeked through the open door and found a body lying in the middle of the floor. He wasn't moving, which was a bad sign, but no blood covered the floor, so things might have been worse.

A howl of pain prompted him to turn just in time to watch Blade rip her dagger out of Gunner's thigh. He collapsed, clutching his leg.

"Gunner!" the shout came from down the street. A quartet of men in leather armor and bristling with weapons forced their way through the gathered gamblers with a combination of shouts and threats.

Robert whistled and when Blade turned his way he pointed at the approaching reinforcements. With a final look at the rapidly bleeding out Gunner, Blade ran over to him. They ducked inside the shop and Robert found a wedge off to one side. He slid it under the door and kicked it in tight.

"That won't hold them for long," he said.

Blade wiped the blood off her dagger and sheathed it. "Let's hope our next plan works out better than our last one. That pirate was a fair fighter, better than his captain."

Robert nodded and knelt beside the prone figure. The man —he assumed it was Sean, but it could have been an employee too—still breathed at least. Robert rolled him over onto his back. Gunner must have clobbered him as he had a knot on his head the size of a hen's egg.

A heavy blow buffeted the door.

"We're out of time, Bobby." Blade knelt beside him and gave Sean a sharp backhand.

The man sat up with a gasp. He looked from Robert to Blade and back. "Where? What?"

"A pirate named Gunner hit you and now his men are trying to break down the door," Robert said. "Another way out of here would be great."

"We also need water," Blade said.

"Who are you two?"

"I'm Robert and this is Blade. We're friends of Archibald's. You're Sean, right? He recommended your services."

"Is he okay?" Sean asked with the sort of desperation usually reserved for a missing kid or sick wife.

"He's fine," Robert said, hoping it was true. Another heavy blow shook the door. "About that exit?"

"Right." Sean tried to stand, wobbled, and was promptly caught by Robert. "Thanks. I'm okay. In the back-right corner there's a hatch that leads to our warehouse and the loading dock. We've got ten casks of water in stock, though I doubt we'll have time to load them."

Blade hurried ahead of them and pulled open a trapdoor. "I smell blood."

Robert wanted to bounce his forehead off the wall.

Behind them the door splintered under a third heavy blow.

"My men," Sean said. "I had three workers down there. Are they…"

"I don't know, but I'm going to find out." Blade disappeared out of sight.

Robert joined her, letting Sean climb down the ladder first then following.

"There's a lock for the hatch," Sean said.

Robert found it and threw the bolt. One more barrier between them and the pirates wouldn't hurt anything.

Shouts of pain mingled with the clash of steel. Sounded like Blade had found someone to fight. At the bottom of the ladder, Robert had to hop over a fresh corpse. Sean stared at the dead man, his face pale. Archibald had said the two of them worked on a pirate ship. He should be more familiar with death than this.

"One of yours?" Robert asked.

"Tan, my foreman. He's been with me for seven years." Sean shook his head. "He had a wife and daughter."

Robert wanted to ask why the hell he didn't take his family and find a better place to work, but the sounds of battle had ended. "Come on. We can't do anything for him now."

They found Blade standing over the bodies of two pirates. The warehouse held any number of crates and barrels. The bodies of two more workers had been thrown like so much trash in a corner. Robert did his best to shield Sean from the sight.

"I think we're good for the moment," Blade said. "How do we load the dory?"

"There's a lift and rail system we use," Sean said. "You need water, right? That's the black barrels against the far wall. Get the side door open and we'll start loading."

Blade sheathed her sword and marched over to an iron ring on the wall. A long door slid open on greased rails.

She'd barely gotten it halfway open when a crossbow bolt thunked into the floor an inch from her right foot.

Robert drew his throwing dagger, ran over to the opening, and hurled it at a man busy cranking the string on a crossbow. The rushed throw missed anything vital, but still sank six inches into the crossbowman's gut.

He fell screaming into the water.

"You okay?" he asked.

Blade ignored him and charged a dripping wet man with an axe making his way down the pier. The lunatic must have leapt into the water and swam over to the private dock.

Three sharp slashes sent his headless body splashing into the water.

"I thought there was supposed to be patrols or security or something," Robert said. "Where's Jerrod anyway?"

Sean shrugged. "I don't know, but if I see him, I'm going to demand the return of my protection money."

Blade rejoined them. "I don't see any more, but that can't last. Do you want to help load or fetch Archibald?"

"I'll get Archibald," Robert said. "If there's trouble here, you're the one to handle it."

She nodded and dragged Sean back inside to get started. Robert grinned and retreated through the warehouse, up the ladder, and out the front door. Looked like they'd dealt with the entire party. Even the gambling pirates had cleared out, leaving the streets empty. He flicked a glance at a large pool of blood, but Gunner seemed to have made his escape.

Pity that. Of more interest to him was the crossbow the man his dagger struck dropped. A single bolt sat beside it. He cranked the string back and loaded it. Having a single shot stunk, but he preferred it to no shots.

He frowned. There's no way Jerrod didn't get word of what happened from someone. For all his talk of no violence in town, he sure didn't seem interested in putting a stop to it.

Well, whatever. Robert turned up the street toward where he left Archibald hiding in the alley. The silent streets gave him the creeps, but as long as no one tried to stab him, he wouldn't complain.

As soon as the alley came in sight, Archibald burst out and ran right up to him. "Sean, is he okay? I heard people talking about a fight."

"He's got a knot on his head, but otherwise seems okay. He and Blade are loading the dory. What say we join them?"

"Yes, please."

Robert and Archibald made the short walk to the outfitter's. As soon as Sean saw him, he left Blade to maneuver the heavy cask on her own and embraced the money changer. They kissed on each cheek then stared at each other as if fearing to find something missing.

For his part, Robert was content to help Blade steady the cask and let the men enjoy their reunion.

"I think they're more than friends," Blade said.

They used the block and tackle to lower the cask into the dory beside the six already waiting.

"Whatever they are or aren't is no business of mine. But I can tell you I've had my fill of this town and the sooner we leave the happier I'll be."

"You'll hear no argument from me."

They went back to collect another cask and found Sean and Archibald waiting hand in hand.

"I'm coming too," Sean said. "We'll never be safe here if Captain Crow is after us."

Robert grimaced. He needed extra passengers like he needed a hole in the head. "We're not exactly sailing into calm waters. You two might be better off on another ship."

"All the others are pirates and many of them allies of Captain Crow." Archibald shook his head. "You're our only hope of getting out of here that doesn't end with us in chains on *The Murderer's Nest*. Please, we'll help any way we can."

"Fine." Robert threw up his hands. "We don't have time to argue about it anyway. Let's get the water loaded before anyone else shows up."

.—✢

L awton paced in his modest cabin aboard *The Glaive* and glared at Gunner. He had little enough room, four paces took him from one end to the other, but if he didn't do something he feared he might strangle his second-in-command. For his part, Gunner offered no excuses for his failure to capture the little rat of a money changer.

In fact, he was still unconscious and his leg still leaked blood on Lawton's floorboards. Two of the men he'd dispatched to help had brought Gunner back near death, a deep wound in his thigh that almost severed the big blood vessel running there. According to their report, the same woman that had sent him fleeing at Archibald's shop had dealt with his second.

He shook his head. Maybe instead of trying to make her a slave, he should offer her a post on his ship. She clearly had better sword skills than any of his current crew. Loath as he was to admit it, Lawton included himself on that list. He'd never fought anyone that good with a sword and he dearly hoped never to do so again.

Lawton didn't even know why the captain wanted the

useless old man so badly. He'd simply ordered Lawton to bring him back, alive if possible. If not, well, that was okay too.

A knock sounded on the cabin door and a moment later it opened revealing the stooped, haggard form of Lotta, their priestess of Dagon and his great aunt. She wore little more than a dark robe that appeared salvaged from the bottom of the ocean. He'd seen beggars with better clothes, but she refused all offers of anything else. The hag served as both the ship's healer and mistress of all matters magical.

She shuffled over and looked down at Gunner with indifferent, watery-green eyes. "What happened to him?"

Lawton shivered at her raspy, gurgling voice. "There was a fight. He lost. I need to finish Captain Crow's mission and I need Gunner to do it."

Lotta put a claw-like hand out just above Gunner's injured leg. A minute passed and nothing happened. In Lawton's experience, when she called on the demon lord's power, it came instantly, did the job in excruciatingly painful fashion, and vanished just as quickly.

At last she looked up. "Dagon disapproves of your mission. He will grant no healing to Gunner or anyone else you send into battle against the woman and her companions."

"Why?" Lawton asked between clenched teeth. If he couldn't count on Lotta's magic, his task just grew ten times harder.

Her harsh laugh made the hair on his arms stand up. "You think he explains his decisions to the likes of me? Whatever you're doing, I suggest you stop lest Lord Dagon grow angry. Should he command it, I will kill everyone on this ship, including you, nephew."

"And will you explain your decision to Captain Crow?"

"Ha! You think I fear that whelp Dantilion Crow more than my master? Dagon's wrath should terrify anyone that sails the seas and you are close to drawing it down on all of us. Leave this place, return to Shadow Point, and tell Crow to forget about whatever it is he wants."

"You know the captain as well as I do," Lawton said. "He'll never stand down once he decides on a path. Certainly not on my say-so and likely not even on Dagon's."

"Then sail far away, nephew, and let my master's punishment fall on his head rather than yours." Lotta shuffled back toward the door and out of sight.

Lawton shook his head. This job just got worse and worse. And now he had to finish it without Gunner. The thought of trying to flee Captain Crow never really crossed his mind. Even if he sailed to the other side of the world, he doubted that would be far enough to escape.

"Sir?" a nervous voice asked.

He looked up from his unconscious, likely dying first mate and found a nervous sailor standing in the doorway. What, in heaven's name, had come up now?

"Report."

"Jerrod's here, sir. He wanted to talk to you."

Lawton thought he'd fully cowed the so-called Lord of Black Rat Cove. Well, this would be a good chance to take out his frustrations on someone whose opinion he didn't care about and whose power he didn't fear.

"I'm coming. Did the rest of the shore party get back yet?"

"Jerrod brought them, sir. Or their bodies anyway. Two are missing, apparently fallen into the cove."

"Then the razor fish will have stripped them to the bone by now." Lawton wanted to scream his rage at the universe, but held it in. Those had been some of his best men and now they were so much fish food.

The two pirates went up on deck. The men all offered nods of respect and in two of the younger men's cases, salutes. He ignored them and went to the gangplank. Jerrod stood at the bottom in his ridiculous top hat. Behind him, two of his thugs waited on either side of a hand cart filled with bodies.

"What's the problem, Jerrod?" Lawton asked. "I thought I made it clear when we spoke that as long as you stayed out of my way, we wouldn't burn your town to the ground."

"The problem?" Jerrod waved a hand at the pile of corpses. "This is the problem. Bad enough I have to let you kidnap a man that pays me for protection, but now you're starting fights in the street and leaving corpses lying around my town. If I do nothing it makes me look weak. How long before I lose all control? I can't have it, Lawton. You've got until sunset to finish your business. If you're still causing problems then, I'll sink your ship and take my chances with Crow."

Lawton stalked down the ramp. He needed no threats from this popinjay.

One of the thugs moved to intercept him.

Lawton backhanded him so hard his knees buckled and he fell on his ass.

He grabbed Jerrod by the collar and yanked him close. "You do not want to cause problems for Captain Crow. I don't care how strong you think your pet monster is, the captain will kill it. Then he'll gut you and feed you to the razor fish, before slaughtering everyone in this miserable shithole you call a town. These are facts, not threats. Keep your mouth shut and stay out of my way and you might live to see the end of the month. Oh, and don't let the bitch's ship leave the cove."

A final shove sent Jerrod staggering back into his second thug.

They had a brief staring match before Jerrod and his men fled, leaving the corpse wagon behind.

Lawton meant every word he said. What he didn't add was

that if he failed, Captain Crow would likely do to him what he threatened to do to Jerrod.

He spun to find the men watching him. "I want every man armed and ready to fight in five minutes. We're going to get that bastard Archibald and heaven help anyone that gets in our way."

CHAPTER 5

The sight of *The Hopeful Journey* floating safe and sound in the berth where he left her filled Robert with relief. Sean manned the tiller of his dory while Robert and Blade rowed. Archibald offered to help, but one look at the little man's scrawny arms made it clear he'd be less help and more hinderance.

A rope ladder clunked on the side of the hull and Thompson shouted, "Is all well, sir?"

Talk about a loaded question. "For the moment, but I doubt that will last. Get the hoist ready, we've got the water along with a couple extra passengers."

Thompson blanched. "Is that okay?"

"I doubt Scaly will care." Robert turned to his companions. "Blade and I need to secure our exit. Can you two hook the casks for Thompson? As soon as you're done, climb on up."

"No problem," Sean said. "And thanks again for letting us join you."

Robert nodded and started up the rope ladder with Blade on his heels. Up on deck, the men were positioning the hoist over the rail. Robert left them to their work and headed for the gangplank.

"How are we going to secure our exit?" Blade asked.

Robert pulled the scale-marked coin from his pocket and let it flash in the light.

"You think he'll honor our arrangement if he's working with Lawton?"

"We'll find out soon enough."

Jerrod's thug remained exactly where they'd left him, lounging against a piling staring off into space, face blank, and mouth halfway open. Robert had seen smarter-looking trees.

"Hey!"

The thug gave a full-body shake, blinked, and stared at them. "What do you want?"

"To leave. I've got Jerrod's gold. Fetch your boss so we can go."

"He's busy. No ships are leaving until morning."

Blade drew her sword and placed the tip under his nose. "That is not acceptable."

The thug gave a nervous wave of his hands. "Hey, easy, I don't have any say in this. I just carry messages and beat people up. Jerrod controls the thing that turns the ships."

"What thing?" Robert asked.

"I don't know, man, I swear. It stays mostly underwater."

"Alright, get lost," Robert said.

"I'm supposed to keep an eye on you."

Blade pressed hard enough to draw blood. "How about I cut your lips off?"

"Okay, okay, I'm going." He shot Robert a pleading look. "Your lady friend is scary."

"You're not the first to say so." He ran off and Robert turned to Blade. "You were right. We're going to need Scaly's help to get the ship turned."

Blade sheathed her sword. "How do you call him?"

"I don't. At least I never have. Maybe I could fire off a light ball underwater. That might do it. Assuming it doesn't attract the attention of whatever thing Jerrod controls."

"Happy thoughts, Bobby, happy thoughts."

She led the way back to the ship and Robert smiled as he followed. A scary lady indeed. But he loved her more than anything.

When they reached the deck Robert asked, "How are we doing?"

"Four loaded, sir," Thompson said. "When do we get turned around?"

"Good question."

Robert walked to the rear of the ship and stared into the water. He'd never cast the light spell underwater, but it couldn't be any harder than doing it in the air. The ether didn't care about wet or dry. At least as far as he knew.

As he contemplated the possibilities, a pair of golden eyes appeared staring up at him. A moment later water geysered up, soaking the deck. Scaly looked down at him and swung his head from side to side.

"I warned you not to get into trouble," the serpent said.

"I didn't. Trouble just showed up. We've got our water nearly loaded. When we're done, can you turn the ship around?"

"Certainly, but don't think using me as a tug will be a regular thing."

That had never crossed Robert's mind, but something else did. "How did you know we needed you? I planned to use a spell to send a signal, but didn't have a chance."

"Dagon spoke to me. It seems one of his worshippers is abroad a pirate ship. She asked for healing to help one of the pirates you fought and he refused. He also sent a warning, but the priestess deemed it unlikely the pirates would obey. Not wanting your mission to fail, Dagon sent me to aid you. It seems I arrived at a good time."

"You can say that—"

"Bobby! Company!"

Robert turned toward the wharf in time to see a force of over thirty pirates approaching with Lawton in the lead. Even Blade would have trouble with that many fighters.

"Finish your loading," Scaly said. "I will delay them."

Robert had no intention of arguing. "Thanks."

He leapt down from the rear castle and ran over to the rail. One cask remained in the dory.

Hell with it. There had to be an island out there with a spring and no pirates. "Archibald, Sean, get up here. We're leaving."

"What about the pirates?" Blade asked.

The answer to her question arrived in the form of Scaly emerging and spraying a stream of water at them with enough force to knock every man down and blast them twenty yards up the boardwalk.

"I guess that works," she said.

"Your guests are aboard and the lines are free," Thompson shouted.

Scaly vanished back underwater and a moment later the ship lurched. Such was the serpent's power that it spun them around in under a minute and started dragging them out into the cove.

"Set the sails!" Robert shouted. "Let's get the hell out of here!"

The sailors greeted his order with enthusiasm and soon men swarmed the rigging. A glance back at the dock confirmed that they had reached a safe distance. Lawton and his men had regained their feet and were glaring at them.

Robert didn't care if they glared themselves blind, as long as *The Journey* got away in one piece.

—⋇—

Asopping wet and furious Lawton stared at the fleeing ship as if he could stop it by sheer force of will. When that sea serpent rose out of the water he'd feared they were dead, but it only sprayed them with water. Granted, it felt like he'd been hit by a horizontal waterfall, but at least no one had been hurt.

"Did Jerrod betray us?" one of the men asked.

The question jarred Lawton out of his funk. He didn't think Jerrod's monster was a sea serpent, but he'd also never seen it out of the water so maybe.

"Let's go ask."

Lawton led the way up the street toward the beached ship that served as Jerrod's office. It sat within sight of the docks, so the walk didn't take long. If Jerrod hadn't betrayed them, then he could use his monster to kill the serpent and stop Archibald from escaping. He didn't even care about getting even with the woman for embarrassing him and killing his right-hand man.

Someone had cut a hole in the hull of the ship, framed it, and hung a door. Lawton slammed his fist into it, drawing a dull thud.

"Open up, damn you! My prey is escaping."

"Good," a muffled voice said. "Why don't you chase them down yourself and leave my town alone? I'll have your ship turned around by the time you reach it."

"I need you to use your monster to stop them. Whoever they are, they have a sea serpent with them. A big one. *The Glaive* wouldn't stand a chance."

"So that's why she's been so scared. She must have smelled

that serpent in the water. Sorry, Lawton, my girl won't go anywhere near that thing."

"Damn him to hell!" Lawton snatched an axe out of the hand of a nearby pirate and tossed him his borrowed sword.

Three hard blows smashed the door down and Lawton stalked through. He found Jerrod cowering behind a cluttered desk.

Four long strides carried Lawton within reach of Jerrod. He grabbed the man by his scrawny neck and dragged him across the desk, sending papers and ink scattering everywhere.

"Listen to me and listen well. You will use your monster to kill the serpent and stop Archibald's escape. If you don't, I'll cut your head off and stick a candle in it for a decoration. Come on."

He wasn't letting Jerrod out of his sight until this business was over, one way or the other.

The group double-timed it across town to the ship. As soon as they were aboard Lawton shouted, "Throw lines! Jerrod, do your thing."

"Stop this foolishness." Lotta hobbled across the deck toward them. "That sea serpent is one of Dagon's servants. Whatever this man you seek is doing, he has the master's blessing. Let him go before you get us all killed."

The crew started muttering among themselves. None of his men were devout, but all of them feared the Lord of Corrupt Oceans. Lotta's word carried serious weight. If he let this go on too long, he might lose them.

"If we're not moving in one minute, I'm going to feed one of you to the razor fish." He glared at Lotta. "Maybe starting with you."

She snorted. "As if there's a creature in the ocean I fear."

Lotta shuffled to the rail and leapt over it. A splash followed a moment later.

Every man on deck rushed to the side. It felt like everyone held their breath until one man said, "No sign of her."

While Lawton hated to lose her magic, he didn't need Lotta undermining his authority. If she couldn't be of use, better for him if she swam back to whatever wet hell spat her out.

He gave Jerrod a shake. "Make with the monster. Throw those lines!"

The crew reluctantly moved away from the rail and got them ready to sail. Jerrod's face scrunched up as he concentrated. The monster needed half a minute, but finally they were turning and heading out to sea.

Lawton looked up at the crow's nest. "Can you see them?"

"Yes, sir. They've got about three miles on us and all their canvas is out. No sign of the serpent."

Once they were away from the dock, the men got busy setting their own sails. The Glaive was a fast ship, but it would take time to catch up.

His angry gaze bore into Jerrod. "Stop them."

"I can't." Jerrod's voice trembled. "She's terrified of that serpent."

"Who's the master, you or the monster?" Lawton asked. "What good is it if the creature can ignore your orders?"

"The magic doesn't work that way. I can compel her to do certain things. But I can't overcome her natural instincts. She's sure if she goes near the serpent, it will kill her. I can feel it through our link. Threaten me however you like, but it changes nothing."

Lawton shoved Jerrod away. "Fine. I'll deal with the creature myself. Load the forward ballista! We're having sea serpent steaks for supper."

Two men hurried to fit a steel-tipped harpoon into the ballista as Lawton stalked across the deck. He took his place behind it and waited. As soon as they got close to that ship, the serpent would rise and when it did, he'd put a spear through its heart.

⋅ ⋯ ✦

R obert stood at the rear of the ship and watched as the pirates slowly closed in. They had every inch of canvas raised and still the enemy ship gained. When he considered what might happen on his quest to wake a sleeping dragon, getting killed by pirates never crossed his mind. And now he found himself on the run from the bloodthirsty bastards. While he rated Blade's combat skills highly, defeating an entire ship of pirates, given the meager help the crew could offer, seemed too big an ask even for her.

Their only hope had ducked underwater ten minutes ago and he'd seen no sign of since. He seriously doubted Scaly would save them in the cove only to abandon them now. No, whatever the serpent went to do must be important. Hopefully he'd finish up before the pirates came into ballista range.

"Excuse me, sir." Archibald stood on the steps leading up to the rear castle seeming hesitant to come the rest of the way.

"What's on your mind?" Robert asked. Anything to distract him was welcome.

"I wanted to apologize. I never dreamed Lawton would go this far to capture me. Try as I might, I simply can't imagine why Captain Crow would want me back so desperately. My skills as a bookkeeper hardly seem to justify all this effort."

"While I appreciate the thought, I suspect Blade and me killing some of his men played a part in his determination. Don't worry, Scaly will deal with them, then we can find a nice safe port where we can drop you and your friend off."

"About that. I spoke to Sean and if you're willing, we'd like to join your crew permanently. If Captain Crow is looking for us, no port will be safe. Better if we keep moving."

Robert debated if they'd be more trouble than they were worth but finally shrugged. "Let's see where we stand when the current crisis is over."

"Fair enough, sir." Archibald pointed. "I believe something is happening on the enemy ship."

Robert turned in time to see the pirate ship lurch hard to the right then back left.

A crunch reached him from a distance and he spotted a flash of green. Looked like Scaly took a four-foot chunk out of their hull.

Another crash and the vessel's keel snapped clean in half. Men leapt overboard and he heard faint screaming.

Robert shook his head. No doubt he'd just seen what would have happened had they refused to follow the serpent's instructions. As good decisions went, playing along with Scaly had to be one of Robert's best.

Half a minute after dealing with the pirate ship, Scaly's head burst out of the water beside their ship. Even after doing all that damage, the serpent's scales didn't have a mark on them.

Robert grinned. "Much obliged. When you disappeared on us, I feared the worst."

"One of my master's priestesses called out to me. She had served for a time on that ship and warned them to call off their pursuit lest Dagon's wrath fall upon them. When they refused, she abandoned them rather than disobey our master. I honored her loyalty by listening to what she had to say."

"Anything I need to know?"

"Only that the one called Crow ordered Lawton to retrieve the human Archibald no matter the cost. Unfortunately, the reasons were unknown to her."

Robert turned to Archibald who cowered in the serpent's presence. "Any ideas?"

"As I said, I have no idea what might have pushed Captain Crow to such desperation."

"Well, it doesn't matter now that Lawton's been dealt with. We're all stocked up with water and can get back to finding the dragon."

"Yes," the serpent said. "I fear our time grows short."

"Did you say you're looking for a dragon?" Archibald asked.

"That's right," Robert said. "Sure you still want to stick with us?"

"It's not that. I remember when I was reading the old captain's charts it mentioned a place called Dragon Isle. It's northeast of Shadow Point, the pirates' home base. The old captain only went there once. Whatever he found must have scared him as he ordered all the ships under his command to stay away and to sink anyone that got close."

Robert and Scaly shared a look.

"A sleeping dragon might have that effect," Robert said.

"Indeed," Scaly agreed. "And if the new captain is aware of what this human knows, it might explain his desire to capture him. Though his interest in the dragon is another matter. Should he interfere with our task, I will show no mercy."

Nothing like having a sea serpent on your side to make the pirate problem seem manageable. "Assuming the compass agrees, I think we have our destination."

"Dagon will be most pleased." Scaly dove out of sight though Robert doubted he'd wander far.

"You have interesting companions, sir," Archibald said. "I thought Lady Blade was the most dangerous of them all, but I can see I erred in my thinking."

"Don't let Blade hear you say that." Robert clapped him on

the shoulder. "Let's take a look at my charts. You can show me where to find Dragon Isle."

He led the way down the stairs. It felt good, knowing where they were going, but he couldn't stop wondering what other dangers awaited.

Whatever they were, Robert feared they'd make Lawton look like a walk in the park.

CHAPTER 6

Though she still couldn't see it, Shara felt the ether gather in her hands. It reminded her of soft clay only dry. The most interesting thing, at least according to Daktari, was that she couldn't make anything that didn't have a lock. Shara had spent an afternoon trying, but after ten failures in a row gave it up.

As she had every day since his arrival, she and Daktari gathered in the small chamber that served as their temporary classroom. On the room's sole desk sat a simple lockbox.

Today, her teacher said she needed to create a lock strong enough to stop him from opening it. Given Daktari's power, that seemed a nearly impossible task. Yet if she failed in this, sealing a void pit linked to a cosmic entity would remain forever beyond her.

So she concentrated, gathered, and compressed ether until it felt heavy in her hands. Molding it like the clay it resembled, she formed chains and a simple lock. The lock didn't need to be complex, but it had to be there. Even Daktari didn't know why. His guess was that since her power revolved around a key, it naturally needed a lock. Her power had a remarkably narrow focus which was what made it so strong.

That made as much sense as anything Shara had imagined.

Her visualization didn't need to be fancy, he said, but it did need to be clear in her mind, the clearer the better. Since she still failed to see the ether, Shara had to rely on touch.

At last, she wrapped the chains around the box and put her lock in place. Sweat poured down her face and she wanted to sleep for a month, but she'd done it.

"How's that?" she asked.

The dark shadow of her mentor fell over Shara, sending a chill up her spine. Though she no longer feared her one-time kidnapper, he still had a presence filled with malice, even if he didn't direct it at her.

"The power of the binding is impressive," he said at last. "I'd need months to make something that dense and you did it in only minutes. The construct is crude in appearance, but given that you made it all by feel, I can find little fault with your work. Now for the real test."

He walked around so they were face to face. Anger no longer twisted his features, but kindness did nothing to soften them either. Shara doubted she'd ever truly figure him out.

When Daktari reached for the box, purple flames sprang to life on his fingertips. An inch from the wood's surface they stopped. He grasped her invisible chains and the flames burned brighter.

Seconds and then a minute passed.

She felt her construct break when his fist closed and her heart sank. Another failure.

"Your best effort yet," he said. "Well done. At first, I despaired of you ever reaching our ultimate goal, but having seen your progress over the last few days, I can say with confidence that you will get there."

Shara brightened. He'd never given her such a strong compliment. "Really?"

He nodded. "That one nearly stopped me. The durability is more than adequate, the problem now is the shape you chose for your construct. The chains offer too many gaps for my magic to attack."

"What should I use?"

He stayed silent for so long Shara thought he'd forgotten about her. At last he said, "For a box like this, I'd say a solid barrier on all but one side. On the final side imagine two pieces coming together with the lock in the center. Try to make it as smooth as possible."

"I need to rest a little longer." She expected a rebuke, but he only nodded.

"I'm not surprised. Given the amount of ether you're handling, it's a wonder your hands haven't melted off. Is there any discomfort?"

"None. It really does feel like soft clay."

"Amazing. Your visualization must compel the ether to take on a form you can understand. I've never encountered anything remotely like your magic in all my studies."

He stared off into space for a moment, like his train of thought had been interrupted. Shara had seen that expression enough times to recognize that he was speaking mind to mind with his ugly little homunculus.

"Is something wrong?"

"Your father is coming and he looks displeased. Since I have done nothing that might upset him, I assume he received some bad news."

Shara frowned. What could have happened now?

T he white stone walls of Sultan's Oasis had never looked so beautiful to Abin, nor so thin. Not that the thickness had actually changed. Only his knowledge of what followed them colored his perception. Prince Nord's head, now attached to a suit of magical armor of tremendous power, still stalked along behind them.

Since Abin and his team left the jungle, Nord had closed the gap so that only an hour or so separated them. He had drawn so close that the ether appeared warped in Abin's magical vision. He'd tried to summon a magical messenger, but the spirits were so scared of Nord that they wouldn't answer the spell.

And Abin didn't blame them. That Nord now had power enough to warp the ether to such a degree terrified him. They had little time to evacuate the sultan and his daughter, assuming Vilos would even take Abin's advice and make a run for it. Trying to reason with Nord would be a waste of time and fighting him even more so. Unless you had some soldiers you wanted dead, the only thing to do was run.

Abin shot a glance at Sergeant Harl. The man slumped in his saddle, eyes half closed. His uniform had collected a variety of sweat stains and other crud. Days of eating in the saddle, resting only the absolute minimum, and generally running for their lives had worn the men down to a nub. Only the fear of what would happen should Nord catch up to them kept everyone moving.

"Someone's in front of the gate," the lead rider said.

Abin snapped his gaze forward. In fact, several someones stood in front of the gate. They remained too far away to iden-tify, but he counted nine. Who would be dumb enough to roast in the sun by the front gate? Not merchants. Even from a distance he could tell they had no wagons.

He'd find out who they were soon enough. Hopefully they'd have the sense to run when he warned them.

Forty-five minutes later Abin finally recognized their welcoming committee. The high priests of all the temples save the Binder's along with three others in dark robes. One looked like the assassins' guild master. He shook his head at the stupid thought. The followers of archangels and demon lords didn't play nicely together.

The priests parted and Abin reined in. While the gates slowly clanked open he said, "You need to run. Prince Nord has joined with a powerful, evil force and is only minutes behind us."

"We are aware," Amane said. "The archangels commanded us to defeat The Void's agent. We will stop him here."

Abin chewed his lip and finally said, "I don't know that all of you combined will be enough. I mean no disrespect, Priestess, but I've seen Nord's new power and it is unlike anything I've ever experienced."

"We are aware." Amane repeated, looking more resigned than determined. "If we fail, use the time we buy to get the princess to safety. She is the key to ending The Void's threat. Hurry now. He's getting closer."

Abin didn't need to be told twice. He thumped his weary camel in the ribs and hurried through the partially open gate. As soon as he passed through, it started clanking shut. Good, the wall guards must have been told to keep them sealed. No people crowded the streets despite the hour. Hopefully word had gone out to stay out of sight and hunker down.

Nord had no reason to want to hurt the people of the city as long as they stayed out of his way.

"Permission to rejoin my unit?" Harl asked.

"Granted. Warn them not to try and interfere with Nord in

any way. Nothing they could do would hurt him, so they'd be dying for nothing."

"I'll be persuasive." Harl nodded and led the other soldiers back toward their barracks.

Abin hoped he succeeded, but whether he did or not, Abin had his own problems to deal with. When he reached the palace, the guards opened the outer gate for him without issue. He drove his exhausted mount right to the palace gates, leapt off, and hurried up the steps as fast as his weary legs would permit.

Again, the guards let him in without issue and he made his way directly to the throne room. He sent a silent prayer to any listening angel that he found Vilos there as he had no energy left to search.

Heaven must have heard him as he found the sultan, not seated on his throne, but stalking around the throne room like a caged lion. A scowl creased his face and he muttered something Abin didn't catch.

"Majesty?"

Vilos turned to face him and smiled with relief. "You've finally returned, old friend. Thank heaven. Though from the state of you I can't think your mission went well. Some things have happened since you left and I need your advice."

"I will be happy to advise you in any way I can, but my report must come first."

Vilos's smile vanished. "Very well. Speak."

Abin told him about Nord and the new power he wielded as well as about the priests guarding the city. "Did they not send someone to the palace to warn you?"

Vilos's face twisted in annoyance. "No, perhaps the recent tension made them think twice. Either that or in their arrogance they think dealing with my brother will be no problem. Whatever their reason, this is the first I've heard about it."

"I beg you to take Shara and flee as far and fast as you can. Nothing will stop your brother, not even the combined might of the high priests. At least that is my opinion. If they prove me wrong, so much the better."

"How did my brother come by this new power?"

Abin shook his head. "I wish I knew. It's the same as what the goblin used to kill our guards, so I'm forced to assume that both the goblin and now Nord serve the same master."

"Perhaps it's The Void the sorcerer spoke of. If it learned of Shara's new power, that would explain much."

Vilos seemed to be talking more to himself than Abin. Thoroughly confused he asked, "The priests mentioned The Void, Majesty. It's not something I'd heard of before. They also advised me to get Shara to safety should they fail to stop your brother."

"I see. As I said, there's a matter I need your advice about. Daktari returned shortly after you left to hunt down the goblin. He came to teach Shara about her power and how to use it. He says she's the world's best hope to seal away an ancient power called The Void before it and its servants can free Balthis and destroy the world. Sounds like the priests agree. That makes me feel a little better about his intentions."

"If this is what you wanted advice about, I fear I have little to offer. How has he behaved?"

Vilos smiled and shook his head. "That's the strange thing. Since he arrived and offered to teach Shara at the palace, I couldn't have asked for a more polite guest. He's been far more pleasant than most of the visiting dignitaries we entertain. Not that we've spent a great deal of time in each other's presence. Shara tells me he's a patient teacher, which is a shock. She actually seems to enjoy their lessons, though sometimes she seems frustrated at her lack of growth."

"Much as I despise what the sorcerer did, I'm forced to

admit that I can think of no one better suited to teach her to use some rare magic. But let us not be distracted. You still need to flee. Daktari should be able to transport the three of you virtually anywhere in the world. He can take you somewhere safe, or at least far enough away that Nord will need months to reach you. As far as I can tell, he's forced to walk everywhere he goes."

"I hate to flee my home yet again, but I will speak to him. As for you, find somewhere to rest, well away from the palace. Clear everyone out. Even if Nord destroys the entire building, the people will be safe. We rebuilt once and we can do it again."

Abin blew out a sigh. Vilos had taken that better than he'd feared. While putting the lives of the sultan and princess in the hands of a one-time enemy rankled, Daktari's power should help ensure their safety, which mattered more than anything.

"I will see to it, Majesty." A distant roar filled the air. "He's here. Please, hurry and escape."

Vilos stood and clapped a hand to Abin's shoulder. "Stay safe, old friend. I'll see you again when this madness is over."

Abin dearly hoped that came to pass. It would mean the world survived.

⸻✧⸻

Daktari stood beside the door to the classroom and waited for Vilos to get closer. The sultan seldom came to visit during their lessons. Despite his repeated assurances that he considered the earlier matter of Vilos's betrayal behind them, there still seemed to be some lingering ill will there. He swallowed a sigh. Some people held grudges, often for far longer than they were useful.

A ripple ran through the ether and a moment later he heard a distant roar. Turning away from the door, he studied the ether. A faint warping appeared and the source drew ever closer. Daktari recognized the shape; someone had used void magic, extremely powerful void magic. It seemed their time here had come to an end.

"What was that?" Shara asked.

"Did you see the ripple?" That would be a first for her.

"No, I felt a weird vibration, like an out-of-tune harp string."

So she really could only interact with the ether by feel. Strange and remarkable. If only he had the time to study her gift properly instead of having to rush.

"A servant of The Void is coming."

Her eyes grew wide and the blood drained from her face. "You can beat whoever it is, right?"

"Doubtful. It looks like whoever has come possesses even greater power than the void knight I faced. That foe cut my magic apart with ease, forcing me to flee. Though galling, the time has come for us to relocate."

Daktari opened the door just before Vilos knocked.

"I hate it when you do that," the sultan said.

"Why should such an inconsequential act bother you so much?"

Vilos waved his hand. "Never mind. Abin has returned and it seems my brother has gained a new, magical body. Given the power Nord displayed, Abin recommends we run for it."

"He is wiser than I expected," Daktari said. *Bane, come.* "It is, indeed, time to leave this place. Fortunately, I have a safe location to which we can retreat. Shara's training is progressing well and soon she will be ready to seal the void pit."

"I will?" she asked in a squeaky, strangled voice.

"Yes. Once you can block my power, it's only a matter of expanding what you can already do to finish the final task. But we can discuss that later." Bane flittered in and landed on his shoulder.

Daktari collected their practice box and slipped it into his satchel. He kept all he brought with him at all times as a matter of course. "Will you be joining us?"

Vilos's face twisted as if he'd like to refuse, but at last he nodded. "I ordered the palace cleared. Nord will find nothing of value when he arrives."

"Then there's no sense in delaying." Daktari concentrated on his rune-marked coin and raised a hand. Ether gathered and swirled and soon a portal formed. "Go, quickly. With The Void's agent twisting the ether, I can't hold this portal for long."

Vilos took his daughter's hand and they leapt through. Daktari followed, a moment later emerging in the bitter cold of the mountains. An effort of will conjured a heated bubble to protect them. He didn't need to maintain it for long. One of the monks opened the secret door that led to the temple.

"Shadow Man, welcome back. Is all well?"

"Not remotely." He bent to retrieve his coin. "The Void has empowered a new champion and I have yet to complete the Divine Key Bearer's training. I will do so at the temple then she will seal the pit."

The monk bowed. "As you say, Shadow Man. Please, follow me."

Shara looked up at him as they passed through the magical door. "Shadow man?"

"It's what the monks call me. They seem to think I'm some prophesied savior since I can use shadow magic. The name is irrelevant save that it makes it easier to come and go from the temple."

The passage through the portal took only moments and they

found themselves in the temple hall. Vilos and Shara gaped around but he ignored them. The decorations were plain enough, no doubt their magical arrival more than the decor startled them.

"Do you wish to speak with Abbot?" their guide asked.

"Not particularly, but I suppose I should update him. What I really need is a quiet room where my pupil and I can study. Preferably one with an adjoining room for her father."

"That is no problem, Shadow Man. We have many more rooms than we have brothers. I wonder sometimes if your predecessor foresaw a larger order than we have now, or if he simply decided bigger was better."

Daktari couldn't have cared less what the first Shadow Man thought as long as his requirements were met.

They walked through the silent halls until the monk stopped in front of a pair of doors that looked exactly like all the other doors they'd passed. He pushed both open revealing a pair of identical monk's cells. The rooms held little beyond cots, tables, and a single chair each.

"Will this do?" When Daktari nodded he said, "I will let Abbot know you've returned. No doubt he will arrive shortly to speak with you."

The monk bowed and took his leave.

"This place is a maze," Vilos said. "How do you find your way around?"

"I usually let the monks guide me." Daktari pointed and the chair from Vilos's room floated out and into the study chamber. "We may as well wait for Abbot to arrive before we resume your studies."

"Where are we anyway?" Vilos sat in the spare chair. Shara looked at him as well, clearly curious.

"The Temple of Soom in the Black Ice Mountains." Daktari conjured a magical chair and dropped into it. Bane hopped down to his knee and he stroked the homunculus between the wings until he trilled.

"I've never heard of either place," Vilos said.

"I'm not surprised considering we're about five thousand miles north of the High Kingdom. I'd never heard of the temple myself before this business with the Divine Key began and I got serious about researching." A knock sounded, saving him from further conversation. "Come in."

The door opened and Abbot waddled in. Daktari would have sworn he'd gotten fatter during his brief absence, but that seemed impossible.

"Welcome back, Shadow Man. Is one of these the bearer of the Divine Key?"

Shara raised her hand like a nervous student. "I am."

"Welcome, my dear. We all have the highest hopes for you. If you can end the threat of The Void for thousands of years, it would truly be a glorious thing."

"I'll do my best, sir."

"Has the situation here changed?" Daktari asked.

"No. The voidlings continue their endless, pointless attacks and we endure the noise as we must." A thud and explosion sounded as if to punctuate his statement. "How fare things in the outer world?"

Daktari told him about Nord and his new armor. "Are you familiar with it?"

"Not specifically, but void artifacts are not unknown to us. I will search the Manuscript of The Void for any references. When will you and the bearer descend to the pit?"

"She needs more practice. At least a few more days. How far is the entrance?"

"Not far, perhaps an hour or two on foot." Abbot shook his head, setting his chins to jiggling. "I still can't believe the first

Shadow Man built the temple so close. Not that I would dare question his wisdom."

"Of course not. Please let me know what you find out about the armor and if you could have some food brought, that would be helpful."

"Certainly." Abbot bowed to Shara and her father. "It is simple fare, but filling. Please enjoy your stay in the temple. Best of luck to you, bearer."

When Abbot had gone Shara asked, "What now?"

"Now we get back to work. You have a world to save after all."

———�֍———

With his new powers, Nord could sense the fear coming off his brother's pet wizard as he and his pathetic soldiers fled. He reveled in their terror of what he'd become. Every day he made sure to gain on them, but only a little. Drawing out the chase amused him and he thought increased his strength.

Or maybe he just needed the time to get used to his new body. He found the enchanted armor's movements far more sluggish than a flesh-and-blood body. He certainly wouldn't have wanted to get in a sword fight with anyone. On the other hand, he seriously doubted anyone with a sword could even scratch him. He also no longer felt hungry, tired, or thirsty. Not surprising since he'd been transformed from man to metal.

Not that he'd want his old body back even if someone offered it to him. For all its faults, the power surging through the armor made even the mighty sorcerer seem weak.

Ahead of him, Sultan's Oasis appeared out of the sands.

From a distance it appeared they'd repaired the main gate. Pity, he'd have to knock it down again.

Nord squinted against the shimmering waves coming off the sand. Yet another good thing about this new body: the heat didn't trouble him in the least. The magic even protected the skin of his face.

Were there people standing around outside the city? You'd think some kind of sight enhancing magic would be included with the armor. Well, whoever they were, they'd soon get out of his way or wish they had.

Distances in the desert often deceived and at his clanking pace it took most of an hour to reach the base of the wall. Now that they were closer, he finally saw who waited for him. A small group of men and women, each of them dressed in fine robes, though some in white and others in black. He sensed their power, but his own dwarfed them by orders of magnitude.

He stopped and crossed his metal arms. "Stand aside. My business isn't with you."

One of the men stepped forward. On his chest he wore an amulet shaped like an upside-down sword, the symbol of Branik the Sword Lord. If this one was a priest, then the rest no doubt were as well.

"In the archangels' names, you are commanded to turn aside. Refuse and face Heaven's wrath."

"Look at me!" Nord shouted. "Do you think I fear Heaven's wrath? Where was Heaven and your precious archangels when I was screaming in pain? Nowhere! The Void take you all!"

He thrust his hands forward and black flames gushed out in a river.

The priest leapt ten feet straight up, avoiding the blast.

A golden blade appeared and hacked at Nord.

The instant it touched his armor it shattered into glowing motes.

He shifted his aim, spraying the black flames at the other priests.

Each of them dodged or vanished as their magical ability dictated. All save one. A single arrogant man raised his own hand and sent blue flames tinged with black rushing to meet Nord's.

He actually felt an instant of resistance before The Void's fire pushed through and reduced the man to nothing.

More spells struck him only to be instantly negated. He lost track of the sorts of magic they used to try and slay him only to fail miserably.

Much like Abin's fear, he reveled in their shock and horror as the power of their collective masters failed to so much as scratch him. Watching the great and powerful reduced to helplessness pleased him a great deal.

He spread his hands apart, trying to burn away a pair of women who ran in opposite directions. When he did, a dark figure appeared right in front of him.

Instead of a spell, he found himself staring down a black metal dagger. It seemed to happen in slow motion. The needle-sharp tip drew ever closer, finally plunging into his right eye up to the hilt.

He roared, more in outrage than pain. In fact, he felt nothing despite having six inches of steel in his brain.

Tiring of the game, he thrust both hands out and sent a wall of fire roaring in every direction.

He felt some of the priests die, but couldn't decide if he got them all. When the flames vanished, nothing remained beyond blackened sand. Maybe some escaped. He neither knew nor cared. The path now lay clear in front of him.

Nord ripped the dagger out of his eye and tossed it aside.

His vision remained exactly the same despite the lack of a right eye. As he stalked toward the closed gates, he expected a pelting rain of arrows, but nothing happened. A quick glance confirmed that no guards manned the battlements. No doubt Abin had ordered them all to safety.

He didn't mind. Regardless of what had happened to him, he held no particular ill will toward men simply doing their duty. Another part of him, The Void part no doubt, wanted to send everyone to oblivion.

When his fingers touched the wooden gate, black flames roared out and disintegrated an opening big enough for him to walk through.

No traps waited on the other side. In fact, King's Way didn't have a soul in sight.

Enough delay. He marched straight to the palace through the eerily silent city. He felt the people watching. Their lives burned like tiny candles and their fear eased his frustration. Soon enough he would have his niece then he would make a new bargain with The Void. Instead of a return to nothingness, he wanted to keep his new body and have a continent to rule. A small-enough price for capturing the one it seemed so concerned about.

Someone had thrown the gate to the palace wall wide open. Again not a single guard opposed him.

Though he no longer had a stomach, a queasy feeling filled him. No way would Vilos simply let him stride through the palace and take his precious daughter. His brother should be fighting tooth and nail to stop him. Wizards, guards, the army, everything should be here.

He shoved the palace doors open and shouted. "Vilos! Face me, brother."

Nothing. He sensed no life in the palace and no magic that might be hiding them.

He stomped through the silent halls to the equally empty throne room. A sense of overwhelming exhaustion washed through him and he sat on the throne before he collapsed.

Now what should he do?

YOU WILL WAIT AND BE READY. WHEN THE GIRL APPEARS YOU WILL WASTE NO MORE TIME. SEIZE HER AND BRING HER TO A TEMPLE OF BALTHIS. I HAVE INDULGED YOUR ARROGANCE LONG ENOUGH.

Nord's head ached and his ears rang from the power of The Void's voice.

"Even if she appears," Nord dared say. "This body is so slow, I'll never reach her in time to do any good."

FOOL! SHE HAS ONLY ONE PURPOSE, TO SEAL MY VOID PITS. WHEN SHE TRIES, I WILL TAKE YOU THROUGH THE PIT.

"You can do that?"

I AM THE VOID! I CAN DO ANYTHING!

Except, apparently, seize his niece on its own.

"I will be ready."

CHAPTER 7

Lawton watched from a raft consisting of an intact chunk of his ship's hull as Archibald's ship sailed away along with his hopes of living through his next encounter with Captain Crow. *The Glaive* had been reduced to so much flotsam. He'd heard about sea serpents of course, every sailor had, but seeing that one's power made him think perhaps Lotta had been right about drawing Dagon's wrath. Besides the piece of hull he'd ended up on, there seemed to be little enough of use drifting around. They'd gotten damn lucky that the serpent only wanted to stop them and not kill them all outright.

A splash and gasp drew his attention to the left. A sputtering Jerrod flailed as he tried to keep his head above water. His ridiculous top hat still somehow remained on his head. Lawton debated letting the little rat drown but then got a better idea. If he laid the blame for Archibald's escape at Jerrod's feet, maybe the captain wouldn't kill him.

He shifted over, grabbed Jerrod by the scruff of the neck, and yanked him aboard his makeshift raft.

"Thank you," Jerrod said between gasps. "I feared I might drown."

"Why didn't you call your monster to save you?" Lawton asked.

"She can still smell the serpent. Until the scent dissipates, she won't come close. What do we do now?"

"Sir!" Lawton turned to see eight men in the ship's dinghy rowing toward them. A pretty sight indeed. "We feared you were lost."

"It'll take more than a sea serpent to kill me." When they got close enough Lawton climbed in, dragging Jerrod along with him. "Are you lads everyone?"

"Everyone we've found so far, sir," one of the men said. "What are your orders?"

Lawton thought for a moment. If the men still looked to him for orders, then he hadn't lost them completely. Slowly his plan crystalized.

"Now we take one more pass around the wreckage to make sure no one else survived. Once that's done, Jerrod's going to have his beast tow us to Shadow Point. We need to report back to Captain Crow."

The guys all shared nervous looks. He didn't blame them. The thought of facing the captain made Lawton nervous as well.

"Is that a good idea, sir?" a different sailor asked.

"Maybe, maybe not, but can you imagine what he'll do if we try to run and he catches up to us later? Better we face it straight on. If we're lucky, hopefully he'll only break up the crew and distribute us on other ships."

He didn't speculate on what he'd do if they weren't lucky. Everyone knew the captain's temper.

They circled the ship one last time and picked up a solitary survivor, the ship's cabin boy, a vicious little monster Lawton held high hopes for.

They watched the sharks circle for most of an hour before they all vanished as one. Lawton didn't need another hint. He took a firm hold on the back of Jerrod's neck.

"That beast of yours does anything other than take us to Shadow Point and I'll snap your neck, get me?"

Jerrod let out an exhausted sigh. "I understand my situation perfectly, Lawton. Your constant threats aren't necessary. Once we reach your base, you'll release me, right?"

"That'll be up to the captain, but as far as I know, you two have no bad blood."

"No. Crow's marauders are good customers and Black Rat Cove doesn't function without me. We have a mutually beneficial relationship."

"Then you have nothing to worry about. Let's get going."

Something bumped the hull and the next thing he knew they were skimming the water far faster than even the fastest sailing ship. Shadow Point waited southeast and at this rate they'd arrive in less than a day.

Lawton knew the beast had to be strong since it turned ships bigger than *The Glaive*, but he never imagined it could swim so fast. If they tamed a dozen of the creatures the fleet would be unstoppable. He immediately thought of Lotta, but he doubted his great aunt would have anything to do with them after they interfered with Dagon's plans, whatever they were.

"Where'd you find this thing anyway?" Lawton asked.

Jerrod got a wistful look. "Before I founded Black Rat Cove, I dove for pearls. One day a shark came sniffing around the grounds. In desperation I swam into a cave and inside found an air bubble. Thanking the archangels, I settled in to wait in the hopes that the shark might find something else to eat. As I looked around, I spotted a glow. It looked like an egg and when I touched it, it cracked open. Out crawled a tiny little creature no bigger than my thumb."

"It seems to have grown," Lawton said.

"Indeed. Perhaps when I touched the egg a psychic bond formed. I can't say for sure. I've even spoken to wizards about it and they hadn't a clue. Anyway, in five minutes she went from the size of my thumb to the size of my arm. An hour after that she'd grown twice as big as the shark which served as her first meal. We've been together ever since."

Lawton grunted. Some people got all the luck. For as long as he could remember, his luck had been nothing but bad. Hopefully that would change soon and he'd survive his meeting with Captain Crow. If he had to throw Jerrod overboard to survive, he wouldn't feel too bad about it.

.—☆

Shadow Point got its name from the shattered lighthouse that sat on a rocky point jutting out into the ocean. Jungle covered the bulk of the island, just like all the other islands in this part of the ocean. None of the pirates he knew bothered with the interior. All the dangerous animals had been eliminated before Lawton joined the fleet, so nothing remained worth hunting.

He shaded his eyes against the sun. Instead of casting light, the broken tower now only cast a shadow. Like most pirates. Lawton didn't have a romantic bone in his body, so he focused on the deep-water bay surrounded by keel-crushing rocks. Catapults defended the opening so any pirate hunter stupid enough to try something would soon end up on the bottom of the ocean.

In the safety of the bay, the pirates had built a sort of dry dock where they could repair ships damaged on raids. Huts and larger buildings dotted the sandy beach. If *The Glaive* had been his first real home, Shadow Point was his second. Lawton tried not to dwell on how depressing that sounded.

From a distance he counted five ships tied up at the piers, including *The Murderer's Nest*, a monstrous galleon with a crew of nearly two hundred and four heavy catapults. He'd kind of hoped to find Captain Crow out hunting, but as usual his luck was sour. On the other hand, at least he wouldn't have to keep Jerrod under lock and key until the captain returned.

One way or the other, his fate would soon be settled.

"I didn't realize the fleet had such a large operation here," Jerrod said.

"We've got the basics, though we lack the diversions of Black Rat Cove."

"I appreciate that as it would cut into business considerably if I had to compete with you."

Lawton snorted a laugh. The late Captain Gray Carnage claimed the island and built the fleet of pirates into the terror of the ocean. He'd been a warrior to his soul and refused to have anything that might weaken the men's spirits on Shadow Point, though being a pirate captain, he understood that the men needed a release now and then thus the deal with Black Rat Cove.

Now the lunatic Crow ran things. He shook his head. Maybe he should have retired with the old timers when Carnage died. Or maybe gone straight. He shuddered at the thought. Honest work didn't pay nearly as well as piracy nor was it as much fun. Most days at least.

But too late now.

"Have your pet leave us about half a mile from the barrier wall. We don't want the lookouts getting nervous and sinking us accidentally."

"An excellent idea," Jerrod said.

A few minutes later the dinghy slowed then drifted forward on its momentum. With two guys on each oar they made good time to the gap between the outcroppings.

"Halt and identify yourself!" the much-amplified voice of the wizard on duty said.

"It's Lawton! I need to speak with Captain Crow."

"Thank heaven," the wizard said, his voice now much lower. "He's been ranting about your mission since five minutes after you left. Given that you're in a dinghy and not *The Glaive*, I can't help thinking you don't have good news. Either way it's none of my business. Proceed."

The guys started rowing again and soon enough they were tied up to the berth reserved for his now-sunken ship. Lawton blew out a breath. He'd served on *The Glaive* for twenty years, first as a mate then as her captain. Losing her to a sea serpent in under a minute stung more than he'd ever admit.

He climbed out onto the dock and brought Jerrod with him. No sense delaying. He'd go straight to *The Murderer's Nest* and make his report.

"Do you want us to come with you?" one of his men asked in a tone that suggested he really hoped not.

"No, lads. If worst comes to worst, better if you're not there. Should I not make it back, you scatter and if anyone asks you never served with me. Understood?"

"Aye, sir. Good luck to you."

Lawton nodded. He'd take every bit of luck he could get.

Only three slips separated their berth from the captain's and less than a minute after tying up they stood at the gangplank. At the top looking down at them stood Dandan, Crow's first mate, a great barrel of a man with sun-darkened skin and not a hair on his body.

"Lawton!" Dandan said. "Thank Dagon you're back. Please tell me you got him."

"Afraid not, Dandan. Archibald gave us the slip with the help of some outsiders. Is he on board?"

"Yeah, pity for you. Come ahead. No sense delaying the inevitable."

Lawton nudged Jerrod ahead of him and stomped up the ramp. He'd barely set foot on deck when a lithe, handsome man dressed all in black emerged from below deck. Captain Crow looked very much like his namesake, right down to the narrow, sharp nose and eyes like black marbles. At his side hung a single-handed arming sword with a cross guard that ended in skulls and a matching pommel.

"Welcome back, Lawton," Crow said, his voice low and cold. It sounded like all the human emotion had been drained out of him. "Did you complete your mission?"

"No, Captain. Archibald escaped with the help of some strangers."

Captain Crow moved closer, his hand drifting near the hilt of his sword. "What strangers?"

"I don't know, but they had a sea serpent with them. Damn thing sank *The Glaive* and took half my crew."

Crow rested his hand on the hilt of his sword and caressed it. "You were right. It seems Dagon has gotten involved."

"That's what Lotta said before she jumped ship. How did you know?"

"What?" The captain looked at him as if suddenly remembering he was there.

"Dagon, sir. Lotta said he wanted Archibald to get away and that we shouldn't interfere. She didn't say why the demon lord cared about the fate of our former bookkeeper, but he wouldn't heal Gunner when she asked."

"I wasn't speaking to you, Lawton. The demon lord's

involvement in this matter is a complication I don't need."
Crow turned to Jerrod. "And why are you here?"

Jerrod nodded toward Lawton. "He dragged me along so
my pet would pull his dinghy here. If we're finished, I'd like to
return to Black Rat Cove."

Crow stroked his pale, hairless chin. "Could your pet not
have stopped Archibald's escape?"

"As I explained to Lawton, she's no match for the serpent.
In fact, it terrified her so much I couldn't even get her to come
close."

"I see. Then you are of no use to me." Crow drew his sword
and black flames ran down the length.

"No!" Jerrod shouted.

A moment later a creature from a sailor's nightmare burst
out of the water. It looked like an eel with claws like a crab.

The monster swung a claw at Crow who calmly slashed his
sword, slicing the claw off at the first joint.

Jerrod and his monster both howled in pain.

The captain took a step closer and swung again, this time
sending a wave of black flames at the monster. They burned
it in half and both pieces slid back into the water out of
sight.

Jerrod dropped to the deck, his mouth open and expression
slack. His chest no longer moved.

"Kill one, kill both, interesting." Crow sheathed his sword
and Lawton relaxed a fraction. "You will join me on *The
Murderer's Nest*. When the time comes, you will have a chance
to redeem yourself. Fail me again, and you can join Jerrod."

Crow kicked the corpse off his deck to splash into the sea.
"Dandan, ready the fleet! We're sailing for Dragon Isle."

Lawton stared into the water. Crow had dealt with the
monster like it was nothing. If he could handle the serpent as
easily, maybe they had a chance.

Dandan clamped a powerful hand on Lawton's shoulder. "Today's your lucky day. Time to get to work."

Lawton didn't feel lucky, but at least he'd survived.

CHAPTER 8

Amane felt the others die an instant before the contingency spell she'd precast whisked her to safety. She gagged and retched in the shadow of the city wall. Traveling through the ether often left her sick and when it happened suddenly in response to a lethal danger, well, good thing she didn't have a big breakfast. Some way away, but still too close for comfort, she felt Prince Nord stalking through the city. His presence felt like a vortex swirling the ether. No doubt that hadn't done her stomach any good either.

At least she sensed no one else dying. She took some solace from that despite failing the mission her patron set her. Closing her eyes, she found her link to the archangel every bit as strong as usual. It seemed her failure hadn't cost her that connection, not yet at least.

She spit one last time and wiped her mouth with the back of her hand. Not exactly behavior appropriate for a high priestess, but today she didn't care.

"Feeling better?"

She spun and found the master of the Reaper's Guild leaning against the wall, one foot flat against it, his black cloak seeming undamaged by the blast. He seemed no worse for the near-death experience.

"How did you survive?"

"That same way you did, I assume; I took precautions. While my master may revel in death, I prefer he not revel in mine, not yet at least."

"Has he spoken to you? The Queen of Coins remains silent. I can only assume that means she expects me to continue to try and defeat Nord, if such a thing is even possible."

"No, the Reaper hasn't spoken to me again. As for the former prince, I'm not certain he's actually alive. I drove six inches of black iron into his brain and he didn't so much as flinch. No living being could survive that."

"I'm willing to take your word for it. When it comes to killing, I doubt I'll find a more knowledgeable expert." She'd meant that last as an insult, but he just smiled and offered a little bow. "If we can't kill him, how do we defeat him?"

"As he is now, I'm not certain we can. No magic we can conjure will harm him and if a dagger to the brain didn't kill him, we can assume weapons are of equally little use."

She frowned. "How do you know all this? The weapons' uselessness is clear, but why assume our magic won't work?"

"I know all this, as you put it, because unlike you fools flinging spells at random, I watched to see what happened. That black armor generates a field that repels the ether. Since all of our spells work through the ether…"

"None of them will reach him. Okay, what if we dropped a building or something on him?"

He shrugged. "Do you know a spell that will drop a building on him?"

"No." She growled a little but if he noticed her annoyance, he gave no sign.

"Neither do I. Priestly magic tends to work in more subtle ways. At least mine does. In fact, I doubt there are more than a handful of wizards capable of such a feat. No, if we are to defeat Nord and complete our masters' task, we will have to wait, watch, and strike at the correct moment."

"But strike how?" She threw her hands up. "You just said none of our weapons or magic can harm him."

"None of ours can, but there are other weapons in the city. I believe the key to defeating him is to separate his head from the armor. To do that, we'll need a mithril blade. Obviously, I have none at the guild. Mithril is anathema to demon follow-ers. I couldn't wield a mithril sword even if we had one."

Amane stared at him. "Don't look at me. I'm no warrior."

"A fact I'm well aware of. I suggest we recruit the champion of Branik's temple. Surely the sword lord's champion will be the finest warrior in the city. With the high priest dead, you could even argue that it fell to the champion to complete their patron's task."

"I can approach the temple and request an audience," Amane said. "But even if I convince the champion to battle Nord, where will we get a mithril sword?"

"Leave that to me. Meet me at the Marble Elephant within sight of the palace's north wall."

Amane nodded. She'd visited the inn many times to socialize with wealthy merchants and nobles, all of whom were eager to receive the queen's blessing. "Very well. What is your name? If we're to work together, it would be nice to know."

"I am Nadir. Pleasure to formally make your acquaintance, Amane."

She felt no surprise at hearing him use her name. Unlike

the assassin, she worked openly in the city. Most people knew her. "I'll meet you at the inn, hopefully with the champion."

—※—

Nadir Graves left the idiot high priestess standing in the wall's shadow and turned toward the guild hall. As the master of the Reaper's Guild, he hated relying on anyone or anything save his own skill, but the assassins had always enjoyed a less-than-cordial relationship with Branik's followers. Strange when you considered they both served masters that wanted them to kill. Granted the archangel tended to favor honorable combat and all that nonsense, but the point still held.

And his problems didn't end there. Just touching mithril without the proper protections would sicken him. Still, he doubted any other metal would do the job. His black-iron dagger, basically the demonic equivalent of mithril, hadn't killed Nord, so only one option remained.

Halfway to the hall a dark figure draped in flowing black robes, his face concealed by a deep cowl, stepped out of the shadows and bowed. "Master, the target has reached the palace and entered. We detected no signs of battle."

"The sultan?"

"Unknown. Our spies didn't see him leave when the court wizard fled. We have also seen no sign of the princess."

"They probably used the emergency escape portal." Nadir smiled to himself. If Vilos found out he knew about the escape portal he'd doubtless be horrified. "A prudent decision given the power of their foe. Return and observe. Under no circumstances make yourself known. Should Nord detect your presence, flee immediately. You're no match for the former prince."

"As you command, Master." The assassin stepped into the shadows.

To anyone else it would seem the man vanished into thin air, but Nadir heard his faint footsteps as he sprinted away. The youthful assassin would have to work on his technique. Silent movement served as one of the foundations of their skill set.

Putting the training of his followers out of his mind, Nadir continued toward the slums. Today even the alleys were empty of bums. Word of the danger must have gotten around. It never ceased to amaze him how well informed the city's poor stayed. He'd found many uses for that informal network over the years, though he doubted any of them knew anything that might make his current problem go away.

Nord would have no reason to bother with the people here. As a former noble, he probably considered them no more valuable than the refuse littering the ground. Nadir had little enough use for people, but his disdain came from a professional place. He had as little use for the rich as the poor. Generally, as far as Nadir was concerned, people fell into two categories, potential targets and potential patrons. And just because you were in the latter group today didn't mean you wouldn't end up in the former tomorrow.

The nobility simply seemed to consider anyone of lower status of lower value. A rather dubious worldview given the value of some of the nobles he'd met.

He reached the butcher shop without meeting another soul. Inside the butcher lowered his gaze. "Master."

"Anything I need to know?"

"All has been quiet." He looked up from his bloody boots then immediately dropped his gaze again. "How did the battle go?"

Nadir snorted. "It wasn't a battle. We couldn't even hurt

him. But I haven't given up. If the Reaper wishes him dead, then die he will, one way or another."

He left the butcher and ducked into the meat locker. One of his wards tingled as he passed through and descended the narrow steps to his office. Inside, his second sat at the desk, no doubt trying it on for size on the off chance he ended up dead.

The slender, beautiful woman sprang to her feet, long dark hair flying, and bowed. "I'm pleased you've returned unharmed, Master."

"You are a terrible liar, Ashera. Ready Team One. We'll be departing in two minutes."

"I thought you meant to complete the Reaper's mission on your own."

Nadir stared at her until she lowered her gaze. "Forgive my presumption, Master. We will be waiting outside when you're ready."

"Good."

Ashera slipped out of the office and Nadir finally allowed himself a faint smile. She so badly wanted to take his place. And while she had the skill to do the mundane tasks of a guild master, she lacked the will to challenge him. Just as well since he still had the Reaper's full favor and would slaughter her in seconds.

He moved behind the desk and touched the wall in two places. A faint red glow appeared and a section of wall vanished. Beyond it, a small niche held a thin folio. He pulled it out and stroked the worn leather. The Book of Secrets. Every guild had one. The book held potentially useful details about the city in which they operated.

Flipping through it he soon came to the page he sought. The El Marids, a merchant family of no particular distinction. Ordinarily they wouldn't even merit a mention in the book, but once upon a time, they had been far richer and more powerful. They also collected rare and valuable items and despite falling on tough times, they'd sold none of them.

Here it was, the Summer Sword. Two-handed longsword with a pommel shaped like the sun. Most importantly, a blade made of mithril, one of only two known to have appeared in the city. And with the second now missing, the only one currently present. With any luck they'd be reasonable and hand the weapon over. If not, well, he and Team One would have little trouble changing their minds.

. —✧-

A mane took a deep breath to steady herself as she approached the white marble wall surrounding Branik's temple. The fortress-like temple looked far more intimidating in the daylight with the sun gleaming off its white walls. Had it truly only been half a day since the high priests all met to plan Nord's defeat? They'd been so full of confidence, misplaced confidence.

Though hardly warlike, the Queen of Coins offered her many potent abilities, all of which proved useless against the former prince. She felt like a petulant child tugging on her father's pant leg, only less effective. She shook her head. At least she survived. None of the other high priests managed that feat. Too arrogant to cast a basic contingency spell no doubt.

Unfortunately for her, all she had to rely on now was the leader of the Reaper's Guild who she wouldn't turn her back on for all the gold in the royal treasury. If she failed to convince Branik's champion to help her, Amane seriously doubted they had any hope of victory.

A guard must have spotted her approach as the front gate opened slowly ahead of her. A pair of underpriests, one man and one woman, both in their midtwenties, dressed in steel-gray robes and sporting amulets with the inverted sword symbol of Branik, waited for her. They bowed as one.

"Welcome, Amane, High Priestess of the Queen of Coins." The man spoke in an even tone, polite but not deferential. She had no authority here and needed to remember that.

"If you have come to tell us of Master Ibreem's death, we have already received word from Lord Branik himself," the woman added.

"I did come to tell you that, but I also need to speak with your champion. The mission given us by our patrons remains unfinished and I require aid to complete it."

"The champion prays in the central chapel and has since word of Master Ibreem's death reached us," he said. The underpriests moved aside. "Enter and be welcome. I will guide you to the chapel."

Amane bowed and fell in behind the male priest. They marched toward the temple, an ugly, box-like building that looked more like a prison than a place of worship. Beyond the doors, a short passage led to the central chapel. It held an altar draped with gray silk, with the sword symbol of Branik embroidered in black. Behind the altar stood a black stone statue of an inverted sword.

Branik's champion rose from one knee and turned to face them. The woman wore shining mail and a gray cloak. On her right hip hung a plain steel arming sword devoid of decoration. It looked like a weapon made for war which made perfect sense given who she worshipped.

Her glowering, angry face showed nothing feminine. "You are Amane, High Priestess of the Queen of Coins. Does courage or arrogance bring you here after you abandoned our master in battle?"

"Neither, Champion. Desperation brings me here. Together we all failed to complete the archangels' quest. Only two survived the encounter. No magic cast through the ether can touch Nord. That leaves a physical confrontation as our only hope of victory. I'm no warrior. In a clash of blades, I wouldn't last a second. You, on the other hand, are the finest sword-master in the city. I ask you to take up your master's quest and help us defeat Nord."

"You speak well, as expected of a merchant. Who else survived?"

Amane kept her face impassive. Now came the part she'd been dreading. "The Reaper's guild master."

"Of course, another coward. I warned Master Ibreem not to go into battle with the followers of the demon lords. He should have mobilized the temple and gone to battle with trustworthy allies beside him. Now you wish me to make the same mistake."

"Our mistake," Amane said with excess patience, "was not understanding our enemy. Had Ibreem brought the entire temple, you all would have died needlessly. Had his pride allowed him to use a basic contingency spell, Ibreem would have survived as well. But it didn't and he's dead. Now those of us who survived must complete the task. Hate the assassin. Blame me for Ibreem's death. I don't care in the least. All that matters is completing the mission. If you refuse to help me, say so now. There are other warriors, even if they are of lesser quality."

"Strong words and correct ones. Were he here, Master Ibreem would tell me the same thing. My grief can wait; Branik's quest cannot. Where is the assassin? I presume he has a plan."

"He's gone to retrieve a mithril sword so you can use it to separate Nord's head from his magical armor. We're to meet him at the Marble Elephant." Seeing her confused expression Amane added, "It's the city's finest inn."

"I know it. Master Ibreem had me accompany him to several events there. I was wondering where in the city he might find a mithril sword. The sultan's enchanted shamshir is the only one I knew of."

Amane shrugged. "Heaven knows. Shall we depart? If we must wait, why not at the inn?"

"So be it. I will use the assassin's weapon to avenge my master or die trying."

⸻

Nadir and his subordinates made their way through the quiet streets toward the El Marid compound. Despite the family's fall from grace, they'd somehow managed to retain ownership of a sprawling estate in the noble district within sight of the palace. The current head of the household, Ali, must know people high up in the government. No doubt that's how he ended up recently marrying the princess's childhood companion. Assuming he did nothing stupid in the next fifteen minutes, Nadir saw a prosperous future for the El Marid family.

They stopped fifty yards from the low stone wall surrounding the compound. No guards patrolled the grounds; the family lacked the funds to hire them. It seemed strange to Nadir, standing out in the open like this in broad daylight. Usually, they did their work after dark, but today they had no time to spare.

Beside him, Ashera kept darting glances over her shoulder at the palace.

"You feel it, don't you?" Nadir asked. "The wrongness of his presence."

"It's the strangest thing," Ashera said. "Like a scratch I can't quite reach."

Nadir understood exactly what she meant, though to him Nord's presence felt more like a hot coal burning in his brain. That certainly had something to do with the Reaper's desire for him to complete his mission. No one would ever consider his master the gentle sort and nothing short of victory or death would lessen the pain. Lucky for Nadir, he had long ago learned to function through any discomfort.

The remaining four members of Team One looked at each other but didn't speak. They were the best assassins in the guild, his personal enforcers, but none of them were priests and they had no connection to the ether. That would be to their benefit today as they'd have no distractions.

"Alright," he said. "The mission is simple. The El Marids have a mithril sword in their possession. We need it. Since we haven't been paid to kill these people, I'd prefer to complete our task without bloodshed. That said, we're on a tight time-line, so do what you must. Ashera, take two and sweep the grounds. The others will join me in the mansion. With any luck we'll find the sword hanging on a wall and we can just walk out with it."

Ashera smiled. "How much do you want to bet they've got it locked up in some vault deep in the basement?"

Her misplaced cheer did nothing to improve his mood. "Wherever it is, we will find it. Now go."

Ashera and her pair sprinted toward the wall and leapt over it without breaking stride. Nadir came right after and headed straight for the mansion. Normally he would have snuck in a window, but again they didn't have time. He kicked the front door in and strode through into a dusty parlor. A quick look around revealed neither servants nor nobles.

"Search everywhere. Bring anyone you find to me, alive."

"Master," they said in unison before sprinting away.

While his subordinates searched the old-fashioned way,

Nadir would employ more magical means. Mithril had a decidedly negative effect on demon magic. All he had to do was suffuse the area with corruption and see where it didn't stick. That would be the sword's hiding place.

Opening himself fully to the chill, dark presence of the Reaper, Nadir breathed out a black fog. The corruption oozed out, spreading in all directions.

He let his consciousness ride along with it. Room by room, floor by floor it spread. One of his team paused as the darkness swirled around his ankles, but quickly resumed his search. A terrified servant in a filthy smock shuddered as the darkness oozed along past her.

He sensed a presence near his body and willed his consciousness back. The darkness would continue to spread on its own. He'd set the parameters of the spell as the house's outer walls and down to the dirt. He'd check the spell's progress in a moment.

Two people stood before him, a quaking, middle-aged man dressed in dark robes and a gray turban and a pudgy young woman in a pale-blue dress. The master of the house and his blushing bride. Perfect.

The assassin guarding them held a short sword easily in one hand. Clearly, he had no expectation of resistance. An arrogant belief in general, but likely correct in this case.

"I'm pressed for time, so I'll get straight to the point," Nadir said. "Among your collection of antiques is a mithril sword. I want it. Now. Comply and I'll leave you unharmed. I swear this in the Reaper's name. Do anything other than comply and I'll cut off your arms at the elbow and legs at the knee leaving you a helpless stump for the rest of your life."

The scent of urine filled the air as a dark stain spread across the front of Ali's robe. Pathetic, but reassuring. If a mere threat loosened his bladder, the odds of trouble dropped to near zero.

"Please," Ali said. "I don't even know what a mithril sword looks like. I haven't visited the trophy room in years."

Nadir checked his spell and found a small area in the rear section of the basement that retained an area of pure ether. The sword had to be there.

"This trophy room is in the back of the basement, yes?"

"Yes. How could you know that?" Ali asked.

"Doesn't matter." The mansion door opened and Ashera entered with her two teammates. "Perfect timing. Ali and I are going to collect the sword. Keep his darling wife company. Should this clown suddenly grow a spine, cut her eyes out."

Ashera drew a double-edged black-iron dagger. "As you command, Master."

"You wouldn't dare," the woman said. "Shara is my best friend. If you hurt me, nowhere will be safe for you."

Nadir glanced at Ali who gaped in obvious horror. Must be difficult when your wife had more guts than you. Still, he couldn't have her thinking her connection with the princess would protect her. That kind of foolishness got people killed unnecessarily.

"Please understand," Nadir said, his voice calm and even. "The princess and her father have fled the city. And if I decide to kill you, no one will ever find your body."

The blood drained from her face, leaving her bronze skin nearly white. Good, clearly she understood.

Turning back to Ali he said, "After you."

Nadir followed the merchant through the house to a set of stairs leading down. His magic had already revealed everything up to the trophy room, so if Ali thought to lead him into a trap, he'd be very disappointed.

Fortunately, just as Nadir had hoped, Ali went straight to

the spot where his spell failed. An archway led to a room filled with pedestals, each supporting a single item. Nadir had eyes for only one item, a sword with a shining metal blade in the center of the room. The sun-shaped pommel and two-handed grip looked exactly as the book described.

But now he had another problem. More than the mithril blade had stopped his spell. The archway had a ward on it. Nadir couldn't tell exactly what it did, but the shape of the ether still looked sharp and considering how long had passed since this family amounted to anything, the wizard that created it must have been a strong one. While protective magics certainly weren't his specialty, he could at least see the spell well enough to know it didn't do anything lethal.

"Is that the sword you want?" Ali asked.

"It is. Fetch it and I'll be on my way, then you can return to your dreary little life."

When he didn't move instantly, Nadir gave him a shove through the archway. The ward didn't react. Likely the wizard had keyed it to allow members of the family to enter freely. Anything else would have made it too much of a pain when they wanted to bask in their glory.

Ali looked back at him and Nadir gave a none-too-subtle gesture at the sword. The idiot crept forward as if fearing something might leap out at any moment and bite him.

He sent a silent prayer to the Reaper for patience and pulled a pair of black gloves out of a pocket sewn into his cloak. They were woven with black-iron threads and should, in theory, let him touch the mithril sword without getting sickened. He'd never tested them however, so their protection remained hypothetical.

At last Ali stood before the sword. It rested on a simple metal stand that held it upright on the pedestal. The merchant looked back again and Nadir stared back. They had a threat that worried the demon lords sitting alone in the palace waiting for heaven only knew what to happen and he had to deal with this moron. It had to be a test. The Reaper was sitting on his bone throne laughing at him.

"Would you get on with it?" Nadir said.

Ali reached for the sword and the moment his hands rested on the hilt something happened. He straightened like he suddenly developed a backbone. The ether swirled and penetrated Ali's body.

Since the merchant couldn't use magic, at least not as far as Nadir knew, the sword had to be enchanted. The Book of Secrets hadn't mentioned an enchantment, but even his predecessors didn't know everything.

"What's the problem?" Nadir asked, not entirely certain he wanted to know.

"You are the problem." When Ali's mouth moved a different voice spoke. A deeper, more powerful voice. His eyes glowed with a golden light.

Nadir understood now. The sword must have housed a spirit of some sort and now it had taken control of the weak-willed merchant.

"You are mistaken," Nadir said even as he got ready to retreat should it be necessary. "The problem is a servant of The Void that needs to be destroyed. Can you not feel his presence warping the ether? We need the sword to destroy that servant."

Ali pointed the sword at Nadir. "Rest assured that once I've dealt with you and the other demon worshippers, I will defeat that abomination as well."

A brief flash in the ether provided his only warning.

Nadir leapt aside as a searing bolt of holy light shot past him.

His flesh crawled, but he took no damage.

Rolling to his feet, Nadir sprinted for the stairs, Ali's pounding footsteps right on his tail.

Focusing as he ran, Nadir projected his thoughts to the rest of his team. *Scatter and retreat to the guild. I will join you when I'm able.*

Trusting his people to do as he commanded, Nadir ran for the front door.

He dodged right, avoiding another blast. Not daring to look back, he burst into the courtyard and went straight for the wall. If he couldn't take the sword, maybe he could lure Ali into fighting Nord for him.

Gathering ether in his legs, he sprang over the wall and went straight for the palace.

"You won't escape me, villain!" the spirit said through Ali. It had to be an angel of some sort, nothing else would say something so cliche. Despite its power, the spirit clearly inherited the intellect of its host.

He dodged down a road running between a pair of sprawling mansions. The palace waited only a few hundred feet away and according to his spies, no one guarded the walls and the gate stood open. That should make his task easier. Any delay would likely end up with him having to fight the spirit and while he felt certain of his victory, it would be a waste of time and energy.

Through the gate and down the path toward the palace he raced like a sand squirrel from a jackal. The closer he got, the more twisted the ether grew. At this rate casting a spell and getting it to function properly would be a challenge.

At last, he reached the open throne room door and there sat Nord on his brother's throne. He scowled at Nadir then looked past him, presumably at Ali.

Nadir dove and rolled under a swipe of the mithril sword that would have taken his head.

When he came to his feet he asked, "What serves the greater good, continuing to fight me or defeating the monster in front of us?"

Ali narrowed his glowing eyes. "I will deal with you shortly, assassin."

With that pronouncement, he raced directly at Nord.

Nadir waited long enough to see Ali dodge a blast of dark fire and land a ringing blow to Nord's arm before he fled. He needed to collect his allies and revise the plan. And he needed to do it quickly. Possessed by an angelic spirit or not, he held little hope that Ali could defeat Nord.

CHAPTER 9

Nord didn't know the next stage after boredom, but as he sat on the throne surrounded by silence and an empty palace, he felt confident he'd reached it. He'd never been an overly patient man and a new body hadn't changed that. He wanted whatever might happen to happen already.

The throne room door burst open. He recognized the man in black that sprinted into the throne room. The fellow that had stabbed him in the eye outside. Nord had assumed he died with the rest of the priests stupid enough to try and challenge him outside the city. Clearly this one knew a few more tricks than the rest. Nord hated dealing with magic users for exactly this reason. You never knew for sure what they were capable of.

He didn't have a chance to rectify his error when another fool with a death wish entered and tried to cut the first fellow's head off with a shining sword. A golden aura surrounded the newcomer, marking him as another magic user. His day just kept getting worse and worse. On the positive side, his boredom had been relieved.

The priest said something to the swordsman who frowned.

Nord didn't care what they discussed. He stood and clanked down from the throne. He'd kill them both. Slowly. Anything would be better than sitting on the throne and staring at nothing.

The swordsman charged and swung his weapon.

Nord raised an arm to block and the blade clanged off his armor, drawing a wince. That hurt. Nothing had hurt him since he fused with the armor.

A blast of void flames sent the swordsman leaping back.

HE WIELDS A MITHRIL BLADE. NOTHING ELSE COULD DAMAGE MY ARMOR. DO NOT UNDERESTIMATE THIS ENEMY.

The Void's powerful voice caused his head to pound so that he nearly didn't raise his arm fast enough to block a second slash. This time he angled it so he struck the flat of the blade. That seemed sufficient to avoid any damage and more importantly pain.

Instead of a blast, this time he sent a wave of black flames roaring out in all directions. He'd burn them both to oblivion.

"You will not defeat me so easily, pawn of darkness," the swordsman said.

Nord looked up to find his opponent flying near the ceiling. Of the second man he saw no sign. No doubt he took advantage of the opportunity and fled. Clearly the priest had a strong survival instinct.

Blasts of flame rocketed up at the swordsman who dodged them easily. As he'd feared when he first bonded with the armor, the lack of mobility made it difficult to hit a speedy target. If he wanted to defeat this foe, he'd need to try different tactics.

Nord grinned. Now this was better. He'd been born for combat. Hopefully the idiot lasted long enough for his niece to reappear.

—✦—

Nadir sprinted from the palace as fast as his ether enhanced legs could carry him. The battle wouldn't last long and if they wanted to take advantage of it, he needed to collect his allies and return to the palace as quickly as possible.

He soared over the palace wall and landed a block from the Marble Elephant. He turned ninety degrees and continued his headlong rush. If anyone had been outside, they would have noticed little more than a dark blur as he ran past.

Skidding to a stop outside a white-washed three-story inn with a stone elephant statue outside, he looked for Amane and Branik's champion. Of course they weren't waiting outside. That would have been too much to hope for.

"Nadir?"

He spun to see Amane and another, taller woman dressed in mail with a gray tabard featuring the symbol of the sword lord approaching from the direction of Branik's temple. A female champion, surprising given the generally male clergy of the temple, but then again, much like the Reaper, Branik respected skill more than gender.

He shook off the pointless thought. They had no time to delay.

"We need to get to the palace, now." He focused on the champion. She had no aura in the ether which meant no magic. "Amane, can you enchant her so she can make it over the wall?"

"What about the sword?" Amane asked.

Nadir started toward the palace. They could talk and run.

"Its current owner is using it to try and finish our mission. I hold out little hope for his survival."

He'd finished his explanation by the time they reached the base of the wall.

"An angelic spirit, how remarkable," Amane said.

"I just hope Branik's champion has a will strong enough to avoid becoming its puppet."

The champion, a rather stern, masculine-looking woman, glowered at him. "Do not worry on my account, assassin. Be grateful that today we stand on the same side. Were it otherwise, I would slay you where you stand."

"Yes, of course." Why did everyone lately seem to think he'd be easy to kill?

He glanced at Amane who touched the champion with glowing hands. The two of them rose toward the top of the wall.

Nadir leapt, clearing it with a foot to spare and landing on the other side. The instant his allies joined him, he led the way to the palace entrance. Nadir enhanced his hearing and could just make out the sounds of battle.

The Reaper smiled. Somehow Ali had survived long enough for them to return.

They hurried up the steps and down the hall to the throne room. A blast of black flames shot out the entryway where a ruined door barely still hung. He stopped short, avoiding getting incinerated by inches.

Nadir peeked into the throne room.

Nord and Ali circled each other, Ali in the air and Nord on the ground. The black flames danced around his hands while the mithril sword remained cocked and ready to strike.

Looked like a standoff. That suited Nadir fine. The more time he had to rest, the better.

He motioned Amane and the champion back, away from

the throne room. When they'd hopefully moved out of earshot he said, "They're still battling. When Ali falls, I need you, Amane, to use your magic to pull the sword to our champion. What is your name anyway?"

"My name is not for the likes of you." How he would have enjoyed cutting the smug arrogance off her face.

"With the ether as twisted as it is, even that simple magic won't be easy," Amane said before he had a chance to get angry.

"We should help him," the champion said.

"How?" Nadir asked. "Magic and ordinary weapons can't hurt Nord. If we go in there, we'll only be in the way and likely dead in short order. If Ali wins, great, but if he doesn't, we need to be ready to act."

"Are all the Reaper's servants as cowardly as you?" she asked.

"Are all Branik's followers as stupid as you?" Nadir countered. "We're not here for an honorable duel. We need to win or risk the world's destruction. How can I drill that thought into your thick skull? Your honor means nothing. Your life, my life, none of it matters more than winning. Hundreds of millions of lives will be on your shoulders when you take up the blade. Think on that before you look down on me with superior certainty."

A pained shout from the throne room shut off the conversation. Nadir hurried back to the door. Ali lay on the floor, the mithril sword a few feet to his left. His right arm was gone from the shoulder down. Black flames flared around Nord as he stood over his fallen foe.

Nadir waved his companions up and pointed at the sword.

Amane's hands glowed faintly in the ether as a thread shot out and wrapped around the sword's hilt.

When Nord pointed his hands at Ali, Nadir said, "Now."

The sword shot across the throne room and the champion

stepped forward to snatch it out of the air. Immediately the same glow that surrounded Ali formed around her.

She leveled the sword at Nord. "Leave him alone and face a real warrior."

For a moment, the ex-prince looked exhausted, but rage quickly replaced it.

His aim shifted and a river of black flames rushed out.

Nadir leapt at Amane and knocked her flat as the black flames shot over their heads.

"Thanks."

Nadir nodded. He didn't especially care if Amane lived or died, but he didn't have so many allies that he would give up one of them so easily.

From the crashes and clangs in the throne room, he assumed their champion had dodged the assault. Good. Hopefully the woman had the skills to back up her arrogance. If she did, they might just win this.

CHAPTER 10

Shara held her breath as she watched Daktari try and overcome the lock she'd placed on the practice box. They'd been at the Temple of Soom for three days and they spent most of each day training in the modest, almost claustrophobic room the monks had provided. She saw her father only at mealtimes. He looked as anxious as she felt, but never said anything to discourage her.

All the training had done her good and her sense of the ether had grown more and more refined. She could shape it into anything she wanted, at least as long as what she wanted included a lock.

A trickle of sweat ran down Daktari's neck and at last he blew out a long breath. "Congratulations, Princess. I can't break the barrier."

Shara perked up at once. "Really? I did it?"

"You did. Now you're ready to seal the void pit."

Her smiled evaporated. "Are you sure? I mean, shouldn't we practice on something bigger first?"

"Where magic is concerned—at least your magic—size is

meaningless. You have access to so much raw ether you could probably seal nearly anything. Remember that and you'll be fine." She wished she felt half as confident as he sounded.

"Right, right, I'll be fine." Her breathing grew shallow and she fought not to pass out. So much rested on her getting this right. If she messed up, heaven only knew what might happen.

No, she knew exactly what would happen, the world would end and it would be all her fault. She couldn't do it.

Shara stood and turned to the door only to find Daktari standing directly in her line of escape.

"Calm yourself." His voice washed over her like a soothing mist. "Still your mind like I taught you. Let the fear go. Even if you fail we're no worse off. The pit has remained exactly where it is, open to anyone, for hundreds if not thousands of years. If you fail, nothing gets worse and you can try again."

"You don't know that. No one knows what my power can do. It's this giant question mark. For all we know if I mess up, I might free The Void from The Creator's prison and destroy all of reality. Have you considered that?"

A thin smile creased his face. "Someone certainly has a high opinion of herself today. Strong as your magic is, do you imagine you can compare to a being that created the entire universe? On the scale of the universe, what you're trying to affect is a millionth the size of a hair. The implications for our world are vast, but the danger to the universe is nonexistent."

"Really?" She needed to believe that more than she could say.

"Really. Come on, let's find Abbot and see where this void pit is. We'll bring your father. He's a fair fighter and if we run into trouble he might be useful."

"I'm sure he'll be thrilled to hear your high opinion of him."

They left the training room and went next door to collect Father. They found him half asleep on the cot they called a bed, a book across his chest. He looked so peaceful she hated to disturb him.

His eyes popped open and he immediately scrambled to his feet. "Is everything okay?"

Shara nodded though she doubted "okay" really described the situation.

"We are preparing to descend to the first void pit," Daktari said. "An extra sword might be useful."

"Oh, I'm coming. But I don't have a sword."

"I'll take care of that once we're outside the temple's wards. Now, let's find Abbot and see what we're dealing with."

They found a nearby monk who led them to the library where Abbot sat with another monk, this one the oldest she'd seen so far, his eyes nearly covered by long white eyebrows. A map spread across the table in front of them. Both monks stood as soon as they entered.

"Shadow Man," Abbot said. "Do you need something?"

"The location of the pit. Shara is ready."

Shara didn't feel ready, but she held her tongue. Doubtless she'd never really feel ready.

"That's excellent," Abbot said. "We've been studying the area and can see no issues with you reaching the pit."

Shara had little experience with reading maps, but this one had the important points labeled. A little square that marked the temple sat in the middle. Dotted here and there throughout the mountains were circles indicating portals. Finally a single black disk a little way away from the square indicated the pit.

"Looks pretty close," she said.

"Distances aren't exactly to scale," Abbot said. "It's about a two-hour hike."

"The army of voidlings surrounding the temple might object to us leaving." Daktari glared at the map as if he could change what it said by sheer force of will.

"They won't even know since the passage is underground."
Abbot's chins jiggled as he chuckled. "There's an access point
under the temple, you can go the whole way without leaving
the tunnel."

"That's convenient," her father said.

"Yes, Lord Soom had great vision. Though whether he actually saw the future or only anticipated the possibility I can't
say."

"What time is it?" Daktari asked.

"About an hour after noon," Abbot said. "Why?"

"If there's a fight, my powers are strongest after sunset.
Though being underground will mitigate the worst of the
light's effects."

"I told you, the voidlings won't even know you're there."
Abbot sounded a little irked that Daktari didn't trust him. He
shouldn't take it personally. Shara doubted he really trusted
anyone.

"I believe you, but I also seriously doubt The Void would
leave one of its points of contact with our reality unguarded. If
we can just walk up and let Shara perform the sealing ritual, I'll
be shocked."

"So are we waiting or going?" Father asked.

"Going," Daktari said. "We'll take our time and arrive in the
late afternoon. That should be a good compromise."

"I'll show you the tunnel entrance." Abbot turned toward a
door in the far wall. "Follow me."

Shara didn't know what to expect, but she was committed
now. Succeed or fail, there was no going back.

Abbot led them to the temple basement, thankfully in a different section from the brain room. He stopped in front of a normal-looking door made of dark wood. Numerous wards far stronger than anything Daktari could imagine the monks creating crackled around the entrance. It wouldn't have surprised him if this room and its magic dated back to the first Shadow Man. If he had the power to lay an enchantment across the entire mountain range, then this bit of casting would prove no challenge.

Daktari swallowed a sigh. How he wished he'd had a chance to meet that long-past wizard. He had no peers today and those even close to his knowledge and power either feared him or wanted to steal his secrets. Not exactly a good basis for a friendship.

Abbot waved his hand and the wards vanished. He pushed the door open and they stepped inside an empty room about the size of the makeshift classroom back at the palace. This room seemed to serve no purpose beyond acting as a buffer between the temple and yet another door that he assumed opened into the tunnel. More wards glowed in the ether around this one. These looked lethal, similar to the ones he used to protect his lab.

"The tunnel lies beyond this final barrier," Abbot said rather unnecessarily. "Once you pass through, I will seal the way behind you. Please do not try and return without letting me know as the protections in place are most dangerous."

"Bane, you'll stay here with our host." The homunculus hopped off his shoulder and settled on Abbot's. "Bane can convey my thoughts to you and vice versa. That will allow us to remain in contact should anything unexpected happen."

"A wise precaution, Shadow Man." Abbot moved toward the door.

"Are you sure about this?" Shara asked. "Maybe I need to practice some more."

"I fear time is not on our side, Princess," he said. "You have made remarkable progress and as long as you remember what I taught you, sealing the pit will be no problem. My final word of advice is, when you think you've made the cap big and strong enough, keep going. You need to use every drop of ether you can command."

She nodded, but didn't seem overly confident. In fact, her hands trembled and she clasped them in front of her to stop it. Daktari sent a silent prayer to any watching archangel, or demon lord for that matter: please let her find the will to do what needs to be done.

Abbot deactivated the wards and opened the door. Daktari led the way into a dark tunnel that quickly sloped downward. A light appeared at his mental command giving them a good look at the roughhewn tunnel. The walls appeared clawed out rather than dug with typical tools. Perhaps a summoned monster had done the work. No lingering magic gave him a hint and he dismissed the question as irrelevant.

Behind them the door shut with a rather final-sounding thunk.

"About that sword," Vilos said.

Daktari concentrated and shook his head. "We're still under the temple and bound by their teleportation ward. Once we put a little distance between us, I'll get it."

He found the walking easy though the pitch of the descent argued that the pit had to be pretty deep. This tunnel couldn't be the only access point. Both the void knight and the voidlings had to have a way to reach it. He hoped their tunnel didn't intersect with any of the others. A fight would draw attention they didn't need. Not that he expected to get out of this without one, but the longer they delayed it, the better.

Twenty minutes of hiking finally brought them beyond the effects of the temple's ward. Daktari paused and held out his hand. Light flashed and Heat's Bane, sheathed in its scabbard, appeared in the air above his outstretched palm.

"There you are. I believe you'll be comfortable using this one."

Vilos took the weapon and offered a grim smile. He made no move to strike Daktari down. Wise of him since the same enchantments still prevented anyone from using the sword against him.

"It's good to have it back," Vilos said at last. "Though I assume this is only a loan."

Daktari no longer especially cared if Vilos had the sword and he had no personal use for it beyond his pleasure at having enchanted such a fine artifact. "If we survive this and the threat of The Void is eliminated, you may keep it."

Vilos shot him a side-eye. "Why? What's the catch?"

"There is no catch. I consider your betrayal behind us. You've suffered the consequences for breaking your word and I'm satisfied. The sword will serve you well in the battles to come."

The sultan still seemed dubious, but his concerns interested Daktari not in the least. He set out again, senses both magical and mundane alert for any danger. The unchanging black stone walls made it difficult to tell how much ground they'd covered, but the twisting of the ether made it clear that they were drawing closer all the time.

At least they didn't encounter any voidlings. Fighting in this narrow tunnel would be difficult, mainly because he'd have to be careful not to catch either of his companions in a magical attack.

An hour later he sensed a larger space directly ahead. This had to be their destination.

A few strides carried them into a large cavern. As he suspected, two other tunnels entered the chamber from the opposite side about fifty feet away. That would be where the monsters came from.

His gaze shifted to the inky pool of absolute darkness in the center of the cavern. His conjured light didn't reflect off the pool, instead it seemed to absorb it. Fascinating, but now wasn't the time to indulge his curiosity.

Bane, let Abbot know that we've arrived.

Yes, Master.

"When you're ready, Princess."

She took a deep breath, centering herself the way he'd taught her. Good, if she remembered that, hopefully she'd remember everything else. Their success depended on it.

Ether gathered around her, starting at the symbol on her abdomen and from there flowing into her hands as she compressed and shaped it. So far everything looked good. The Void's presence didn't seem to affect her magic at all.

"Something's coming," Vilos said.

He tore his gaze away from the magic on display and checked the tunnels. A moment later two ogres lumbered into the cavern from the leftmost passage. He couldn't tell from a distance, but it seemed unlikely they weren't voidlings.

"I thought you said they were all besieging the temple?" Vilos whispered.

"I'm certain I said I *think* they all are. Clearly I was mistaken."

The ogres stared at them with comically stupid looks of surprise. If The Void summoned them, then they should have known intruders were waiting. Since they clearly didn't, that meant The Void didn't control them directly.

Vilos leveled his sword. "I'll deal with them."

Daktari lowered Vilos's arm. "Don't waste your magic. A little chill won't bother them."

The ogres' roars were cut off when blades of shadow magic streaked in from all directions, cutting the monsters into quivering lumps. Instantly they tried to regenerate, but next came the flames, white-hot and nearly blinding. When they faded, only blobs of void energy remained and they quickly vanished into the stone.

Good. He'd feared that the stone wouldn't absorb them so close to the source.

"That was easy," Vilos said.

"Yes, but now The Void is fully aware of our presence." Daktari suspected it knew from the moment they stepped into the chamber, but if there was any doubt, they'd eliminated it. "I don't know how long it will take, but you can be sure something much worse will be on its way."

Vilos grunted but forbore comment.

Shara, fully focused on creating the seal, remained silent. That pleased Daktari a great deal. Hopefully they could hold off whatever nasty thing showed up long enough for her to complete her task.

⁕

Daktari glanced away from the tunnels to check on Shara's progress. The ether in her hands looked denser than anything he'd ever seen and still more poured out of the Divine Key every moment. Maybe, just maybe, they had a chance of success. He only wished she'd hurry. They'd seen nothing since he destroyed the voidlings ten minutes ago, but deep down he knew something else would show up. Still, he dared say nothing lest he disturb her concentration.

He turned back to find Vilos looking at him. Not glaring, just looking; it made a nice change of pace. "How's she doing?"

"Well. The cap grows larger and stronger by the second. At this rate I'm certain it will succeed in sealing the pit."

Vilos shook his head. "This is too heavy a burden for her."

"You see her with a father's eyes. Look deeper and you will find a woman with stores of determination that will surprise you. I knew back when she was alone in my lab, and she still mastered her fear. You do her no favors by denying that strength."

"I don't need parenting advice from you."

"Nor would I offer it. But the truth doesn't change simply because you dislike it."

A rushing sound filled the air and new twists formed in the ether.

Vilos snapped around, sword at the ready.

A moment later the black knight galloped into the chamber on his flying horse of black flames. He held his blazing sword, drawing a grimace from Daktari. That weapon had already proven capable of cutting his spells to pieces. He'd been thinking about how best to handle it. He had a theory, but hadn't tested it yet.

The knight leveled its sword at Shara and charged.

Vilos stepped forward to meet it.

Heat's Bane slammed into the black sword and Vilos went sprawling. He did force the knight to change course and swing around for another run.

The mithril blade took no damage and Vilos scrambled to his feet, seemingly ready for round two.

Daktari would never deny his courage, but the knight had too big a power advantage. That, at least, he could do something about. Opening a microportal to Heaven, Daktari drew out divine energy and wove it through Vilos's body, making him stronger and faster than he'd ever been. The delicate spell tried to twist out of control and he feared it wouldn't last as long as usual, but for the moment, it should help even the odds.

The black knight wheeled around and dove at Vilos. This time when the swords clashed, the sultan held strong, even pushing his opponent back and to one side. Though it never made a sound, Daktari couldn't help thinking it looked frustrated. The thought pleased him very much.

His pleasure aside, he still needed a way to deal with the knight permanently. Abbot said the best way was to force it to touch the ground. Since it appeared that the stone still absorbed void energy, that strategy should work.

"Can you hold it off on your own for a minute?"

"What does it look like I've been doing?"

Daktari took that as a yes and placed his hand on the wall near the tunnel exit. The stone resisted, but soon enough he forced ether into it. Inside he found it lousy with void energy. No surprise given where they were. As long as his magic worked, nothing else mattered.

An oval outline appeared and he started slicing with a disk of shadow magic. In less time than he'd feared, a chunk of stone popped loose and floated beside him, suspended by tentacles of ether.

He nearly dropped the stone when a massive ethereal cap appeared above the pit. A quick glance at Shara revealed her face twisted in concentration as she tried to force the two pieces of the cap together and lock it shut.

"No!" Vilos shouted.

Somehow the knight had slipped past him and now raced directly toward Shara.

Time to test his theory.

The chunk of rock he'd cut loose shot out at the knight.

The black sword rose and hammered into the stone.

Nothing happened. Three hundred pounds of rock crashed into the knight, driving him across the room, and slamming him into the far wall.

Daktari kept up the pressure. Through the ether he felt the knight's mass decreasing by the moment. It might not be the ground, but apparently the wall would do.

It took most of a minute, but at last he felt nothing between the rock and the wall. He let the stone drop and found only the black sword remaining.

A gasping Vilos staggered over beside him. It seemed the augmenting spell had run its course. Usually it would last an hour, but down here it looked like the spell maxed out at five minutes.

"Where's the body?" Vilos asked.

"I'm not certain there was one. The sword may have created both horse and rider out of pure void energy. Fascinating and troublesome if true. Keep an eye out. I need to deal with the blade permanently."

"How?"

"I'm going to bury it in the stone."

Vilos turned back to the tunnels and Daktari focused on the sword. For the moment it appeared as nothing more than a finely made black sword devoid of markings with a one-handed grip and upswept guard. When he looked closer, he found a trickle of void energy oozing out into the ground to be instantly absorbed into the rock.

Nodding to himself, he sent ether into the stone and found the smallest area he could affect. The sword's magic made it difficult to work too close so he ended up cutting a section of floor far bigger than he needed.

With a final heave of effort, he flipped the chunk of stone upside down, sword and all. It would take someone truly powerful to lift that boulder. He doubted even an ogre had the strength to do it.

A little squeak of pain drew his attention to Shara. During their fight with the knight, her face had turned pale and sweat plastered her clothes to her body. He checked the progress of the cap and found it about halfway complete. Another two feet and she'd have it.

"It's fighting me." She clenched her teeth and squeezed harder, gaining another three inches.

"You're doing very well. We've eliminated the only threat that can reach us without running for hours. Keep fighting. The Void knows you're stronger, that's why it's trying so hard to break your will. Don't let it. Your father and I will make sure nothing reaches you."

She offered a grim nod and pressed her hands together even harder.

Bane, what are the monsters around the temple doing?

I'll check, Master.

"Is she okay?" Vilos asked.

"Yes. Far better than I thought she'd be given that she's fighting a cosmic entity. And you? My enhancement spell can leave a person a bit under the weather."

Vilos growled. "I'm fine. What happens now?"

"That depends on your daughter. We can only protect her. She must fight the battle on her own."

Master, the monsters are milling around like they don't know what to do. The monks seem confused.

Tell them we destroyed the black knight. I suspect it acted as their controller.

Yes, Master. Are you almost done?

I'm not certain, but we should be close.

"The voidlings have lost their purpose. As I hoped, the

knight controlled them like puppets and without him they don't know what to do."

"What does that mean for us?" Vilos asked.

"With any luck it means Shara can take her time and work in peace and we can rest."

Vilos snorted. "Since when did we have good luck?"

He had a point, but this one time, Daktari decided he'd hope for the best.

CHAPTER 11

Nadir didn't know whether to be impressed or annoyed. Branik's champion had fought Nord to a draw that had lasted for better than two days. Neither of them showed the least sign of fatigue despite the endless battle. Nadir and Amane had taken turns watching over the match while the other rested in an empty room nearby.

All around the combatants, the throne room looked like a war zone. Huge holes had been blasted in the floor and ceiling, the throne resembled a melted pile of slag, and the less said about the once-fine carpet, the better. Even worse for them, despite surviving everything Nord had sent at her, the champion hadn't yet come close to making a decisive blow to his neck.

Nadir had explained what she needed to do, so clearly ignorance didn't cause her failure. Nord's defenses were simply too good.

"How long are they going to keep this up?" Amane asked. "I'm exhausted just watching."

She certainly looked exhausted. Her once-fine robes were stained with sweat, torn, and wrinkled. The under-priests probably wouldn't let her in her own temple as she appeared now.

"I don't know, but as long as the champion lives, we at least have a chance at victory. Not a good chance, I've decided, but a chance."

"And if she dies?"

"Then I'm out of ideas. In my years of service, I've never received a command from the Reaper that I couldn't carry out, but this might be the first."

Amane's laugh was bitter. "This was the first time the Queen has spoken to me, outside of an augury, since I became high priestess. And it seems I'm going to fail her in a spectacular fashion."

A crash and screech dragged their attention back to the throne room. Nord had the mithril sword by the blade in one hand.

Even as the black flames rushed out, the champion yanked, slicing the fingers off Nord's right hand.

A futile effort in the end as an instant later the flames consumed her utterly.

A least she did some damage. The sight of Nord's fingerless hand gave Nadir hope that the monster could be defeated.

They just needed a new plan.

Nord turned and stared right at them.

Uh-oh. Nadir thought they'd found a concealed location to watch the battle, but it seemed he'd been mistaken.

He and Amane sprinted out of the way an instant before the black flames rushed through the space they'd occupied a moment before.

"Come back and fight, you pests!" Nord roared after them.

Nadir neither responded nor slowed. Part of him desperately wanted to flee and forget this madness, but his mission hadn't changed. They raced down one hall, turned, and hurried up a second. Only when he had a few walls between him and Nord did Nadir finally stop and gasp for breath.

"Is he coming?" Amane asked.

Nadir cocked his head and listened with ether enhanced ears but heard nothing beyond their heavy breathing and racing hearts. "No, I don't think so."

"What do we do now?"

Nadir wished he had a good answer. "Unless you have another master swordsman capable of wielding a mithril sword, I'm out of ideas."

Every hair on his body stood up as power filled the air. Nord hadn't done anything like this before and, worried as he was, he had to see what the monster was up to now.

"Stay here."

She didn't argue as he slipped back the way they'd come.

The power continued to grow as he got closer to the throne room. When he peeked around the corner, he caught a glimpse of dark energy surrounding Nord before it vanished along with the man himself.

The air finally felt calm and the ether already worked to repair itself. That meant Nord hadn't turned invisible or something to trap them, he truly had vanished.

But to where?

—⋇—

Nord didn't blame the surviving high priests for running. After the trouble they'd caused him, he wanted to melt their flesh away an inch at a time. He glanced down at his right hand, now fingerless. He'd thought this body indestructible, but clearly mithril was his weakness. At least he felt no pain.

There had been a moment when it first happened that something like pain ran through his metal flesh, but The Void quickly suppressed it.

He took a step to pursue his tormentors.

BRACE YOURSELF.

He got no other warning before darkness rose all around him and he found himself falling through it. A vague sense of motion ended when he rose straight up and appeared above a dark disk in the middle of a cavern.

Vilos and Daktari stood facing him while the princess stayed some distance behind them, her eyes closed and a look of intense concentration on her face. This must be his lucky day.

"Everyone I want to kill all in one place. How convenient."

"Brother," Vilos said. "There's no need for us to fight. I did my best to help you and will do so again."

Of all the stupid nonsense. Nord's eyes narrowed when he noticed Heat's Bane in Vilos's hand. Another mithril sword, what horrible luck.

"Don't waste your breath," Daktari said. "He's fully consumed by The Void. There will be no reasoning with him."

Nord swung his gaze to the sorcerer. "You did this to me."

Daktari shrugged as if his suffering was no big deal. "I warned you there would be consequences if you betrayed me and yet you did it anyway. I partly expected it, you understand. It's part of your nature. Yet the breathtaking stupidity you displayed still came as a surprise."

STOP TALKING, KILL THEM, AND FETCH THE GIRL. YOU'LL NEVER HAVE A BETTER CHANCE.

"Shut up. I've been looking forward to this and I won't be rushed by you or anyone else."

Nord leveled his still-intact hand at Daktari and loosed the black flames.

He let the torrent continue long enough to destroy an army. When it stopped, he found his target unharmed behind a floating chunk of rock.

"Pathetic." Daktari pointed and a screaming pain ran through Nord's brain. "Strike now while he's distracted."

He barely saw Vilos charging in through the pain haze. He raised his already damaged arm just in time to intercept Heat's Bane. The enchanted edge bit half an inch into his forearm, sending another wave of agony through his body.

A backhand swipe sent his brother flying.

Everything went black and when his sight returned the pain had vanished. He straightened, his mind clear of anger and pain. It felt like he'd returned to oblivion only he retained control of his new body.

HUrry.

A soft moan sounded before Shara collapsed.

"She's done it, let's go," Daktari said.

"You're not going anywhere." Nord shifted his hand into firing position.

Before he could loose the flames, Daktari's boulder slammed into his chest and sent him flying across the cavern to crash into the wall.

When it finally fell to the ground, he found his targets gone.

"No!" He slammed his fist into the stone.

I warned you not to fool around. They've fled for the surface.

"Your voice sounds quieter. Never mind." He took a step then stopped. "Which tunnel did they take?"

You know, if you used some of the powers I gave you that don't revolve around destruction, you wouldn't have to ask. Concentrate and you'll sense them. As to my voice, your niece has sealed this pit and blocked half my strength. Now only the pit where you emerged remains. Should that one fall, your armor will stop moving and the pain you knew before we met will return.

Nord grimaced. He really didn't want that pain coming back. "I need to catch them."

You're too slow as you are, but I can help. To your right you will find an ill-fitting disk of stone in a shallow depression. Lift it and you will find one of my swords. You can use it to create a mount of enchanted flames. With that you will have no trouble catching them.

He found the spot easily enough. Hooking the fingers of his left hand in the crack took a little more effort but at last he heaved it aside. Underneath rested an arming sword with a black blade. He'd never been much good with his left hand, but under the circumstances he had little choice.

When he swung it, his enhanced strength made it feel weightless. Following The Void's earlier advice he concentrated and soon sensed three people fleeing up the left-hand tunnel. At his unspoken command, a horse made of black flames appeared beside him.

Catch the girl. Once you have her, I can bring you both to the last pit. From there it's only a short walk to Balthis's temple. All will not be lost if you hurry.

Nord leapt on the horse's back and found it solid.

He'd catch them alright. He'd catch them and make them pay for this most recent humiliation.

⋅—✦⋅

Daktari glanced back but saw no sign of Nord. The boulder he'd slammed into the man—assuming calling him a man still applied—had fallen away moments ago, freeing him to give chase. And he would, Daktari harbored no illusions about that.

Beside him Vilos carried Shara over one shoulder like a sack of potatoes. Hardly dignified, but no doubt easier on his arms. He had no idea how long it would take to reach the surface, but hopefully his power would have recovered enough by then to allow him to open a portal out of here.

"Why didn't we retreat to the temple?" Vilos asked.

"The wards were designed to stop voidlings. They disintegrate the host allowing the enchanted rock to absorb the void energy. Nord's body is nearly indestructible. He'd smash through the doors, wards and all, then slaughter everyone in the temple likely including us. Once I've recovered my strength, I'll transport us all back to my lab where we can rest."

"When will she wake up?"

Daktari's gaze shifted a fraction to the unconscious young woman. When would Shara wake up? An excellent question, one he unfortunately had no idea how to answer. The stress of handling that much ether had to have taken a toll on her, but as far as he could tell, she'd suffered no physical damage. Likely it was just mental exhaustion.

"She'll wake up when she's recovered. How long that might take I can't say. She's young and strong, try not to worry."

Vilos snorted. "You might better ask the sun not to rise in the east than ask a father not to worry."

A vibration ran through the ether, twisting it for a moment. Over the last few days he'd gotten good at reading those vibrations. "Your brother is coming."

Vilos looked back, but of course saw nothing. That would likely change all too soon.

"You hurt him before, can you do it again?"

"No. All I did was end the spell binding his soul to his head. It caused some discomfort but little else. I hoped it might end the fight immediately, but it seems The Void now binds him to the mortal realm."

"Wait, Shara sealed the pit. How can The Void still protect Nord?"

"Simple, there must be another pit. Despite Abbot's confidence to the contrary, I assumed there had to be more than one. The Void has acted in too many directions at the same time for it to be otherwise. The question is, where is the second pit?"

"I think I know," Vilos said. "When Abin first encountered Nord he found him in the jungles south of the High Kingdom. That must be where The Void transformed him into whatever he is now."

"You may well be right." Another, stronger vibration twisted the ether behind them. "For now we need to get out of here in one piece."

"I see a light up ahead."

"Thank heaven." Outside, the ether should be clearer and safer to use. Daktari risked a glance back and caught a glimpse of movement. "He's close. As soon as you clear the opening dodge right and press your back to the mountain."

A few seconds later they ran out of the tunnel mouth. Vilos went right and Daktari left. A moment later Nord flew out on the back of a familiar black horse made of flames, a dark sword clutched in his remaining hand.

So much for keeping it safe by burying the thing.

Daktari raised a hand and a portal began to form.

Nord banked through the sky as he tried to reach them.

"Go!" Daktari shouted as soon as the portal stabilized.

Vilos leapt through.

Only ten yards separated him from a power-diving Nord.

Daktari almost felt the sword swish by as he jumped through the portal.

He closed it with a thought and stared up at the ceiling of his lab. They'd made it, if only by a hair.

CHAPTER 12

As *The Murderer's Nest* powered its way northeast through the ocean, Lawton didn't exactly know what to do with himself. Captain Crow had retreated to his cabin as soon as the fleet cleared Shadow Point and Dandan spent all his time at the helm. Neither of them gave Lawton any orders and the rest of the crew shied away from him lest his bad luck infect them, so he ended up standing in the prow beside the ballista and above the skeleton mermaid figurehead. He told himself that he could act as an extra lookout, but in truth he simply wanted to avoid drawing anyone's notice.

He no longer cared about Archibald or the woman that embarrassed him. Whatever the captain wanted to stop them from finding interested Lawton not in the least. He had one goal now: survive. Whatever he had to do, whoever he had to betray, he meant to get out of this mess with his head firmly attached to his shoulders. And when he did, he'd find Lotta and apologize for not listening to her. Assuming she'd even speak to him.

"Land ho!" the lookout called from the crow's nest.

He squinted out over the water and spotted a little patch of green and brown that marked the distant island. He'd heard of Dragon Isle, all the men had. The old captain had made it clear that should any of them get near the island and he found out about it, they'd die in a horrible fashion. Given the old man's reputation, no one tested him.

Looked like that would soon change.

"Lawton!" Dandan's voice carried over the rush of the water.

He hurried across the deck and joined the first mate at the helm. "Yeah?"

"Take the wheel and hold her steady. I need to let Captain Crow know we've nearly arrived."

Lawton took over and despite his best intentions asked, "What are we doing here?"

"Following orders. Best you keep that in mind." Dandan made his way below deck.

Lawton shook his head. Clearly Dandan didn't know either. Probably no one but Crow knew their true purpose, assuming their lunatic captain knew himself. And no one would ever convince Lawton they only wanted to stop Archibald. That skinny little money grubber couldn't threaten a herring, much less the fleet. No, Crow had a secret up his sleeve.

Well, as long as that secret didn't get Lawton killed, Crow was welcome to shove it in the deepest, darkest place he could find. Lawton had a couple ideas in mind, but suggesting them went against his not-getting-killed plan.

Dragon Isle grew gradually clearer as the distance narrowed. Lawton saw no sign of any other ships which meant they'd arrived first. Assuming anyone showed up, they'd regret the decision. The fleet would make short work of a single ship.

Captain Crow finally came out on deck followed by

Dandan. The captain had a jade amulet in his left hand. He stopped by the mainmast and spoke clearly. "*Taker* and *Hellfire*, circle around and patrol the far side of the island. *Rampage*, take the north end. *Slaughter*, you've got the south side. We'll anchor up offshore to guard the beach."

Crow pocketed the amulet and muttered something to Dandan who trotted up to the helm. "He wants you."

Exactly what Lawton didn't want to hear. He let Dandan take over the wheel and descended to the main deck. "Sir?"

"The time has come for you to make up for your mistakes, Lawton."

That didn't sound encouraging. "How am I to do that, sir?"

"You will lead a shore party to protect the cave. Should, by some act of demon or angel, our enemies make it past the fleet, you will be the final line of defense. I would do this myself, but someone needs to stay here in case that sea serpent you mentioned shows up and attacks. I have no confidence that anyone else could deal with it."

"No question about that, sir. That thing sank *The Glaive* in minutes. What's so special about this cave, sir?"

"That is not your concern. All you need do is keep anyone from entering. Take ten men. Surely even the she-devil you mentioned couldn't defeat so many on her own." Crow put a hand on Lawton's shoulder and squeezed hard enough that he feared the collarbone might break. "Don't fail me again. Better for you if you die protecting that cave than fail and survive. You understand?"

"Perfectly, Captain," Lawton said in a pained voice. "Don't worry, no one will get past me. I'd have had them before if not for that damn serpent."

Crow barked a laugh and released him with a slap on the back. "Things happen and that's a fact. Once we deal with Archibald and his interfering friends, we can get back to business as usual. If their ship survives, maybe I'll rename it the *Glaive 2* and let you command it. How about that?"

Lawton didn't know where this sudden good cheer came from and he didn't trust it in the least. That said, he'd take it over the brooding, threatening version of the captain all day long.

"I'd like that, Captain, thank you. Do I need to select a team?"

"No, I've taken care of that already. Once we anchor up, all you need do is row to the island. You'll find a path that leads to the interior. Just follow it and you'll come right to the cave. Remember, no one goes inside, not them and not you and your team."

"Understood, sir. I need to hunt up a new axe. Permission to go below and raid the armory?"

"Granted. The rest of your team is already down there gearing up. I've explained that you're in charge, but it couldn't hurt for them to meet you before you land."

Lawton saluted and turned for the stairs. Absolutely barking mad, but if the captain wanted him off the ship before the sea serpent showed up, he didn't plan to complain.

At the bottom of the steps, he turned right and opened the next door on his left. Ten grizzled veterans were busy buckling on leather armor and choosing weapons from the many racks. They looked up from their tasks when Lawton entered. He stared down each man, making sure they saw no fear and understood he'd take no shit from them. He'd led men like this long enough to know that any show of weakness would be the end of his authority.

He found a double-bitted axe three racks in, hefted it, and nodded. The balance felt good though it lacked the weight of his old weapon. "Meet me on deck as soon as you're ready."

With that he retreated the way he'd come. Having a weapon

in hand felt good, but he harbored no illusions about his chances should he be dumb enough to take a swing at Captain Crow. Any man capable of casually taking down a monster like the one Jerrod commanded could handle Lawton without batting an eye.

Dragon Isle had gotten bigger while he claimed his weapon and the other ships had broken off to patrol their assigned sectors. Anyone that showed up wouldn't stand a chance. He grimaced. Unless they had a sea serpent. If Lawton had cared about the fate of his fellows, he might have worried about their survival.

An hour later found the ship anchored a mile or so offshore and Lawton and his team rowing for the beach. The best part about being in charge was not having to do any rowing yourself. He sat in the front of the dinghy and studied their destination.

The sandy beach looked like the sort of place you'd bring your lover for a tryst. The jungle beyond it loomed dark and forbidding. An odd combination, but he just shrugged. Appearances meant nothing. He'd take whatever they found and deal with it.

A hundred yards from the beach he finally spotted the path they were supposed to follow. It looked like little more than a game trail, narrow and overgrown. Seemed like no one had been here since Captain Slaughter years ago. What did the old man find to make all this fuss worthwhile?

Lawton didn't know and doubted he ever would. Perhaps the secret passed from captain to captain. Though he doubted that given how much Slaughter hated Crow.

The front of the dinghy hit the sand and they leapt out. Two men pulled the boat clear of the waterline and Lawton led them toward the path. As soon as they crossed into the jungle, the temperature dropped twenty degrees. He shivered. The chill came from more than the shade.

"Where are the birds?" one of the men asked.

Lawton noticed the silence then. No birds, no monkeys, no nothing, not even a breeze. It felt like they'd stepped into a dead zone. Only the perfectly healthy trees dispelled the impression. On the plus side, there seemed to be no mosquitoes either.

"Doesn't matter." Lawton shook off the strange feeling. "Let's find this damn cave and set up camp. Heaven knows how long he's going to keep us here."

Aside from a few dangling vines, the narrow path stayed remarkably clear. They marched through the dim jungle for he didn't know how long before the path widened into a clearing at the base of a hill. A cave so dark it didn't look real gaped in the hillside.

He needed no one to tell him he'd reached his target.

"Get set up." Lawton left them to pitch tents and dig a fire pit while he walked closer to the cave.

He had no intention of going inside. Even if Crow hadn't ordered him not to, one look at that unnatural darkness would have been enough to warn him off. Still, he wished he knew what waited beyond opening. The absolute darkness hid everything even a step past the threshold.

He turned away. Only a lunatic would fight his way past the fleet to reach this creepy place.

Of course, there were plenty of crazy people in the world. Lawton felt like he'd run into most of them over the past week.

⊶—✧

A few days of sailing through the smooth seas made it clear that Dragon Isle was their destination. The magic compass pointed right at it every time Robert checked. According to the charts, they should arrive within sight of it in a few hours. Scaly had swum ahead to scout out the situation and hopefully find them a good spot to go ashore. A little bit of good luck should see them to the dragon's lair by the end of the day.

He smiled to himself as the spray moistened him, warding off the worst of the heat. Who would have thought that finding a dragon's lair with the dragon still hopefully inside, would be good luck? Under different circumstances he would have happily stayed as far away from a sleeping dragon as possible. He hoped this wasn't one that breathed fire first and asked questions later.

"Bobby."

He turned to find Blade sauntering across the deck toward him. She had her silver-steel sword at her hip and wore her usual pirate outfit. A lovely sight indeed to start his day.

"Good morning." He kissed her and put an arm around her waist.

"Have you spoken to anyone at the palace yet?"

"Afraid not. The crystal ball seems to be working okay, but no one is completing the connection on the other side. Which is strange since Abin told me once that they always have someone on duty in the scrying chamber. Hopefully another war hasn't broken out."

"I hope she's okay."

"The kid's tougher than you think." Robert grinned as he thought about Shara. "I bet she's busy studying with whoever's supposed to teach her to use her magic."

"Our guide is approaching!" the lookout called.

Scaly had taken to swimming just under the surface so they could see him before he arrived. The sailors all appreciated the gesture, though Robert couldn't deny his surprise that the serpent had bothered.

"Hopefully he found us a nice white-sand beach in a cove devoid of coral or jagged rocks that might damage the hull." A tropical paradise with a dragon's lair seemed unlikely, but you never knew.

"I'll bet on a dark jungle filled with bloodthirsty monsters," Blade said.

"Come on. We already did that on Serpent Island."

Scaly's head popped out of the water, cutting their banter short. "Bad news."

Of course. "Nowhere to land?"

"Worse, the pirates arrived ahead of us. They've got the island surrounded and the largest ship is guarding the best landing site."

"The best landing site," Robert said. "That implies you found a less than ideal but still useable location somewhere else."

"Yes, on the far side of the island. I recommend you change course north and swing well wide of the eastern side. Two of the smaller ships are guarding that approach, but they will be no problem for me."

"Sounds like a plan." Robert turned to Thompson who manned the wheel. "Adjust our course due north."

He got a salute and soon enough they'd shifted course to circle around to the far side of the island.

"I will remain close for the time being." Scaly dove out of sight.

"There was a time I would have found that more threatening than comforting," Blade said.

"Me too. Strange, isn't it, what you can get used to?"

JAMES E WISHER

"I got used to you."

Robert put a hand to his heart. "You wound me, woman."

He grinned, enjoying her teasing. Robert figured he'd best savor every moment as soon enough they'd be back in the thick of trouble.

⸱—✧

Dantilion Crow paced on the deck of *The Murderer's Nest*. He'd been doing so for hours despite knowing how nervous it made the crew. Their nerves didn't concern him. He'd had no word yet from any of the other ships. He judged that sailing from Black Rat Cove to Dragon Isle should have taken only a little longer than their own journey from Shadow Point. That meant the target ship should've arrived by now. Assuming it was even coming.

It is. Dagon's servants must not be allowed to reach the cave.

"How can you be so sure?" Dantilion still didn't fully understand the entity that spoke to him through his sword. It called itself The Void and it granted him immense power in exchange for performing the occasional task. And the promises it made about his future made his mouth water with greed.

The dragon is their only hope of victory should my plan succeed. Why else would they rescue the only person outside the fleet that knew where to find the isle?

Dantilion didn't have an answer to that and so kept quiet. The hunting hadn't been great lately anyway. A few days or a week guarding the island wouldn't matter.

You will guard it until either my plan has succeeded or Dagon's servants are dead. Is that clear?

He bristled. Taking orders had never been his strong suit—that's how he ended up a pirate after all—and taking them from an inanimate object felt ridiculous.

"We can't just sit here forever. Eventually my men will get bored. And bored pirates are nothing but trouble."

Pain ran through his thigh where the sword rested and traveled up his leg to his hip continuing on to his chest where it wrapped around his heart with a grip like iron. He stopped and staggered, leaning against the mainmast to keep from hitting his knees.

The Void had never done that before. He didn't even know it could.

You will do as I say. If your men become a problem, they can be converted to voidlings. You can also be converted to a mindless puppet. The only reason I refrain from doing these things is that you are more use to me as a thinking bearer. Should that change...

The sword's voice trailed off along with the pain in his chest. Perhaps he'd been kidding himself, thinking he commanded the sword and not the other way around. Sure, he knew it had a mind of its own, sort of, but the power and promises it made far outweighed anything else.

Now he wondered, quietly and only in the very back of his mind, if he'd made a bad bargain.

Dantilion would have to be extremely careful as he moved forward lest he wind up as dead as Jerrod.

A faint warmth spread through his leg and for a moment he feared the sword had heard his thoughts and deemed them rebellious enough to carry out his threat. Then he remembered the amulet he'd put in his pocket earlier.

Blowing out a breath and calming himself he pulled the amulet out and said, "Go ahead."

A scream and shout echoed in his head. "The sea serpent is attacking the *Hellfire*. We're going—"

The connection went dead. That would only happen if the bearer died along with it. According to the old captain's notes, the only place a ship could land on Dragon Isle was the beach behind him. That being the case, why would the serpent attack the others and not them?

It's a ruse to draw you away and let them reach the dragon.

Dantilion nodded. Possibly, but maybe the servants of Dagon had information they lacked. If a second landing point existed, the enemy might slip right around them. Did he dare risk it?

No, even if they did land, Lawton and ten of his best fighters waited to deal with anyone that came ashore. Without the serpent to help them, his men would handle them easily.

Good. Our enemies are growing desperate. They know my victory is inevitable. An animal's death throes can be most dangerous.

Dantilion wanted to believe that, needed to, but so far they hadn't acted in ways that suggested desperation to him. He only hoped that if the sword miscalculated, it didn't blame him.

—✦—

D ragon Isle actually looked a bit like a dragon, or at least what Robert thought a dragon would look like if it curled up like a cat and wrapped its tail around its head. He'd never seen one and had no particular desire to. The island had a vague crescent shape with a stony ridge like a spine in the middle. That's where they'd find the cave no doubt. The rest appeared covered with thick, hopefully not monster filled, jungle.

He'd ordered the ship to anchor up a few miles away from the eastern shore. Now they just had to wait for Scaly to finish clearing the way for them to land. Robert checked his short-sword and throwing daggers and found them exactly where he'd left them five minutes ago when last he checked.

He pulled out his farseer and studied the shoreline. He

didn't know what Scaly had in mind, but nothing he saw indicated a safe place to land. The entire coast was sheer cliffs at least fifty feet tall and the thick jungle started immediately at the top. Honestly, it surprised him that the pirates bothered to patrol the area. Even with the help of a sea serpent, he didn't know how they'd get to the top.

"All secure, sir," Thompson said.

Robert put the farseer away. "Good. Remember, at the first sign of pirates, weigh anchor and get out of here. If they're trying to secure the island, I doubt they'll pursue you, at least very far."

"Aye, sir." Thompson's face twisted like he wanted to say something more. Finally, he blurted out, "Don't you want a bigger shore party? Just you and Miss Blade against heaven only knows how many pirates doesn't sound like very good odds."

"No, it doesn't, but she'll go easy on them if they surrender." Robert grinned. "Seriously though, the goal is to avoid a fight. A big shore party will make more noise than the two of us. Hopefully we can sneak right past them."

"And if you can't?" Thompson asked.

"Then we'll deal with that when we have to. No offense, Thompson, but I've seen you guys training with Blade. How long do you think you'd last against a pirate?"

"Not long, sir, I admit it."

Robert clapped him on the shoulder. "I appreciate the offer, truly, but I need you and the men to look after the ship. It's what you're best at and I trust you to do it right."

"We won't let you down, sir."

"Here he comes!" the lookout shouted.

Robert spotted Scaly swimming toward them, his head and about twelve feet of body out of the water. The serpent had a chunk of wood in his mouth and he spit it out while Robert watched.

He joined Blade on the main deck as Scaly drew up beside the rail.

"How'd the hunting go?" Robert asked.

"I sank all but the big ship guarding the beach."

"Why spare that one?" Blade asked.

"I caught the stink of void energy as I neared. Since I have no idea exactly what sort of item they have, I deemed it prudent not to push my luck. Especially since they show no signs of leaving their post."

"Great," Robert said. "I had a look at the coast and that cliff face seems awfully high, even for you."

"Yes, that's why we're going under it. I found some under-water tunnels during my scouting run. One of them leads to a pool in the interior. I can carry you right to it, but you'll have to swim the final fifty yards as I won't fit."

Robert scowled and turned to Blade who shrugged and said, "We don't have a ton of choices."

She had him there. "Okay, if we're going to do this, let's do it. Thompson, you have your orders."

"Aye, sir. First sign of trouble we'll get the *Journey* to safety, never fear."

Robert had plenty of fears, but none of them involved the ship. He turned back to the serpent. "So how are we going to do this?"

Scaly lowered his head so it was even with the deck. "Climb aboard and hold on tight."

Right. He took a deep breath and jumped. The scales on his head were rough and provided good handholds. Blade joined him, landing in front and working her fingers into a crack between the scales.

"You good?" When she nodded he added, "We're ready."

Scaly didn't hesitate. Fast as an arrow, the serpent shot toward Dragon Isle. They covered the few miles separating them in less than a minute. On the way they passed a scattering of floating wood and bodies, the remains of one of the ships the serpent sank.

A few feet from the cliff wall Scaly said, "Take deep breaths. On my command, take one last breath and hold it."

Despite all the time he spent on the water, Robert hadn't done much diving. Most of the sailors tried to avoid getting in the water since they knew all the things that lived there.

"Now."

Robert took one last deep breath and the next thing he knew they were underwater.

The water rushed past, trying to rip him from his precarious perch. He held on for all he was worth, checking every once in a while to make sure Blade hadn't lost her place. Not that he needed to worry. She had a stronger grip than he did.

Soon enough he spotted the entrance to the sunken tunnels. Scaly shot through the mouth and everything went pitch dark.

Robert crouched as low as he could, fearing at any moment a rock formation might scrape him off. Eventually his lungs started to burn and still Scaly showed no sign of slowing.

Desperation grew by the moment as bright spots swam before his eyes.

Finally a shaft of light appeared ahead of them. Scaly stopped directly under it. Robert got the hint and kicked off, swimming with all his might.

Bubbles burst from his nose a second before his head broke the surface. He sucked in a great lungful of hot, humid jungle air. Blade joined him a moment later also breathing hard. They treaded water for a few minutes, gathering themselves and looking around.

They'd emerged in a pool surrounded by tall trees that cast shadows over everything. The only sound was their soft splashing.

"Let's not do that again," Blade said.

"Fine with me. Shall we swim for shore and try to figure out where to go from here?"

She said nothing, only pulling for land with long, graceful strokes. Soon enough they hauled themselves, dripping and soaked, onto solid ground. It felt good to get out of the water, but now the hard part began.

Robert pulled out the compass and fed ether into it. The pointer snapped around pointing west and a little south. They'd overshot the target. Oh well, a little backtracking wouldn't hurt anything.

"Did you notice how quiet it is?" Blade asked.

"Yeah, that's never a good sign. I've got a bearing. What say we get this over with?"

She nodded and Robert set out in the direction the compass indicated. Despite the density of the jungle, the floor stayed reasonably clear, making the walking easy. It reminded him a little of the forests back north, assuming you forgot about the heat and humidity.

He would've liked to talk with Blade as they hiked, but didn't dare risk the noise given the danger of pirates hearing them in the quiet jungle.

After an hour of marching without seeing or hearing anything beyond the trees he paused and checked the compass again. This time his knees wobbled, but he didn't fall. Hopefully he wouldn't have to check it a third time.

A quick adjustment to their course got them on the right line again.

Blade gave him a worried look, but he grinned and set out, determined to find the damn dragon and wake it up.

After another hour walking through the seemingly endless jungle, he heard a faint noise. He stopped, caught Blade's attention, and touched his ear. She cocked her head. After a moment of listening, she nodded and eased her sword out of its scabbard.

They snuck along on light feet and Robert hardly dared to breathe. He never thought he'd miss all the hooting and hollering of the monkeys, but some cover noise would have been nice right about now.

A hundred yards further on he finally made out voices. "How long is the captain going to make us wait here?" one man asked.

"Until they show up or he calls us back to the ship." That sounded like Lawton. Looked like Scaly didn't finish the job after all. Pity. "If you want to complain, I'm sure Captain Crow will be thrilled to hear what you have to say."

No one had any comment after that and silence fell once more. Robert didn't recognize the name Crow, but when his father had traded, they usually stayed further west, focusing on the High Kingdom and lands to the north.

He pointed to the ground and they crawled closer. Peeking around a particularly large tree, Robert counted ten pirates gathered around a cook fire. They were as rough looking a crew as he'd ever seen. Every one of them sported scars, well-used armor, and an assortment of weapons. He harbored serious doubts even Blade would be able to defeat them all even with his modest help. At least he saw no one on guard duty. In fact, they looked more bored than alert.

Beyond them a dark opening in the nearby hill loomed. That had to be the target. The pirates had camped directly in front of it and he saw no way to sneak past them.

He'd need to come up with a particularly good trick to even the odds.

Robert studied the clearing and surrounding jungle. Luring an animal into their camp wouldn't work as he'd seen no sign that any animals lived here. And they were way too far inland for Scaly to come to the rescue.

His gaze landed on a standing dead tree about six inches around with a top full of dry fronds. A slow smile spread across his face and he eased over beside Blade so his lips were only an inch from her ear. "Think you could cut that dead tree down with a single blow?"

She nodded at once so he whispered the rest of his plan. Blade offered no objections and started crawling back out of sight to circle around.

A painful half hour later he spotted her standing beside the tree, sword drawn. Robert gathered himself, caught her eye, and nodded.

Her silver-steel sword sliced through the trunk like nothing and Blade shoved the tree as it fell, guiding it right into the pirates' fire.

The pirates leapt to their feet shouting as the dry fronds caught and burst into towering flames.

Taking advantage of their surprise, Robert sprinted right for the opening. Blade did the same, pausing only an instant to cut down a pirate that had awareness enough to try and stop her.

Robert made it through first. As soon as she joined him Blade spun to face the clearing.

"Go," she said. "I can hold them here."

Robert didn't know what worried him more, leaving Blade alone or going into the inky darkness by himself.

His dilemma resolved when something swirled in the darkness before reaching out and engulfing them both.

CHAPTER 13

Vilos sat in a chair made of magic, dozing on and off, but never really sleeping. Any moment he expected the thing to collapse into motes of light and dump him on his ass on the cold stone floor. He'd hoped to never see this wretched place again. Yet here he sat, a guest rather than an invader.

To be fair, what really kept him awake was concern for Shara. She slept like the dead and only the steady rise and fall of her chest assured him that she remained among the living. She hadn't so much as flinched since they arrived in Daktari's lab some hours ago.

At least he assumed it had been hours. Time meant little in the dim cavern. Speaking of the sorcerer, he'd seen nothing of Daktari since he went to sleep. It seemed no matter who you were, using magic took a lot out of you.

He reached out and touched Shara's wrist. Still warm, still a strong pulse. Good signs one and all yet he found himself little reassured. For all his life he'd done everything in his power to protect her. Now they faced something his army and advisors couldn't deal with. He felt helpless and hated it.

"She will wake when she wakes." Daktari's voice nearly had him out of his chair and reaching for his sword before he remembered they were on the same side for the moment.

"I'm going to put a bell on you." Vilos settled back down. "What's our next move?"

"I've spoken to Abbot via Bane and he agrees that there must be another pit. The voidlings have shown no sign of collapsing. They've also seen no sign of your brother. In any event, we can't do anything until Shara recovers and that may take some time given how much ether she manipulated. I suggest we speak to your wizard and see what he can tell us about the second pit."

"I won't leave her here alone."

"Your daughter is safer here, protected by my magic, than she would be anywhere outside the temple."

"Speaking of the temple, why didn't we return there?"

"Because as I told you earlier, the wards protecting them wouldn't stop Nord. He'd batter his way through the doors in minutes. I didn't want to give him an excuse to attack the monks. The knowledge they're guarding is priceless. Nord doesn't know this place, assuming you didn't tell him."

"I told him nothing." Vilos crossed his arms. "Do what you will, but I'm staying here until she wakes."

Daktari massaged the bridge of his nose. "As you wish. Did you at least explain that we were no longer enemies?"

"Abin knows, as does the rest of the palace guard. Besides, after your first visit, no one would be foolish enough to attack you."

"Then I will go speak with the wizard and see what I can learn. You must be hungry." Daktari reached into his satchel and pulled out a pouch and water skin that looked too big to fit in it. "It isn't much, but it is better than nothing."

Vilos took the pouch and peeked inside. Dried meat and biscuits. Right now that struck him as a feast.

"Good luck."

Daktari nodded and vanished.

· —✧

Nadir had lost track of exactly how long ago Nord vanished. Some hours certainly and he showed no sign of returning. On the plus side, since he still hadn't come up with a way to defeat the monster, the extra time gave him a chance to consider his options. On the downside, he still had to destroy Nord or face the wrath of his master. Much as he feared Nord, he feared the Reaper considerably more.

Utterly exhausted from the battle and channeling so much ether, both he and Amane decided to simply rest in the palace while they tried to come up with a new plan. She had promptly fallen asleep on a short couch leaving him to do all the planning. Not entirely unreasonable on her part. Had they been considering a new business venture, the high priestess of the Queen of Coins would be a valuable asset. Anything combat related, except healing and some indiscriminate offensive spells, and she offered little.

He rubbed his tired eyes and stood. Maybe a bit of pacing would get the ideas flowing. He considered himself the foremost expert in the High Kingdom when it came to assassinations, but he doubted Nord still actually lived in any recognizable sense of the word. That made killing him difficult.

His gaze shifted to the mithril sword resting on the floor beside Amane's couch. He'd thought that would solve his problems, but he'd run out of wielders. Maybe if he just sent wave after wave of noble idiots against Nord one of them would get lucky.

A humorless, bitter laugh slipped out. As plans went, he'd had better.

Footsteps from outside froze him midstride. Given the number and lightness of the steps, it had to be normal people. Probably the palace guard coming to find out if their intruder had vacated the premises.

Should they flee? No, at this point he needed someone else to bounce ideas off of. Besides, as high priestess, everyone knew Amane, so they should have no fear of getting arrested.

He shook her shoulder and Amane groaned before opening her eyes. "What?"

"Company coming. I need you awake and alert."

Her eyes bugged out. "Nord?"

"No, regular people I believe, coming to scout out the situation. Let's enlighten them."

She scrubbed a hand across her face and the ether surged through her. He knew that spell. In fact he'd used it several times himself lately. It washed away exhaustion and let you function despite being tired. Useful, but eventually you paid a price for it.

Amane stood, looked down at herself, and grimaced. "I'm not exactly at my best."

"As long as they recognize you, nothing else matters."

She led the way toward the palace entrance while Nadir stayed half a step behind. To be safe he cast a basic protection spell, just something to turn aside a stray arrow if one of the guards got jumpy. To survive several encounters with Nord only to end up killed by a random guard would get his soul laughed out of the Reaper's hell.

They reached the entry hall a moment before Abin and

about a hundred heavily armed soldiers stepped through the open doors. The two groups stared at each other for a second before Abin said, "High Priestess, Guild Master, I assume if you're here and not fighting for your lives, Nord has taken his leave."

"He has," Amane said. "Though to where I can't say. He vanished in a column of darkness several hours ago."

"Perhaps we might discuss the situation somewhere more private," Nadir said.

"Good idea." Abin turned to one of the soldiers. "Sweep the palace and get guards up on the walls. I doubt we have anything to worry about, but I'd like to get the security situation sorted out sooner rather than later."

The man saluted and started barking orders. Nadir led the way back to the throne room. It seemed like as good a place as any for them to chat.

As they passed Amane's couch Abin asked, "Where did that sword come from?"

He reached to pick it up but Nadir said, "Don't touch it. Not unless you want to end up possessed by the spirit of an angel."

Abin snatched his hand back. "It seems we have a great deal to share."

They reached the ruined entrance to the throne room and Nadir stopped cold. Alone in the empty room stood a man in a dark robe that practically seethed with magical power.

"Daktari?" Abin asked. "Are His Majesty and the princess well?"

Nadir allowed himself to relax. Abin seemed to regard the stranger as an ally, though from his cool tone not a friend.

"They were as of a minute ago. I left them resting in my lab. Shara has succeeded in sealing the first void pit."

"What's a void pit?" Nadir asked.

Daktari turned his cold gaze on him. In all his time serving the Reaper, even as an acolyte under the guidance of the last guild master, Nadir had never had someone look at him with eyes like that. He actually shivered before getting himself under control.

"Who are you?" Daktari asked.

Abin must have sensed the tension as he said, "Excuse me. Daktari is tutoring Shara in the use of the Divine Key. Amane is the high priestess of the Queen of Coins and, um, this gentleman is the master of the Reaper's Guild. They, along with the other high priests, were tasked by their patrons to defeat Nord."

"A difficult task indeed. I assume you were the ones that severed his fingers."

"That honor belongs to the late champion of the sword lord," Nadir said. "It seems Nord is vulnerable to mithril."

"That's useful information. Since you're both still alive, no doubt you intend to do battle with Nord again."

"Unless the Reaper tells me otherwise."

Amane just offered a glum nod.

"Very good," Daktari said. "I don't have so many allies that I'll turn away more."

"Would you answer my question?" Nadir asked.

"Hmm? Oh, the void pit. They are holes in reality that allow the cosmic entity known as The Void to interact directly with our reality. Ordinarily it is fully sealed within The Creator's prison and thus limited to interacting with us indirectly. Dreams sent to those open to his message, that sort of thing. The pit allows for the creation of monsters and artifacts powered by void energy. The weakest of the creatures are voidlings. Nord may be the strongest of them currently on our world. Though whether he is currently monster or artifact is open for debate."

Nadir grimaced. The Reaper had told him little about The Void, only that Nord had to be destroyed. Now he wondered if he had the power to accomplish his task.

Daktari, seeming unaware or indifferent to his concerns, turned to Abin. "The reason I've come is to hear more about the void pit you found in the jungle. When she recovers, I will need to take Shara there to seal it."

"You're talking about that hole in the earth where Nord emerged with his armor?" Abin said. "It's in some incredibly ancient ruins; they're so old only a few standing stones remained. We had to fight our way through some goblins filled with this dark ooze that wouldn't die until I burned them to ash."

"Voidlings," Daktari said. "The ether will be too twisted to appear directly in the ruins. Is there anything nearby I might use as a reference?"

"We passed a temple dedicated to some demon or other. The place reeked of corruption and we quickly moved on."

"Impossible," Daktari muttered.

Nadir looked from Abin to the sorcerer. He'd completely lost track of what they were discussing. "Is there something you can do to help us defeat Nord? Having him out of the way will certainly make your task easier."

"I can't think of anything," Daktari said. "Once the second pit is sealed, Nord will lose access to The Void's power and his armor will quickly cease to function. Once that happens his soul will be freed from his head and he will truly die. May he rot in whatever hell awaits him."

Nadir considered that. Would his master be satisfied if he simply helped seal the pit and let Nord die that way? It seemed a bit out of character for the Reaper, but then again, as long as the job got done and the threat was eliminated, that should be enough.

A sense of approval flooded him. He could almost see the Reaper on his throne nodding in satisfaction.

When his focus returned to the throne room, he stared with wide eyes at the illusion of a door surrounded by Infernal runes, crude skulls, and flames. "Who is Balthis?"

"How do you know that name?" Daktari asked.

"It's written in Infernal directly above the door in your illusion."

"I suppose that makes sense given it's his temple. Balthis is an elder demon trapped by the archangels long ago. It seems he's made a pact with The Void and seeks to become whatever the demonic equivalent to a voidling is with the intention of destroying our world and no doubt as many others as he can manage."

"That's the entrance to the temple we saw," Abin said. "I'm surprised you were familiar with it."

"I visited the place not so long ago myself to rescue a tome of ancient lore. We may well have missed each other by only a few days. At any rate, having the temple so close to the pit is a problem. Should anything go wrong, it would only take minutes for Shara to be taken to the temple and used to free Balthis."

"This is what the Binder feared and why he ordered the princess's death," Amane said. She'd been so quiet Nadir had almost forgotten about her.

"Without a doubt." Daktari ran a hand over his bald head. "Perhaps the best thing would be to fly south and land in the ruins."

"When you go," Nadir said. "Amane and I will join you."

He expected an argument, but the sorcerer just nodded.

"I'll come too," Abin offered.

"No. Your magic is too weak to be of much use," Daktari said. "You'd just—"

Daktari stopped in midsentence and cocked his head as if hearing something inaudible to the rest of them. "Someone has breached the wards of my lab."

"Who could have done that?" Abin asked.

"I can only think of one person," Daktari said.

Nadir didn't need two guesses to know who. "Let's go!"

·—⟫

Nord galloped south on the back of his flaming horse. He'd found that since picking up the void sword, as he thought of it, his powers seemed sharper and he felt more in control of them, especially the nonviolent ones. For instance, his niece's presence shone like a beacon in the High Kingdom. That surprised him at first, but running home made perfect sense. Especially given that, without the sword, he would've had to walk all the way.

A moment of concentration allowed him to home in on her again. He nudged his horse a little east, toward the Chaos Hills rather than the capital. If they hadn't gone to Sultan's Oasis, they must be in some hideout of Daktari's. No doubt something crackling with protective magics capable of killing most anything stupid enough to cross them.

He grinned. Such things bothered him no more than a cobweb.

Do not get overconfident! You have already failed me twice.

"Because of circumstances beyond my control. My enemies ran rather than fight me. I cannot be blamed for that."

Pathetic excuses and now my power is halved because of your arrogance. Get the girl and bring her to Balthis's temple. No more playing around.

Nord resented the idea that he'd been playing around. He'd done his absolute best to carry out The Void's instructions. He snarled away his annoyance. Shara waited somewhere directly below him.

Urging his mount toward land he focused harder. A little further north maybe?

There! A cave guarded by a magical barrier. That had to be it.

He landed just outside the entrance and let his horse vanish. For the first time he actually felt a little weak. He wouldn't have imagined that possible.

Remember, your power is my power and now it has been cut in half. A little caution and humility wouldn't hurt you any.

Even before gaining his new power, Nord had never known humility. Caution, on the other hand, he had some experience with.

Gathering void energy around the sword's blade he slashed it toward the cave.

Wards sparked and vanished leaving the entrance clear.

"Satisfied?"

No response from The Void. He shrugged and stomped down the tunnel toward where he sensed Shara.

A modest hike into the earth brought him to a cavern filled with stone tables covered with magical junk. Shara lay sleeping on one of them.

Nord stepped into the cavern.

Something gave off a bright flash and pain ran across his chest.

When the next flash came, he barely raised his sword in time to block it.

Now that his vision cleared, he found his brother facing him holding Heat's Bane. The shining mithril blade seemed to glow in the darkness.

"You will not take her, brother."

"Do you really think you can stop me, Vilos? As I am now,

you're nothing more than a pest. Stand aside and I'll let you enjoy however long the world has left."

Vilos tightened his grip on Heat's Bane. "You will not take her."

"You always were a stubborn idiot." Nord sent a wave of black flames rushing at his brother.

Vilos dove under them and slashed at Nord's shins.

More pain ran through him as the sword sliced deep into his metal flesh.

The blow didn't sever his feet, but it did weaken his legs.

Snarling, Nord summoned a wall of black flames all around him. Next he opened a gap facing Shara. Vilos once more stood directly in his path.

Let's see him stop this.

Nord extended the wall in all directions, not stopping until he reached the edge of the table holding Shara's sleeping form.

He opened another gap and barely raised his sword in time to turn aside an overhead chop that would have split his head like a melon.

Vilos stood on the table, a foot on either side of Shara who remained sound asleep. Out of the corner of his eye Nord noticed the top of the wall of flame flickering and growing thin.

You are near to the limit of what power I can spare for you.

Having limits on his power had never appealed to Nord. But sometimes you had to deal with a less-than-ideal situation.

He reshaped the flames from the wall behind him into a disk and sent it flying at Vilos about knee high.

Vilos leapt right and ended up standing on the cavern floor a few feet from the table.

That was enough.

Nord took all the flames he could muster and formed a dome around him and Shara. He had a vague sense of Vilos pounding the flames with ice magic, but his efforts fizzled without result.

Setting his sword down, he scooped Shara up onto his shoulder, her limp form little more than a feather to his enhanced body. When he'd collected the sword, the flames closed in around him.

Finally. I admit I'd begun to doubt you could complete the task.

Nord appeared an instant later in a familiar dark cavern. This was where he'd gained his new body.

Correct. A few miles east of here sits a temple of Balthis. Take her there and place her in front of the altar. The demon will do the rest.

"I may do that," Nord said. "But first we need to discuss my future."

Your future rests in endless oblivion once this world is destroyed. Now go!

"I doubt that's the deal you made with the demon. When he gets here and destroys the world, there's no way he will be content to live in oblivion for all eternity. I want whatever you offered Balthis or I'll snap Shara's neck right here and you'll never free the demon."

Arrogant little human. You were nothing but a head screaming in agony until I had you brought here. Balthis is an elder demon, a far more useful champion than you. Perhaps a reminder of what you used to be will help focus your mind.

Nord screamed as the old pain came roaring back. Every nerve felt like someone had pressed a red-hot torch into it.

Focusing through the pain, he dropped Shara to the floor and raised the void sword.

When he tried to bring it down he found his body refused to obey. Instead, he set his sword down and started to pick her back up.

"NO!"

He fought The Void with everything he had. His body

didn't stop, but its movements grew jerky and slow. What should have taken seconds took nearly five minutes, but still, The Void succeeded in getting Shara up on his shoulder.

A moment later they were rising up and out of the cavern. He landed in the clearing surrounded by distant jungle. His body turned toward where he sensed a huge mass of corruption. That had to be the temple.

His foot rose to take a step toward it and Nord fought with all his will to stop it.

He failed, but that one stride took nearly ten seconds.

Pointless. How long can you maintain your focus through the pain? You torture yourself needlessly. Oblivion welcomes you with open arms. No pain, no worry. Just let go and you can enjoy precious release.

"You will grant me continued life and power in your service or this will be the slowest march in history. I want whatever you promised the demon."

He took another ponderous, fifteen-second stride.

Even if I were inclined to bargain with a worm like you, when your world dies, you're too weak to survive the end. Nothing will survive save the demon. Accept that and your fate.

Nord clenched his teeth against the pain and managed to slow the next stride so much that it took half a minute. He may be doomed. And if so, his brother would doubtless say he deserved his fate, but he wouldn't go down without a fight, not even to a being as powerful as The Void.

· ⋯✧

Daktari tried to open a portal to his lab and failed. Too much void energy swirled around the room to allow the connection. He immediately switched his focus to a spot just outside the cave and the portal opened.

The assassin sprinted through first followed by Abin and a reluctant Amane. Daktari stepped through last, closing the portal behind him. As he feared, all his wards had been obliterated. No surprise there, void energy excelled at destroying anything, especially anything associated with ethereal magic.

He led the small group down the entry tunnel. No sounds of battle reached him. Either Nord had fled or Vilos was dead or disabled. He hoped for the former as losing her father would make Shara's task that much more difficult.

Vilos sat on the floor of his lab seeming unharmed and cradling Heat's Bane. Of the princess and Nord Daktari saw no sign. Abin and Amane hurried over to the sultan while Daktari studied the lab with his magical senses. The ether had only just begun to restore itself meaning Nord hadn't been gone long. Even better, he knew where they had to be going.

Still, they had very little time.

"You said we'd be safe!" He turned to find a furious Vilos on his feet looking ready for a fight.

"I assumed you would be. Nord gave no indication he could track Shara before this. Perhaps he gained the ability from that sword." Daktari shook his head. "The nature and limits of void magic are still very much unknown to me and likely everyone else in the world. The question before us now is, do we argue amongst ourselves, or do we go at once to rescue your daughter?"

"We go at once," Vilos said. "My sword hurt him, at least a little."

Daktari turned to Amane. "Can you consecrate a temple dedicated to a demon on your own?"

She started at the question. "No. No more than one of the demon lords' servants could desecrate one of our temples on their own."

"This temple isn't dedicated to one of the lords of Hell, but an elder demon. He can speak to you in the altar chamber and invoke some minor magical effects. It appears he was worshipped by goblins."

She shook her head. "Even then I'd need a group of at least four other priests and several hours to invoke the ritual. Several undisturbed hours."

"My assassins will protect you from whatever the jungle can vomit out," the guild master said.

"Good. Return to Sultan's Oasis and gather your teams. I'll collect you in the palace courtyard. How long do you need?"

"An hour should do it," Amane said and the assassin nodded.

"Very well, one hour."

Both priests closed their eyes and chanted. The assassin vanished in a flash of hellfire and the priestess in a burst of holy light.

"What's that all about?" Vilos asked. "We need to rescue Shara."

"We will, but we also need a backup plan. If the temple is purified, they can't take Shara there to free Balthis. Given our luck fighting your brother so far, I'm not confident in winning."

Vilos grimaced but nodded. "He seemed a little weaker this time, but still overwhelmingly powerful."

"Doubtless the drop in power came from the fact that Shara reduced his power supply by half. Shall we see if we can locate them and free your daughter?"

Vilos straightened and hefted his sword. "I'm ready."

"As am I," Abin added.

Daktari concentrated on the spot near the temple where he appeared when he claimed the final Manuscript of the Void volume. He would have preferred to go directly to the pit Abin described, but the ether would be too warped to risk a portal there.

The ether connected with his chosen location easily and they all went through to face whatever nightmare awaited them.

CHAPTER 14

obert staggered a step when the darkness receded. Or maybe receded wasn't the right word. He still had no idea where he'd ended up despite the faint purplish glow that filled the space. He might have been in a giant underground cavern. Certainly the ground under his feet felt like stone. If this place had a ceiling, it rose high enough that the light didn't reveal it. Same with the walls. He heard nothing beyond his own ragged breathing.

"What the hell just happened?" Blade asked. "Where are we?"

"The answer to both your questions is, I have no idea. At least there aren't any pirates."

"Or exits. And somehow I don't expect any slimy lightning eels to show up and lead us to the way out."

"No, I expect not." Robert shrugged and shouted, "Hello?"

"I told the last human that I didn't wish to be disturbed." A voice so deep it hurt Robert's ears seemed to come from everywhere and nowhere at the same time, much like the light.

"My apologies for disturbing you, sir. Do I have the honor

of addressing our world's guardian dragon?"

"You have better manners than the last human at least. Yes, I am Soom. Why have you ignored my wishes and come here?"

Robert took a deep breath. Time to make the sale. "The world is facing a great crisis. The Void is active once more and has made a pact with an elder demon named Balthis. They are trying to use the Divine Key to free that demon so it can bond with The Void and destroy our world. Many people are doing their best to stop this from happening, but as a last resort, we were dispatched to wake you and request your aid should the demon be freed from its prison."

"Hmmm." The deep, bass rumble made Robert's bones ache. "I had hoped that sharing the secrets of shadow magic as well as enchanting the Black Ice Mountains would be enough to let you humans deal with The Void and its machinations on your own, but an elder demon and the appearance of the Divine Key is no doubt too much for even the current Shadow Man to handle."

Robert's hopes rose. "So you'll help?"

"It seems I have little choice. I am as bound to this world as you mortals. If it is destroyed, I die as well. If Balthis is freed, I will fight him."

"Great." Robert beamed. "There are also some pirates, one of whom has a void artifact."

"I said I will fight the demon should it become necessary. I am not here to solve all your mortal problems."

Robert winced but pressed on. "The thing is, we don't really have a way to deal with void magic. Even our sea serpent guardian is scared of it."

"It is wise to be so." The purple light gathered and brightened about fifteen paces away, slowly shifting into a human-sized figure dressed in a dark robe. He looked a little like Daktari.

"I thought you were a dragon," Blade said.

"I am," Soom said. "As such I can appear in any form I wish. I assumed that you humans could better deal with me in this guise. My true shape can be overwhelming. Anyway, you must understand that void magic is powered by a sort of cosmic energy. As such, it can only be opposed by another cosmic energy. Shadow magic is the ideal sort to use as it combines both divine and infernal energy. But even then, the tiny amounts a mortal can channel are often too weak to overcome it. It is clear to me that neither of you is capable of wielding shadow magic even had we the decades of training necessary to teach you how."

"Then what do we do about the pirates?" Robert asked.

Soom pointed at Blade's sword. "That weapon, what do you call it?"

Clearly "a sword" wasn't the answer he wanted and Robert doubted he wanted a proper name either. Then he understood. "It's called silver steel. It can cut through damn near anything."

"Silver steel," Soom said. "A good name. It has mithril mixed in with the steel, that's why it's so strong. It also makes the weapon perfect for my needs."

The sword leapt out of Blade's hand and floated over to Soom. Purple energy gathered around it and soaked in until it lost its shine and became dull and black.

"There. I've enchanted the metal to absorb void energy. You should be able to handle the enemy artifact now." The weapon floated back to Blade who gave it an experimental swing.

"It feels no different," she said.

"Why would it?" Soom asked. "Magic adds no weight to an item. Now you'd best be getting back. Rest assured that I will be keeping a close watch and should Balthis approach this world, I will be ready."

"You can beat him, right?" Robert asked.

"I don't know. I've fought nothing as powerful as an elder demon. At the very least I can buy you time. Beyond that, I make no promises."

Robert grimaced. Not exactly what he wanted to hear.

"What about the pirates?" Blade asked. "There's a mess of them waiting for us outside the cave entrance."

Soom cocked his head. "They are still there. I can transport you somewhere safe."

"Our ship is anchored off the east coast of the island," Robert said.

"That's fine. I'll send you to the edge of the eastern cliff face. From there you are on your own."

Darkness wrapped them again and the next thing Robert knew he and Blade stood on the cliff face looking out over the ocean. The drop to the water had to be fifty feet and it looked even more intimidating from up here than it had from the ship.

"Did that go as you expected?" Blade asked.

"I had no idea what to expect, but we lived through it, so I'm calling that a win. Not going to lie though, I'd hoped to find the dragon more willing to directly help. Wonder if Scaly's watching. I really don't want to have to swim all the way back to the ship."

"One way to find out." Blade leapt off the cliff.

Robert sighed, pinched his nose shut, and jumped after her.

⁕

Dantilion Crow had never been good at waiting. Usually if he wanted something he'd find out who had it, smash their head in, and take it. But he couldn't do that now since he had no idea where to find the thing he wanted, in this case the thrice-cursed ship that helped Archibald escape. His sword told him the ship would come here eventually, but eventually might be today or it might be next month.

If he had to wait that long, he might lose his mind.

It won't be months. My other agents are close to completing the final stage of the plan. If they aren't here in the next day or day and a half, it won't matter if they ever show up.

Dantilion forced himself to stop pacing. He stood in the forecastle and stared at the island. Nothing about it screamed, "I'm important." It looked exactly like a hundred other little jungle islands scattered around this part of the world.

He took a breath and focused. A day or two at most. That didn't sound so bad. The sooner this business ended the sooner he got his reward. And while he hated waiting, he loved rewards.

You are much like my other servants. All of you so willing to trade your entire world for personal gain. It's one of the few things I can rely on you mortals to do.

"You know the fleet's creed. My mind is an open book to you, right?"

It is and I do.

"Then you know I believe the strong are free to take whatever they can from the weak. If the people of this world were stronger, they'd stop us. If they don't, then the world deserves its fate. It's that simple."

The sword's laughter echoed in his mind. Dantilion didn't know what it found so amusing and didn't especially care. The creed of the fleet had served him well for thirty years and he'd follow it until hell claimed his soul.

Hours of tedious silence passed. No one approached him on the forecastle and the minimal conversation remained muted. The only downside to having a crew that feared you was a lack of people willing to chat. Despite his near uselessness, Lawton at least had some spine. Maybe he should have sent Dandan to the island and kept Lawton around for company.

A vibration ran through the sword and up his back.

Your men have failed. The dragon is awake.

He was going to gut Lawton and feed him to the sharks. "How can you know that?"

When a being as mighty as the dragon wakes, it's enough to make the ether shift.

"How long do we have before the thing comes roaring in breathing fire and generally laying waste to everything in the area? How do I kill it?"

Kill it? The power I can project into your sword is nothing to a dragon. But don't worry, it won't make a move against us directly.

Dantilion ran a hand through his hair. "What do you mean? What's the point of waking the thing if it won't do what you need?"

As a last resort. You fail to understand the scale of power we're dealing with. The dragon could easily reshape a continent if it loosed its power indiscriminately. It won't act unless the world itself is in danger. Most likely it has empowered a champion, one of Dagon's servants, I'm sure. That at least is an enemy you can contend with. Find the dragon's champion and kill him.

Finally, some action. "With pleasure. Where do I find him?"

His question brought only silence, but Dantilion didn't panic. Often the sword went quiet when doing something magical. Perhaps it needed to concentrate just like a person. It would speak when it had the answer he needed. Ever since he found the sword, it had never failed him and he remained confident that it wouldn't fail him now.

Half an hour later his faith was rewarded.

The dragon's champion has appeared on the far side of the island. Hurry, before they escape.

He didn't need to be told twice. "Alright you lot, weigh

anchor and set the sails. The enemy has made their move. Now it's time to crush them once and for all."

The crew leapt to obey. They didn't like waiting any more than he did.

Dandan hesitantly approached. "Captain, what about Lawton and the rest of the shore party?"

"They failed me, Dandan. Failed me most miserably. Now we have to clean up their mess." He shook his head. "Let them rot on this wretched island. It's a kinder death than I would have normally offered."

"Aye, Captain."

Dandan returned to the helm and soon enough they were underway. Dantilion's blood sang. He lived for this, the hunt and then the kill.

⋅ ⟶ ✧

Lawton hardly believed his eyes when the woman from Black Rat Cove came running out of the jungle. He'd been so surprised by the tree falling into the clearing and bursting into flames he didn't even react before she'd killed one of his men and ran into the cave. One of the other guys said a man entered ahead of her, likely her companion from the cove.

That was ten minutes ago and he still didn't know what to do. They couldn't see more than ten feet into the cave and none of the men wanted to go in after them. Lawton debated to himself whether he'd be better off taking his chances in the cave or with Captain Crow. Neither option appealed to him, but sometimes the devil you knew was better than the alternative.

But not today.

"Who wants to report to the captain and who's coming

with me into the cave?" Lawton asked.

The men, hard, grizzled hands all, stared at him like he'd asked if they preferred the hangman or headsman.

"The captain will kill us," one of them said.

"I'm not going in that cave," another said.

Lawton shrugged and grabbed his axe. "I'm going in the cave. Come with me or go back to the ship. I don't care which you choose, but anyone just standing here staring into space when I get back will get a taste of my axe."

Lawton pulled a chunk of burning branch out of the fire to serve as a makeshift torch and stalked off toward the dark opening. That threat assumed he'd come out alive and in any shape to fight. Right now, such a thing seemed far too optimistic.

The guttering flame pushed the darkness back a little bit, just enough for him to see the rough stone floor and the distinct lack of tracks in the dust. Those two had to have come this way. There was no other way for them to go since they didn't come back out. Lawton knew little enough about magic, but this stank of it.

Something crunched behind him and he turned to find four member of the team following hesitantly behind. One of them carried a second torch that made little difference in dispelling the darkness. Still, he felt better having backup.

Assuming they found anyone to fight.

"The others went back to the ship," one of the men said.

"Their choice." Lawton kept moving forward. This damn tunnel had to end somewhere and when they got there, they'd find their prey.

Or so he'd assumed. Twenty minutes later a light appeared ahead of them and the group emerged into the clearing where they started out.

"How the hell?" one of the guys asked.

"Magic," Lawton growled. Probably the same magic that whisked the woman and her companion away.

"So what do we do?"

"What can we do? We go back to the ship and pray to any listening angel that the captain doesn't kill us all."

That pronouncement drew every bit as much enthusiasm as Lawton expected, but the truth remained unchanged. He shouldered his axe and set out at a dull trudge down the path back to the beach. One after the other the men fell in behind him.

The walk back took about ten minutes at their reluctant pace. When he emerged from the jungle Lawton stopped and stared. *The Murderer's Nest* had her sails up and was sailing north at a rapidly accelerating pace. The men that had gone ahead waved and shouted for them to come back. As if they actually wanted to face the captain.

"They're leaving without us," one of the men said.

Lawton nodded, but didn't speak. He didn't know what to say. Had their luck just gotten better or worse?

Robert hit the water feet first and descended a good ten feet before swimming to the surface. He found Blade treading water a few feet away, a big grin splitting her face. He loved her more than he could say, but she really did get too excited about anything dangerous.

"Well, we survived," Robert said. "I can't deny my surprise about that. What did you think of Soom?"

"I don't like people messing with my sword, but otherwise he seemed okay. I hope we won't even need his help, but it will be nice knowing he's watching our backs."

Robert grunted. From the sounds of it, the dragon intended

to do nothing but watch, at least for the moment. Too bad. With his help, they probably could have wrapped things up in a few days.

Scaly emerged in a gush of water. "Did you wake the dragon?"

"Sure did." Robert gave him a brief rundown of the meeting. "Is that what Dagon expected?"

"Neither Dagon nor his Chosen shared their expectations with me. My job was to get you safely here."

"Don't suppose we can get a ride back to the ship?" Robert asked.

"Very well, one last favor before we part ways." The serpent lowered its head and they climbed aboard. "I have never worked with humans before. You have proven more useful to the mission than I expected."

A bit of a backhanded compliment, but Robert would take it. "Thanks. As man-eating sea monsters go, you've been decent company as well."

Scaly let out a rhythmic hiss and it took Robert a moment to realize he was laughing. Robert barely stifled his own chuckle at the idea of a sea serpent with a sense of humor.

They only needed a couple minutes to reach the ship. When his feet hit the deck Robert let out a sigh of relief. They'd done their part, now it fell to others to finish the job.

Scaly dove out of sight, probably off to report to Chosen that they'd completed their task. He found he'd miss having the serpent watching over them. Creepy or not, Scaly made a person feel safe out at sea.

"Thompson, weigh anchor and get us out of here."

"With pleasure, sir," his second said. "Where to?"

Robert glanced at Blade, but she just shrugged.

"Back to Tao," he said at last. "I find I need a little rest and the rent is paid on our house for another three months."

"Think you should try and reach Abin on the crystal ball?" Blade asked.

"You read my mind. I want to know how the kid is holding up."

They went below deck while the crew got busy. It felt a little anticlimactic, just going home after talking with a dragon that looked like a man. Somehow Robert had imagined something a little more spectacular from a meeting with a legendary being.

Inside their cabin he found his crystal ball resting in its holder right where he left it. Not that he expected the thing to have wandered off on its own, but with magic you never really knew. He sat on the cot in front of it and rested his fingers on the smooth, cool crystal. Ether flowed between him and the device and he focused on Abin and his scrying room.

Several minutes passed with no response so he released the spell. When he did, he became aware that they'd gotten underway. Good, Thompson was as efficient as always.

"Still nothing?" Blade asked.

He shook his head. "I don't know what's going on, but there's a serious problem in the High Kingdom."

"Try Kent," Blade said.

Robert snapped his fingers. "Why didn't I think of that? He's bound to have some idea what's going on."

He reactivated the crystal ball and focused on Kent's new company wizard, Benri. Robert had only spoken to the man a handful of times, but he seemed an okay sort. Hopefully Kent didn't trust him as completely as the last fellow.

It took only a few seconds for Benri to complete the connection. The wizard's swarthy, bearded face filled the ball. "Robert! It's been a while. Looking for more merchandise?"

"Not just now. I need to talk to Kent if he's handy."

"Let me check."

The ball filled with darkness, but the connection remained strong. Robert hadn't learned that trick yet. Kind of a low priority at the moment.

"What's going on?" Blade asked. She couldn't see anything without being connected to the ball and he'd yet to learn how to add a second person to the link.

"Benri's gone to fetch Kent. Hopefully he's not in an important meeting or something."

Turned out he wasn't and five minutes later Kent's distorted face rather than Benri's filled the crystal.

"Hello, sir," Robert said. "I was hoping you might know what's happened in Sultan's Oasis. I've been trying to get in touch with the palace, but haven't succeeded in weeks."

"Nor have we," Kent said. "I'm debating sending a team to investigate, but I don't want to poke my nose into something and make it worse. What did you hear last?"

"Maybe I should just fill you in from the beginning." Robert took a breath, sent a silent prayer that Kent didn't think he'd gone mad, and started talking. When he finished he added, "Unless you can think of something more useful for us to do, we're headed back to Tao."

"A dragon, huh? Interesting. I look forward to hearing the details in person, assuming we all survive. The last thing I heard from Vilos was that a goblin had stolen Nord's head and he'd dispatched a team led by Abin to get it back. When I contacted him for an update a few weeks later I failed to reach anyone. As for what you can do, nothing comes to mind. Returning to Tao seems as likely a move as any."

"A goblin stole Nord's head? And I thought my story was crazy." Robert grinned. "You know how to reach me if anything changes. We're glad to lend a hand any way we can."

"Sir!" Thompson shouted from on deck. "We need you!"

"I've got to go. Thanks for the information." Robert disconnected. "Thompson sounded rather upset."

"No kidding." Blade headed for the door. "You coming?"

He wanted to say no and hit the cot for about ten hours' sleep. "Yeah, right behind you."

Up on deck the sails were set and they were just getting under way. Every sailor's gaze was turned south. Robert looked himself and cursed the universe.

The big pirate ship, the one Scaly was afraid to attack, had rounded the island and now bore down on them, every yard of cloth out.

Fear washed his exhaustion away and Robert ran up to the helm.

Thompson tore his gaze away from the approaching ship. "She just appeared out of nowhere."

"How the hell did they even know we left the cave? Never mind. Can we outrun her?" Robert asked already knowing the answer.

"Not a chance in open water. That galley's got too much sail for us. We're nimbler, but I don't know these waters well enough to try something fancy."

"That's what I figured. Heaven's mercy, why can't we catch a break?"

"Orders, sir?" Thompson asked.

"Put out everything we've got and run for it. They'll need a couple days to close the gap. Maybe we can lose them in the dark." That sounded pathetic even to him.

"We'll fight to the end, sir. Not a man here wants to get captured by pirates."

Robert clapped him on the shoulder. Hopefully it wouldn't come to that, but he didn't have high hopes.

CHAPTER 15

Kweeg let out a long, contented sigh as he stretched out on a pile of soft furs. A trio of females, their wrinkled green skin glistening in the torchlight, emerged from another part of the cave with trays loaded with fresh meat. Only the best cuts for Kweeg. He smelled monkey, rat, and best of all man flesh. His mouth watered and his stomach rumbled.

When the metal man picked him up and tossed him into that black pit, Kweeg had trembled and expected many awful things. What he hadn't expected, despite his master's promises of a reward, was the actual reward. Who would have thought that there was a nice cozy cave with females and the best meat at the bottom of the nasty hole?

He should have trusted mighty Balthis. Kweeg did everything his master said, so naturally he'd received his reward. That's how things were supposed to work. That his master's other servant had delivered the rewards roughly meant nothing. Balthis did everything roughly. No doubt all demons did. Just because Kweeg would have happily betrayed another goblin and kept all the meat and females for himself didn't mean Balthis would. Goblin females and fresh meat probably didn't even appeal to a demon.

So he settled back and watched his females while anticipating the tasty meat.

"Kweeg!" a deep, dark voice said.

The females fled with his meat and Kweeg cowered on his bed. "Master? Kweeg didn't mean to doubt you."

"Of course you did, you're a goblin. A weak, miserable little goblin and yet of all my servants, you are the only one not to fail me."

Kweeg sat up and puffed out his chest. "Kweeg is mighty Balthis's humble servant."

"And now you must serve me again."

Kweeg slumped. Again? He already traveled to a nasty human city to fetch a head, what could his master want now? And more importantly how long would it take to get back to his females and meat?

"Some humans are coming, Kweeg, and they want to take your reward."

Kweeg leapt to his feet. "Take Kweeg's meat? Never!"

"We will make sure they can't threaten your reward again."

"Yes! Kweeg will kill anyone that tries to steal his meat." He frowned. "What do I have to do?"

"Outside, my servant, the one you rescued, is fighting to set me free, but he's losing. Where he fails, you must succeed."

Kweeg's excitement withered. The giant metal man was losing and his master wanted Kweeg to step in? Even with his master's magic, Kweeg had no hope of winning. He looked around for a way out, but the females had sealed the opening to the meat locker.

Where could he run?

"You don't need to fight them, you coward," Balthis said.

"While they're busy, you can swoop in and seize the prize. All you must do is bring a particular human girl to my temple and place her near the altar. Surely you're not afraid of a mere girl?"

"Kweeg isn't afraid." He should be able to manage a girl for the few miles separating the pit from his old home.

"Not that temple," Balthis said. "Powerful enemies stand between you and it. You'll need to bring her to the next closest, on Serpent Island."

Kweeg blinked his big yellow eyes. He'd never heard of that place. He knew what an island was and that they were surrounded by water. Swimming with a prisoner wouldn't be easy, especially since Kweeg didn't know how to swim.

"Never fear, little goblin, I have left you a gift in the chamber above, a sword that will allow you to control even more of my power. And you don't need to worry about finding the island. One of my other servants will meet you on the ocean and take you the rest of the way."

Kweeg found himself floating up through the darkness, his cozy cave vanishing from view. He steeled his nerve. If the nasty humans had their way, he'd never get back to his perfect life. Kweeg refused to let them ruin everything he'd worked so hard for.

He popped out of the pit and dropped to the stone floor. A few feet to his right, a sword nearly as long as he was tall sat forgotten in the dim light. Kweeg needed both hands to lift it and when he swung it nearly ended up on his backside.

"Not to complain, Master, but this sword is too big for Kweeg."

Darkness gathered around the sword and he nearly dropped it. It slowly shrank until the blade measured about a foot and the handle fit neatly in his hand. "Thank you, Master. How do I use this wonderful thing?"

"Be patient a moment," his master said.

A few seconds later black flames ran along both edges of the blade. Kweeg nearly dropped it again, but quickly recognized the flames as the same as those that he used to gather around his hands.

Then something more amazing happened. More flames rushed out and the next thing he knew they had formed into a horse.

Kweeg frowned. Goblins couldn't ride horses, they were too big, like the sword used to be.

Lightning stabbed his brain. "I said be patient!"

"Yes, Master." It seemed the demon remained cranky. Assuming it was ever anything besides cranky.

The horse melted into a puddle of black flames then reformed into a jaguar. Kweeg's eyes widened. One of the big tribes had warriors that rode the huge black cats into battle. He never imagined getting a chance to ride one himself.

Hesitantly he approached the beast. "Nice cat. You will be friends with Kweeg?"

"Stupid! It's not a real jaguar. It's a magical construct made by the sword. Now climb on its back and capture the girl. I will be waiting for you at the second temple."

Balthis's presence faded from the back of Kweeg's mind. Despite what his master said, he still tiptoed over to the jaguar. The beast never flinched as he climbed up on its back. The moment he'd settled himself, the black cat launched itself into the air.

Kweeg screamed then remembered that it was supposed to carry him over the water so naturally it flew.

He spotted the circle of light above him and tightened his grip on the sword. Kweeg had never failed his master and he wouldn't start now.

✦

Vilos had never been to the jungle and he hoped to never come again. Only Heat's Bane's magic kept the air from stifling him. He felt terrible for Abin who broke out in a sweat the instant he set foot out of the portal. If the heat and humidity bothered Daktari, he showed no sign. Vilos figured he had a spell for every climate no doubt including underwater or the top of a mountain.

He took in the walls of greenery, the nearby temple, and dismissed them as irrelevant. "Where is it?"

Daktari and Abin both pointed east and they set out. Heat's Bane carved them a path with wide, effortless swings. Even so it took nearly an hour before he spotted a familiar black figure standing in a clearing ahead. Everything around Nord looked dead and judging from the expression twisting his features, his brother was in considerable pain.

Vilos only had eyes for Shara, who appeared to be still asleep, slung over Nord's left shoulder.

He charged, sword raised.

A wall of black flames sprang up to block him.

He stopped a foot short of getting his face burned off.

The flames only reached seven feet in the air, far less than during their previous battle. Had Nord gotten weaker or was this some sort of trick?

Vilos turned to Daktari who wore a thoughtful look.

"How do we get through?" Vilos asked.

"I'm not certain. Something's wrong with him. It feels like the link between your brother and The Void is out of sync. I assume that explains his pained expression."

"Is that what I'm feeling?" Abin asked. "Nord seems so much weaker now."

"Sealing one of the void pits no doubt made a difference as well, not to mention he no longer has that sword."

Vilos had been so focused on Shara he missed all of that. "Do you have a plan to get my daughter or not?"

"I'm working on it," Daktari said. "Nord isn't going anywhere, at the moment anyway."

Vilos ground his teeth, but what choice did he have? On his own he had no hope of saving Shara and the sorcerer was right, the standoff might last for heaven only knew how long.

In the end, the answer came faster than he'd feared.

"We'll approach him from three sides," Daktari said. "Vilos, stay where you are. Abin, circle around to the far side. I'll try from above."

Daktari rose six feet as Abin circled around. Vilos hated not knowing what was happening.

"What do you see?" he asked. "Is she okay?"

"Yes, Shara appears unharmed. The flames don't form a dome. "I'm going to try and lift her out. If the flames shift to stop me, you two need to be ready to move."

Vilos tensed. He'd be ready alright.

⸻

Daktari stared down at Nord and debated how best to retrieve the princess. She rested over his shoulder and he had his arm loosely wrapped around her. Lifting her out wouldn't pose a problem, but moving Nord's arm enough to free her would. His void enhanced metal body resisted magic like nothing Daktari had ever encountered.

Perhaps if he used shadow magic. That had proven at least somewhat effective in previous encounters with The Void's minions.

Purple light gathered around his magic. Before he could

cast the spell he had in mind, Nord's arm shifted on its own and Shara sagged, nearly falling to the ground. Was Nord trying to help them? He would have dismissed the idea out of hand once, but given the apparent rift between the former prince and The Void, the possibility couldn't be ignored.

Whatever the case, he needed to act quickly.

A band of energy formed around Shara and she started to rise.

She groaned, opened her eyes, and looked up at him. "Daktari? Where am I? What happened?"

"Stay calm, child. I'll have you out of there shortly."

As if to mock him, the black flames surged up and sealed off the opening, severing the threads he'd used to lift her.

"This way, Princess, hurry," Abin said.

Daktari rose so he could see over the flames. His view cleared just in time to see a goblin mounted on the back of a huge cat made of black flames run Abin through from behind.

Shara screamed.

"I'm coming!" Vilos roared and sprinted for the far side of the flames.

The goblin grabbed Shara and hurled her across the front of his mount.

Spears of shadow magic streaked in only to be blown apart by a burst of black flames.

The goblin raced into the air just ahead of a swipe from Heat's Bane.

Daktari flew after them, determined to reclaim the princess.

Fifty feet from the clearing the goblin sent a wave of flames at him. The void energy disrupted the ether, sending him hurtling toward the ground.

Daktari landed in a heap, uninjured thanks to his many

surviving defensive spells. When he regained his feet, the goblin appeared as little more than a black dot in the sky.

They'd lost her again.

"Daktari! Help!" Vilos knelt beside the fallen wizard, his hands pressed to the man's stomach. When Daktari had joined him he asked, "Can you heal him?"

"Yes, but unlike with divine healing there'll be a price."

"I'll pay it. Do what you must."

"No, Majesty." Abin gasped the words out, blood leaking from the side of his mouth. "You're too important."

Daktari ignored the touching scene and began a simple necromancy spell. Unlike what most laymen believed, necromancy dealt with far more than the raising and controlling of undead. He extracted a modest fragment of life energy from Vilos, drawing a pained hiss, then used it to repair a large vein in Abin's abdomen. The little energy remaining he spread evenly throughout the injured wizard's body.

Much work remained to be done, but at least Abin was out of immediate danger. He gestured again and the wounded man rose on a disk of ether. "He's out of danger. It won't be long before I can summon the priests. They are better equipped to deal with a serious injury."

"What about Shara?" Vilos asked.

Daktari didn't have a chance to answer before the wall of flames vanished and Nord crashed to his knees.

"The Key Bearer is on her way to release my champion." The words came out of Nord's mouth, but he didn't speak to them, The Void did. "Soon your world will be nothing but a memory."

"Vilos?" That sounded like Nord. "Are you there, brother?"

Vilos shifted around, moving gingerly, until he stood where his brother could see him. "Where is that goblin taking my daughter?"

"A temple of Balthis. I don't know where. I thought The Void would give me the power to conquer and rule forever."

"The Void only destroys," Daktari said. "If you truly wanted to rule, you shouldn't have betrayed me. The Broken Kingdom would still be yours now."

"Rub it in, why don't you. It seems betrayal is all I'm good for and now I'm paying for it."

"If you have anything to say to him," Daktari said. "Say it quickly. The void energy sustaining his soul has nearly run out."

Vilos blew out a long sigh. "Despite our differences, you are still my brother. I forgive you your crimes. Go in peace to whatever fate awaits your soul."

"You're a better brother than I deserve. I hope you get her back." Nord's eyes glazed over and Daktari felt his soul leave his body.

"Do you know what will happen to him?" Vilos asked.

"Of course and so do you. After the life of murder and conquest he's lived, he'll end up absorbed into the essence of Hell and making the demons just that much stronger."

Vilos glared at him. "You're hardly a saint yourself."

"Did I ever claim to be? I assure you, I know my fate very well indeed and have made arrangements to mitigate it. I suggest we summon the priests and try and figure out which temple of Balthis the goblin has taken Shara to."

"Robert and Blade." Abin's voice came out as little more than a pained whisper. "Remember when he contacted us? He said they'd found a temple of Balthis."

"Yes! On an island somewhere near Tao. How do we contact them and find out exactly where?"

"I will handle it," Daktari said. "But first, this temple needs to be purified, otherwise we may find ourselves rushing from island to jungle trying to catch whoever has her at the moment."

"There's no time!" Vilos looked like he wanted to grab Daktari by the robe and shake him. Fortunately for his continued health, he refrained.

"Yes there is and we're going to take as much as necessary. This needs to be done right. We need to purify every temple and seal every pit. Once that's done, Balthis can't return to this world and join with The Void. If we rush around like idiots, it only benefits our enemies."

"She's my daughter."

"I am aware of that. Why do you think I'm not letting you make any of the decisions?" Daktari pointed and a blade of shadow magic separated Nord's head from the black armor. He assumed the armor needed a head to make it function otherwise why go to all the trouble of collecting Nord? It didn't seem like The Void had any more use for it, but why take chances?

He led the way back toward the temple. Vilos could follow or not as he preferred. Though in this place he didn't have so many choices.

First the priests, then Shara. She still had another pit to seal and nothing could happen to her before she did.

CHAPTER 16

Robert hadn't left the rear castle of his ship in hours. Noon had come and gone, but he only drank a cup of water for lunch. His eyes were glued to the pirate ship growing rapidly larger behind them. They still had maybe half a mile on their hunters, but that wouldn't last the day. Their luck, such as it was, appeared to have run out. In two hours or so he figured that catapult on the pirate's forecastle would start launching boulders if they were lucky and weighted chains if they weren't. If they lost the sails, that would be it.

The click of approaching boots forced him to drag his gaze away from the enemy ship. Blade carried an apple in each hand and wore a determined look.

"You need to eat something." She tossed him an apple and took a bite of her own. "You won't be much help if you faint."

Robert caught the fruit and bit down. A little soft but still sweet and juicy. "Thanks. My appetite shrinks the closer they get. How's the sword?"

"The balance hasn't changed and it's as sharp as ever." She

drew it and held up the now purplish-black weapon. "Whatever Soom did, he didn't change the way it feels."

"Good. I'd hate it if you had to learn a new sword in the middle of a fight for our lives." Robert finished his apple and tossed the core overboard.

During his snack the pirates had gained another fifty or so yards.

"Come on." Blade grabbed his arm. "Let's go down to the armory and pick you out a new crossbow. It'll distract you."

Robert seriously doubted that, but he didn't want to argue. His obsessive watching hadn't slowed the pirates down in the least, so let the lookout do his job.

"They're turning!" the lookout shouted.

What?

Robert spun back around. Sure enough, the huge galleon had begun to turn west and south.

"They had us dead to rights with no way to outfight or outrun them. Why in heaven's name would they suddenly give up?"

"Are you complaining?" she asked.

"Of course not, but I can't help wondering what called them away. I mean, after the pirates failed to stop us from reaching Soom, they seemed pretty determined to kill us. What changed?"

Blade shrugged. "The more important question is, what do we do now?"

"Uh, sir?" The ship's errand boy, a lad of about sixteen, hesitantly approached.

"What's on your mind?" Robert asked.

The youth kept staring at Blade, a perfectly natural response for any man with a pulse. Robert stepped into his line of sight.

"Focus, son. Did you need something?"

The errand boy gave himself a shake. "Yes, sir. When I went downstairs, I saw a light coming from under your cabin door. I didn't go in! But I thought you'd want to know."

"Someone's trying to reach me. Tell Thompson to keep us on this course just in case the pirates change their mind."

Robert left the boy and hurried across the deck with Blade at his side.

"Abin, you think?" she asked.

"Or Benri. I can't think of anyone else that would know how to contact us."

When Robert opened the door to their cabin, the light streaming out of his crystal ball nearly blinded him. It had never glowed that bright any of the other times Abin tried to reach him. He squinted and groped around until his fingers touched the cool surface of the ball.

An effort of will connected him and he found himself facing Daktari. Robert's throat tightened, but he forced himself to speak calmly. "This is a surprise. How can I be of service?"

"How much do you know of events in the High Kingdom?"

"I spoke to Kent not long ago and he mentioned a goblin stealing his brother's head. Beyond that, I have no idea."

Daktari filled him in on Nord's new body, the sealing of the first void pit, and Shara's subsequent kidnapping. So much had happened and he struggled to take it all in.

"We assume the goblin that took her is the same one that stole Nord's head. We further assume that the creature is taking her to the temple of Balthis you mentioned. At any rate, that's the only other temple we know about so if she's not there, I don't know where else to look."

Understanding dawned on Robert. "This goblin, it used a sword with void magic, right?"

"Yes, I believe it was the same one Nord carried for a time. It seems the former prince had a falling out with his new master. Hardly surprising given the man's treacherous nature. Why?"

"Because we were just fleeing for our lives from a pirate ship and someone onboard had a void artifact. What are the odds the pirates are off to meet with a certain goblin?"

"The odds are excellent. Can you catch their ship before they reach the island?"

"Doubtful. But we can arrive a few hours behind them. If we take a direct line we might arrive first, but if they change course, we might lose them completely. That's not a risk I'm eager to take with the kid's life."

"No, stay with them. Vilos and I will join you as soon as we're able. A group of priests are currently purifying Balthis's temple so he can't use it to return."

The connection broke and Robert blew out a long breath. He found dealing with Daktari...intense.

"What's going on?" Blade asked.

He told her. "Looks like the kid's in trouble again. Sometimes I think she has worse luck than us."

"An impressive feat in and of itself. We're going to rescue her." That last was a statement not a question.

"Of course, and Vilos and Daktari are coming to lend a hand. That sorcerer terrifies me, but I'd be glad to have him on my side in a fight."

"I'd be glad to stay as far away from him as possible."

"No kidding. Let's get up on deck and tell Thompson to change course. I'm sure he'll be delighted."

"Let me go!" The human female screamed and pounded Kweeg's leg with her little fists.

It didn't really hurt, but her screeching had begun to give

him a headache. She'd been carrying on since he grabbed her. The flames on his jaguar's back had wrapped around her body, so she had no hope of getting away.

Kweeg glanced down at the water far below. Even if the stupid human got away, where did she think she could go? He hadn't seen any land since they left the jungle and started across the ocean.

She started in on a fresh round of screeching.

"Quiet! Kweeg has had enough! No more noise!"

She twisted to look up at him. "Let me go and you'll have quiet."

"Kweeg would happily let you go. A fall from this height would make you nice and tender. But mighty Balthis needs you to set him free, so you'll have to stay with Kweeg."

"Then you'll have to listen to me scream my lungs out." She took a deep breath.

Kweeg snarled, drew back, and punched her in the side of the head with the fist holding his new sword.

She went limp and his heart nearly stopped.

Humans weren't that weak, were they? A punch from a goblin like Kweeg wouldn't kill one. Would it?

He put his free hand down beside her nose and felt a soft breath across his skin.

Praise Balthis, she lived.

He shuddered to think what his master might have done if he'd accidentally killed the one that he needed to set him free.

But she was fine. Or fine enough anyway.

Now, where did he need to go to find his fellow servant of Balthis? The jaguar adjusted course as soon as he thought about it. "Good cat. Take Kweeg where he needs to go. I have to get there before this noisy human wakes up."

His mount didn't speed up, but it did fly along about ten times as fast as a goblin could run. Kweeg had never moved this fast. Not even that time he ran into a big snake in the top of a tree and fell out. He wished he'd had his new sword that day. The tribe would have praised him had he brought in snake meat. Instead they laughed at his bruises.

If he'd still had a tribe, he would have let his cat eat the ones that laughed. Come to think of it, they were all older and had died years ago anyway. He smiled to think of his dead tormentors. Kweeg outlasted his entire tribe and now look at him. Servant to a mighty demon and armed with a magic sword.

The jaguar started to fly toward the water.

Kweeg let out a very unheroic shriek and kicked the cat's ribs. "Not down, stupid cat. Up!"

As with his earlier request for speed, the cat ignored him.

When his panic subsided, Kweeg spotted the ship. He knew nothing about ships beyond the fact that they traveled across the water. This looked like a big one with many sheets of cloth to catch the wind. He felt a power identical to his coming from down there. The one that would take him to Balthis's temple must be aboard.

Kweeg pet the cat's head. "Kweeg is sorry he called you stupid."

The jaguar landed on the ship and vanished without a warning, dumping Kweeg and the human girl on deck. Many armed humans surrounded Kweeg, but none of them had the power. Still, in Kweeg's experience nothing good came from having so many humans around.

He brandished his sword and black flames ran up the edges. The humans flinched back then parted to let another man through. This one carried a sword liked Kweeg's, only longer, at his waist.

"When I was told to abandon my hunt and transport a fellow sword bearer, I never imagined a goblin landing on my ship. I'm not sure how we'll ever get the stink out."

The humans all laughed at Kweeg who snarled then sniffed. He didn't smell so bad. He'd expected a better welcome from a fellow servant of Balthis.

"And this is the Key Bearer." The nasty human turned his attention to the unconscious female. "Pretty enough, but certainly nothing remarkable."

"She's noisy," Kweeg said.

"I'm sure any woman finding herself in your company would be equally shrill." The human turned to one of his fellows. "Dandan, lock her up and put a guard on her cell."

"Aye, Captain." A burly human with skin the color of teak scooped the female up and carried her away.

"Where are we going?" Kweeg asked. "My master said you knew the way."

"To Serpent Island. Everyone that sails in this part of the ocean knows it. Horrid place full of poisonous snakes. No one lives there and I've never heard of any buildings on it. Though I've also never set foot on the heaven-forsaken rock, so I can't say for certain. Do you have a name, goblin?"

"Kweeg. What about you, human?"

"You may call me Crow." The human glared at the still-gathered men. "What are you lot staring at? Back to work."

The hard-looking men scrambled away. They feared their leader. That was good. Only a weak leader wasn't feared by his followers.

When Kweeg looked back he found Crow's sword pointed at his head.

"Now that you've brought the girl, I wonder if I can kill you." A few seconds passed and nothing happened. What had the human expected? Kweeg was Balthis's champion. Crow was only providing transportation. "I guess not."

Crow raised his sword and studied it. "Have you noticed

that your sword is getting weaker? I find that there's very little extra power lately."

Kweeg only got his sword a little while ago and didn't know what to say. "It made the cat that brought me here and gutted a wizard that tried to stop me. I didn't need it to do anything else."

"I suppose not." Crow sheathed his sword. "Make yourself comfortable. It will take some time to reach the island."

The human wandered off leaving Kweeg alone in the middle of the ship. Kweeg found a shady spot near the barkless tree growing out of the floor and sat down. First a human city and now a human ship. Balthis must be truly testing his faith.

He shot a furtive look at the sky. No demon glowering down at him. Kweeg wiped the sweat from his brow. With mighty Balthis you never knew when a lightning bolt to the brain might strike. His eyes quickly grew heavy and his last thought before sleep claimed him was the hope that the humans had meat somewhere on the ship.

⋅—✣

Shara woke to a throbbing headache. The stink of the goblin had been replaced by something else, something damp and moldy. She forced her eyes open and looked around. Not that she saw much, wooden walls, wooden floor, and a door made of iron bars. It looked like one of the cells back home in the dungeon. It also seemed to be moving. Her stomach churned and she clenched her jaw against a wave of nausea. Heaven help her, the goblin had brought her to a ship.

How in the world did she end up in a cell on a ship? The last thing she remembered was flying on the front of the goblin's strange mount. The thing looked like a cat made of black flames. Whenever she saw something like that she first thought of void energy, but why would The Void give power to a goblin? Surely it could have found something better. They had been over the ocean, so a ship did make sense. At least as much sense as anything made lately.

She winced against a particularly painful twinge in her head. When she touched her temple, she found a lump that felt like a quail egg. That shriveled little runt had actually hit her. If she ever got her hands on it, she'd ring that goblin's scrawny neck.

Using the mental exercise Daktari taught her along with deep breathing she calmed her stomach a fraction and pushed the pain to the back of her mind. With her focus restored, she stood, wobbled, and took a step toward the door. With her power, a simple lock wouldn't hold her for a second.

The angry-looking, broad-shouldered man standing across a narrow hall from the cell, on the other hand, would be a much bigger problem. He leered at her, revealing a mouthful of crooked yellow teeth.

On second thought, instead of opening the lock, maybe she should make it stronger. A few seconds with the ether and nothing short of a battering ram would open the door.

Feeling as secure as possible under the circumstances, Shara offered her best smile. "Where am I?"

"The brig," the man said.

"Yes, I guessed that on my own. I meant where in a grander sense."

His browed furrowed as he tried to figure out what she'd just said. Slowly understanding washed over him. "You're in the brig of *The Murderer's Nest*, the best damn pirate ship sailing the seas."

Pirates, marvelous. At the rate she was going, every group in the world would have a turn holding her prisoner.

CHAPTER 17

Dantilion had been a pirate for many years. He'd
sacked villages, captured ships, and killed men
beyond counting. But the one thing he'd never
gotten used to was being the prey rather than the predator. He
stared out over the water at the white speck following in their
wake.

He couldn't remember ever abandoning a chase, certainly
not when they were so close to catching the prize. But this?
Having his former target turn and hunt him? The sheer insult
of it galled him. They should thank Dagon he'd gotten other
orders and sail as far and as fast from his sight as possible.
But no.

*They're irrelevant. Get to the island and free Balthis. Once that's
done, I doubt even the dragon would be enough to save this world.*

The Void didn't understand. The lack of respect bothered
Dantilion more than anything. It felt like a rabbit nipping at
the heels of a wolf it had just escaped. He needed to snap back
at them.

187

"Would you like the farseer, Captain?" Dandan held out the extended cylinder.

Dantilion turned away from his first mate. "No need. We know who the fools are and they're too far away to threaten us. How's the girl?"

"Obviously unhappy with the situation, but she's not pitching a fit or anything."

"Probably happy to escape the goblin. Speaking of the ugly green rat, I saw him go below deck. What sort of a mess is he making?"

"Cook says he demanded meat then found a dark corner to eat it in."

Dantilion grunted. "As long as he stays out of the way, I guess that's fine."

"What are we going to do with the goblin?"

"Nothing. It serves the same power I do. Unless that changes, I can't kill it and if you try, I'm liable to need a new first mate."

"Captain!" the lookout called down from the crow's nest. "Something's happening on the enemy ship."

He snatched the farseer out of Dandan's grip and put it to his eye. An orange ball had formed on the enemy's bow.

It's magic. Get ready to defend yourself.

Dantilion ripped his sword free. A moment later the fire-ball came rushing toward them.

A vertical slash sent an arc of black flames to meet the spell.

Both of them exploded in a mix of sparks.

"If they have a wizard that powerful onboard, why didn't they attack earlier?" Dandan asked.

Dantilion had no idea and The Void offered no hints.

Kweeg came scrabbling up on deck, a half-eaten strip of jerky in its mouth. It sniffed the air before coming to join

Dantilion in the rear castle. Dandan quickly made himself scarce.

"Kweeg smells magic."

That the goblin could smell anything over its own stink amazed Dantilion. "Yes, we were just attacked by a wizard on the ship chasing us. Would you be kind enough to fly out there and sink their ship, or failing that, destroy their sails?"

Kweeg put a hand on the void sword thrust through his belt. "Mighty Balthis says not to bother, they're too far away for it to matter."

Dantilion clenched his teeth. If they did nothing, he'd have to stay on watch for any incoming spells until they reached Serpent Island. They were making good time, but they still had at least two days' sailing ahead of them.

"Kweeg thinks the sword is running out of magic." The goblin spoke in a low voice, obviously hoping no one else would hear.

Dantilion had come to the same conclusion, though how a being as powerful as The Void could run out of power escaped him.

I am not running out of power. The problem is, with only one pit, I can only push so much energy through. It's like trying to force the ocean through a pinhole. I have already cut off my other servants on this world to power your swords to the extent I have. Should the second pit be sealed, you'll find out what limited really means.

Dantilion hated the sound of that. "It seems we'll have to take turns warding the ship against enemy spells."

"Kweeg will take the night watch. Goblins see better in the dark anyway."

Dantilion forced himself to nod. Leaving the fate of his ship to a goblin. He never imagined he'd see the day.

✦

R obert stayed well back as Daktari loosed another fireball at the distant pirate ship. He'd been firing the things off at seemingly random intervals since he and the sultan appeared on deck a day previous. It didn't look to Robert as if the spells had even gotten close to hitting home. He considered that a good thing since he had no desire for the ship to get burned down with Shara still inside. Judging from his anxious looks, her father had similar thoughts.

When the most recent spell got smashed to bits, Robert worked up his courage and strode up to the sorcerer. Daktari looked at him with those cold eyes and quirked an eyebrow.

"What's the point of this? You can't seem to penetrate their defenses."

"Of course I can't. Ether-based magic is virtually useless against void energy. My goal is to force the sword bearers to use their power to thwart my spells. It's subtle, but I can feel their power lessening. Compared to Nord, these two are weaklings."

"Then why not just fly over there and kill them all?"

"Remember, I said compared to Nord. They are still tremendously strong. Besides, I can't portal us over because of the distortion caused by their swords and if we flew, they'd send us crashing into the ocean. No, the trick will be striking as soon as I can see the island. We'll hit them on the beach, before they can reach Balthis's temple."

"They have us rather badly outnumbered," Robert pointed out.

Daktari just snorted. "Ordinary pirates without void energy are no threat to me."

That made Robert feel much better.

The pointless casting lasted into the night and kept going all morning. Later in the afternoon a green dot appeared in the distance. That had to be Serpent Island. His best guess said they had a good four hours more and the pirates maybe one. If they were going to make a move, they needed to do it now.

As if reading his mind—there was a scary idea—Daktari called, "Anyone willing to fight, join me on deck."

Robert let out a breath and left his post in the forecastle. He wasn't much use in a fight, but he had to try and help the kid. Blade joined them as well, of course, along with the sultan. None of the sailors would be going. In fact, Thompson had orders to keep his distance until Robert signaled all clear with his light spell.

So it would be the four of them against a ship full of pirates and two void magic users. Sounded like a fair fight.

"What's the plan?" Robert asked.

"I will fly us to the island, keeping well wide of the pirate ship," Daktari said. "Once the enemy lands, I will eliminate the ordinary pirates. Blade will defend us with her empowered sword and should a direct fight with the enemy sword bearers be necessary, it will fall to her to handle it."

Blade just nodded and if it came to a sword fight, Robert had no doubt who would come out on top.

"What about me?" he asked.

"You and Vilos will secure the princess. There are bound to be some guards protecting her. Once you have her, don't hang around and watch the fight. Put as much distance between you and them as possible. I'll find you after."

Daktari looked at them one after the other. When his gaze settled on Robert he tried to swallow, but found his throat too dry. He hadn't been this nervous when the kraken dragged them down to meet Dagon's Chosen.

If they screwed up, the kid didn't have a chance.

D antilion stared at the beach in shock. They were close enough now that he had no trouble making out the two figures standing there waiting for them. A slender man in a black robe with purple trim and a woman holding a sword with a dark blade.

Two people. The sheer arrogance of the act stunned him. Who did they think they were dealing with? Even without the men they left on Dragon Isle, he had fifty hardened fighters not to mention his void sword. He could probably wipe them both out from here with a single swing.

Don't underestimate them. Even from here I can sense powerful shadow magic.

He'd find out for sure.

Dark flames gathered along his blade and he slashed.

An arc of flames shot out toward the waiting pair.

The woman took a step forward and raised her own sword.

His attack struck the odd-looking weapon and vanished without a trace.

I warned you. She must be the dragon's champion. Only he has the power to so totally defeat my own. You'll need to kill her up close and personal.

"It would be my distinct pleasure."

He smelled Kweeg before the goblin spoke. "What's happening?"

"Enemies are waiting for us. I will take a shore party to deal with them. You stay here and keep anyone from taking the girl."

Kweeg cocked his head as if debating whether to accept the order or not. "Kweeg will stay. No one can steal Balthis's prize while he is here."

Dantilion dearly hoped the goblin's bragging amounted to

more than words. They were so close to winning he almost tasted it.

"Dandan! Get as close you can then drop anchor. Everyone else, prepare for battle! Ready the longboats! We'll show those fools what happens to those who dare oppose the fleet."

The men roared, clearly eager for a fight.

Dantilion gave a predatory smile. They were good men, the best in the fleet. Not that they had a fleet anymore. Of course, that didn't really matter since the entire world would be gone soon.

It took half an hour for Dandan to get the ship secured. The men immediately started piling into the four boats. Dandan himself belted on a cutlass and moved to join the party.

Dantilion shook his head. "Keep a skeleton crew and make sure no one tries to reach the girl."

"Captain?"

"Do you think I'm going to trust our fate to a goblin?" They both looked to where Kweeg stood in the shadow of the main-mast picking his nose. "He may have a void sword, but he's also clearly an idiot. Assume someone will try and sneak aboard during the fight and deal with them."

Dandan's face fell but he nodded. "Aye, Captain."

Dantilion left his best man to oversee the ship and went to join the shore party. They hit the water and the men started pulling hard for the beach.

Halfway there, the first scream rang out.

He turned to see purple blades falling out of nowhere, cutting his men to pieces. In seconds the first longboat had a crew of corpses. The robed man must be the same wizard that attacked them earlier. He needed to protect his crew.

I have power enough to protect your boat, but no more.

Dantilion didn't like it, but he had no other choice. Raising his sword, a dome of void energy formed above them. It made everything look like it was in shadows, but he could still see clearly. Unfortunately, what he saw was the remaining ships getting cut to pieces.

Instead of hitting the beach with a force of forty men, he'd have ten. And little hope that those ten would be enough to handle the wizard.

Kill the wizard first then overwhelm the woman with numbers.

A sound strategy.

They hit the beach and Dantilion leapt out of the longboat. The woman stood directly between him and the wizard, sword raised.

A wave of black flames got instantly absorbed by her sword.

He grimaced. How long had it been since he fought a fair battle? Not since he found the void sword certainly.

The pirates surrounded the pair, but no one seemed eager to close in.

Maybe a bluff.

He leveled the sword at them. "Surrender and I promise no harm will come to you."

The woman laughed and the wizard offered a thin, silent smile.

Then the first pirate screamed. All around him his surviving men started to sink into the sand.

Dantilion started to summon the flames to sever the wizard's magic.

They barely started to form when the woman charged.

Her first slash came in so fast he got his sword between them with inches to spare.

Dantilion backpedaled. Turning aside her furious assault took every bit of skill he possessed. All thoughts of saving his men fled in the face of the woman's savagery.

He never even considered summoning the black flames.

Her sword darted for his throat.

A desperate leap carried him a hair's breadth out of range.

As soon as his feet hit the sand he lunged, a low strike aimed to gut her like a fish.

The woman danced out of the way.

He hissed in pain as her counterattack opened a shallow slice on his back.

Pain and rage fueled him.

He met her next blow and locked their swords. Pushing hard he forced her back a step.

A crashing left fist grazed her face, and staggered her.

Eager to seize the advantage, he attacked.

Dantilion stumbled with his first step, his toe caught on a little ridge of sand.

He barely registered what happened before her sword cut right through his heart. The void sword slipped out of his hand and he collapsed as the world went dark.

⸱—✦⸱

Robert and Vilos started swimming as soon as the pirate longships hit the water. Lucky for them that the pirate ship had anchored about as close to the island as possible without running aground. He didn't worry about Blade. With Daktari on her side, the pirates wouldn't know what hit them.

All his focus stayed on swimming, a task he'd never especially enjoyed, but that he'd made a point of mastering. The sultan surprised him. A man that ruled a desert kingdom shouldn't be this strong a swimmer. Assuming they lived, he'd have to ask where he learned.

A hundred yards separated them from the hull when the first screams rang out. Sounded like Daktari had found some unprotected targets. Robert shuddered and put his face down.

He had no pity to spare for any man that would sacrifice an innocent girl to a demon. At least when *he'd* kidnapped her, Robert hadn't really intended to hurt Shara.

Finally, they reached the ship and treaded water as he tried to catch his breath. From their hiding place he could just make out a single longship still afloat. A dark aura protected it. No question which boat carried the void artifact.

"How do you want to get up on deck?" Robert asked. "We could climb the anchor chain, but that's awkward at best."

"Don't worry," Vilos said. "I'll get us up there no problem."

The longship hit the beach and Robert said, "Whatever you're going to do, now's the time."

Vilos reached into the water and came up with his sword. It sparkled in the sun and the next thing he knew they were shooting up on a pillar of ice.

As soon as they were even with the deck, Vilos jumped off and cut down a pirate with a look of dull surprise on his face.

Robert drew a throwing dagger and followed. He figured the best way to do this was to treat Vilos the same way he would Blade. Basically stay out of the way and stick a knife in anyone trying to sneak up on him.

Speaking of which. Robert's arm whipped forward and his dagger sank into the chest of a pirate drawing a bead on Vilos with a crossbow. Never one to let good fortune pass, Robert hurried over and scooped up the crossbow. The pirate gurgled at him but offered no other resistance.

Screams and shouts from the stern drew him away from the dying pirate. Vilos had frozen three men solid and cut a fourth in half.

He might not have Blade's pure skill, but an enchanted mithril sword quickly made up the difference.

Vilos grabbed a dark-skinned man by the throat and slammed him against the rear castle. "Where is my daughter?"

Robert hurried to join them, careful to keep an eye on the rest of the ship. There had to be more pirates around here somewhere.

"You're going to have to let him breathe if you want an answer," Robert said when he reached the rear castle.

Vilos growled in the back of his throat. From the sounds of it, he'd rather strangle the man than get the information he wanted. Robert didn't really care. They were on a ship, how long could it take to search the whole thing? That said, if they were going to search, he'd prefer to get started as soon as possible.

Vilos finally let the pirate go. The man gasped for air and pawed at his throat.

"Best answer the question before he changes his mind," Robert said.

A croak emerged from the man's mouth. He coughed and tried again. "We locked her in the brig. Below deck."

"Is she okay?" Vilos asked.

The pirate nodded. "The captain needed her intact for whatever he planned to do on the island."

"What about guards?" Robert asked.

"Just one outside the cell to keep her from breaking out."

Robert glanced at Vilos and cocked an eyebrow. "Shall we go get her?"

"Yes." Vilos slashed his sword across the pirate's neck, sending his head falling to the deck. "Do you disapprove?"

"Of you killing a pirate? Hardly. My father was a merchant. He hated few things more than pirates." Except maybe bandits, which Robert moonlighted as for a few years, but probably best not to point that out just now.

They left the dead man to slump to the deck and ran for the stairs leading below. Vilos led the way, sword raised and glittering. Some magic would probably defend him from any attack, so Robert happily let him go first.

At the bottom of the steps, they found themselves in a dimly lit passage. The modest light came from crystals embedded in the ceiling that filtered sunlight downward. He'd seen them a few times though the *Journey* had none.

"Shara!" Vilos bellowed.

So much for sneaking up on the guard. Of course, if he heard the bodies thumping to the deck, he probably already knew someone was coming.

"Daddy!" came a muted reply from the right-hand passage.

Vilos charged after her. Robert followed a safe distance behind.

"Stop right there!" A rapidly backpedaling pirate brandished a less-than-impressive cutlass at them.

Vilos waved the sword, encasing the unlucky fellow from head to toe in ice.

The sultan finally stopped and stared. Robert joined him and found Shara standing behind heavy bars staring back, tears streaming down her face.

"Hey, kid. We've got to stop meeting like this." Robert grinned. "You okay?"

She wiped her eyes and smiled. "I'm fine. It seems to be my good luck that everyone that kidnaps me needs me alive."

Vilos grabbed the door and rattled it in its frame. "Hang on, sweetheart, I'll get you out of there."

He raised his sword like he planned to hack the door apart. And given his mithril blade, he probably could do exactly that.

"It's okay." Shara moved closer and gently touched the lock before pushing the door open. "I'm the one that locked it. I didn't want the pirates getting any ideas."

Vilos scooped her up with his free arm and held her tight. A

198

touching scene for sure, but this was hardly the place for a reunion.

"What say we make ourselves scarce?" Robert said. "I've had about enough of pirates to last me a lifetime."

"I second that," Shara said.

Vilos set her down and Robert led the way back toward the stairs. Hopefully Blade and Daktari had finished up with the other pirates. He wanted to get back to the *Journey* and put as much distance between them and this miserable island as possible.

He'd barely managed two steps when a high-pitched shriek filled the air. He half turned only to get flattened by something heavy.

A hard twist got him on his back in time to see a goblin dragging a kicking and screaming Shara away.

The heavy weight turned out to be Vilos. He'd been stabbed in the back about waist high.

Cursing the universe and goblins in particular, Robert dragged himself out from under the sultan. He looked from the bleeding wound to Shara.

"Help her," Vilos gasped.

That clinched it. He collected his dropped crossbow and ran after them.

When he was halfway to the goblin it raised a sword lined with black flames.

Not good.

Robert got ready to dive, but instead of frying him, the little monster blew a hole in the side of the ship.

It leapt out, dragging Shara behind.

He ran to the opening. A black mount of some sort had formed and now it carried the goblin through the sky toward the island with Shara behind him. Robert raised his crossbow, but didn't dare shoot lest he hit the princess.

Blade and Daktari would have to save her.

Robert hurried back to Vilos and studied his wound. It looked pretty bad, but if he bound it and stopped the bleeding, the sultan might survive long enough to reach a priest. How he would survive hearing his daughter had been captured by a goblin for the second time, Robert didn't know.

* —✦

The woman's skill impressed Daktari and he'd seen some of the finest fighters in the world. The pirate she killed knew his business as well, but it hadn't really been an even match. In fact, he doubted the outcome would have been different even if her sword didn't negate the void flames.

"I didn't need your help," Blade said.

He raised an eyebrow.

"You used your magic to make him stumble at the end. No way did a swordsman as good as him trip on his own."

Daktari smiled, his already high opinion of her skill rising a notch. "I'm impressed you noticed. I had no doubt you'd win, but we're in a bit of a rush here, so I thought I'd speed things along. Frankly, I would have killed him directly, but the void energy makes my magic less effective if deployed directly. A little bump in the sand, however, is no problem."

An explosion from the pirate ship cut off whatever argument she planned to make next.

"Bobby!"

She took a step toward the water just as a small figure riding a black mount emerged from the opening in the ship's hull. A slender figure lay draped across the front of the mount.

Daktari snarled. Unbelievable. The goblin had her again.

He conjured hands of shadow magic in the hopes of freeing Shara, but a blast of void energy blew them to pieces.

The goblin flew deeper into the island and started to descend.

He must have reached the temple.

"Come on!" Daktari moved next to Blade and conjured a bubble around them.

"No! Bobby might be hurt. I need to get to the ship."

"If we fail, the whole world dies. I can't deal with the goblin's void magic without you."

They rose a foot off the ground and flew toward the jungle.

She hammered her sword against the bubble, hacking chunks out of it. "Let me go!"

Blade hacked again. At this rate she'd ruin the spell and send them both tumbling to the dirt.

"Enough! If he's dead, you can't help him and if he's not a few minutes won't matter. We rescue the princess then help your friend. And if we're lucky we stop the return of the most dangerous being you've ever imagined."

Blade slumped and stopped hacking at the bubble. Thank heaven for small kindnesses. Free of that distraction he sped up, smashing vines and branches out of his way with equal disinterest. The temple site lay just ahead, sitting like a tumor of corruption rotting the land.

When they reached the heart of it, he stopped and dissolved the bubble. A dark dome surrounded a pile of tumbled stone. Despite its condition, he had no doubt the link to Balthis remained strong.

Blade stalked over and slammed her sword into the dome.

No reaction.

"It's not void energy," he said. "But pure corruption. We've failed. Shara is connected to Balthis and soon the elder demon will be free."

"Then we can check on Bobby."

Daktari nodded. Unless they found a way into the temple, he could do nothing.

The bubble reformed and they flew straight up and out to the damaged pirate ship. He went right through the blasted side of the hull and landed in what looked like the remains of the brig. Robert knelt next to Vilos, seemingly unharmed. The sultan, on the other hand, looked rather the worse for wear.

As soon as the bubble vanished, Blade ran over and knelt beside Robert. "Are you okay?"

"Yeah, aside from a few scrapes. The sultan, on the other hand, got stabbed in the back by that little wretch. He's got the kid."

"I know," Blade said. "They reached the temple."

"Shit!"

"Indeed." Daktari stood over the pair. "How about you two move aside and I'll see if I can stabilize him?"

They stood and backed away as he sent a thread of ether into Vilos's body. Remarkably, the sword had missed most of the vital organs and major arteries. On the downside, it had severed Vilos's spine. A little fire magic cauterized all his wounds and stopped the bleeding. He wouldn't die, but would remain paralyzed from the waist down until they found a priest to heal him.

Assuming the world survived.

He stood and turned to find Blade and Robert facing him with serious expressions.

"There's another way into the temple," Robert said. "The underwater tunnel we escaped out of. I don't know the current state of the cavern, but it might be worth a look."

"It certainly might. Are you two coming?"

They both nodded.

"What about him?" Blade nodded toward the still-unconscious sultan.

"He's stable, but anything more will require the attention of a priest. My magic isn't well suited to healing."

"No kidding." Robert glanced at Heat's Bane as if debating taking the weapon.

"You may as well grab it," Daktari said. "I can teach you how to unleash its magic as we fly. Though such rapid instruction will leave you with a headache."

Robert snatched up the sword. "If the worst that happens is I end up with a headache, I'll call that a win."

Daktari surrounded them with another bubble and they flew out into the clear blue sky. "Which way?"

Robert pointed toward the far side of the island. When they reached a wall of towering cliffs he said, "Under here somewhere. I'm not sure exactly where we emerged."

The bubble splashed into the ocean and Daktari conjured lights. A minute or so of searching revealed the entrance of a tunnel. "Here we are. I'll begin your instruction."

Robert groaned and clutched his temples. Daktari ignored his pain and shot into the passage. It took only seconds for them to emerge in a dank cavern filled with jagged rock formations jutting up. He stopped near a pile of broken stone that appeared to have fallen from above. The heart of Balthis's corruption lay directly overhead.

"That was unpleasant," Robert said. "Still, I see why this sword is so valuable. Never thought we'd find ourselves back here."

Blade put a hand on his shoulder. "Are you okay?"

"Yeah, sure. The worst of the pain is gone."

"Good. I intend to break through. Ready yourselves. The goblin will likely attack as soon as we appear."

The top of the bubble shifted, transforming into a cone that started to spin.

Gathering his will, Daktari sent them crashing into the ceiling.

Stone blasted apart on impact and they kept rising.

A few seconds later they emerged into the fallen temple. Not much remained, but the altar appeared intact and Shara lay on it, unmoving. The Divine Key on her abdomen shone like a second sun.

He dissolved the bubble and an instant later an arc of black flames streaked out from the rubble.

Blade shifted to absorb it with her sword.

Robert sent icicles into the ruins, but no scream of pain answered.

For his part, Daktari ignored the exchange and hurried over to Shara. He got within ten feet before the density of the ether forced him to retreat. As he feared, now that the process had begun, he had no power to stop it.

Balthis would be free.

Robert and Blade continued to chase the goblin through the temple's shadows. It was a waste of time. It had played its part. The little beast could have only a single task remaining and they dared not let it succeed.

"Fall back to me!" he shouted.

Both of his allies looked his way and frowned. He feared for a moment they would ignore him, but at last they joined him beside Shara.

"What?" Blade asked. "We can't let that green-skinned rat get away."

"The goblin is irrelevant. All that matters is protecting Shara. I can't stop the process. Once Balthis is free, our only hope is that she can seal the final pit before he reaches it. Then all we have to deal with is an elder demon rather than a void empowered elder demon."

"Is that all?" Robert asked. "And here I thought we might be in trouble."

．--✴·

K weeg screeched in frustration and immediately hurried to the left so the incoming icicles would miss. He kept shooting fire at the humans and the female blocked them. How could he kill the enemies of mighty Balthis like this?

If he could have separated them, then maybe, but they just gathered around the other female and kept watch.

They are cleverer than some humans. They know the only way to stop my ultimate victory is to seal the second pit, so they focus all their effort on protecting the one capable of doing so.

"What should Kweeg do, Master?"

Retreat for now. They may grow overconfident when they leave the temple. If not, I have another plan in motion.

If his master wanted Kweeg to retreat, he would happily do so. Only fools fought when they didn't have to.

Sneaking back to the darkest part of the temple, Kweeg drew on the sword's power to carry him up and out of the small opening above. The humans must not have seen him and soon he flew on the back of his jaguar far above the island.

He looked up. Was his master already on the way? Kweeg didn't know, but he looked forward to receiving whatever extra reward freeing the demon would earn him.

CHAPTER 18

Shara felt like a ruptured dam as ether flooded through her. Try as she might, nothing so much as slowed the flow. Some other power had seized control of the Divine Key. It had to be the demon. Even from this distance she felt its darkness and corruption. Even at his worst, Daktari felt like a pure-hearted angel compared to this creature.

And her gift would now set it free on the universe. Deep down she wondered if maybe it would've been better for everyone if Saladin had succeeded in killing her.

The darkness grew stronger, feeding on her despair. Shara forced it out of her mind. Whatever it took, she would see this creature either dead or back in its prison. Through their connection she felt its amusement.

Laugh now, you monster, but we'll see who laughs last.

The thought had barely formed when the torrent of ether cut off. Shara's awareness of her body returned and she looked up into the worried faces of Robert, Blade, and Daktari. Then she remembered her father.

"Is my father okay? The goblin stabbed him."

"He's been badly hurt, but I stabilized him," Daktari said. "If you're up to it, we need to get back to the second pit so you can seal it before Balthis merges with The Void."

"Yes." She swung her legs off the stone table and stood. The room spun but quickly stopped. "I sensed that monster on the other end of our link. How can something so vile exist?"

Daktari shrugged. "For every pure thing there's something corrupt. It's the nature and balance of the universe as well as the founding principle of shadow magic. The constant battle between light and dark drives everything forward. Without one or the other, all of creation would stagnate. But that's a philosophical debate we have no time for right now."

Daktari conjured a bubble around them and they flew up, smashing through the ceiling and out into the light. He soared down to the pirate ship and through a hole in its side. As soon as they landed, she ran over to her unconscious father.

Shara touched the side of his neck and found a pulse. Thank heaven, he still lived.

"Your old man is tough, kid," Robert said. She finally noticed he carried Heat's Bane. "Just borrowing it until he's strong enough to use it again."

Robert shuddered and his throat worked as he swallowed.

"Are you okay?" she asked.

"I don't know. Something just happened."

"I can't believe it," Daktari said. "The dragon has risen and sealed the planet off from magical transportation. That means Balthis can't simply teleport directly to the void pit."

He pointed and her father rose a foot off the ground.

"That buys us time, right?" Blade asked.

"Some, but he will be here soon. Then it will be up to the dragon to hold him off long enough for Shara to seal the pit." Daktari pointed and a portal opened. "Quickly."

Shara hurried through behind Robert and Blade. She

emerged in a clearing not far from an ancient temple. Ten priests sat around outside of it while a larger group in black kept watch on the jungle.

She spotted Amane and ran over. The high priestess looked up at her with dark, exhausted eyes. Shara almost hated to ask her to do anything else, but Father needed help and he needed it now.

"My father has been stabbed. If you can help, please, I beg you to do something for him."

Amane looked like she wanted to cry, but that passed quickly and she levered herself up. At a shuffle that seemed far too slow to Shara, she made her way over to the magical gurney Daktari had conjured.

Speaking of the sorcerer, he had his head cocked and she suspected he was speaking with his homunculus.

Amane raised both her hands and a glowing cocoon formed around her father.

"What's that?" Shara asked.

"An isolation spell. It will protect him while slowly healing his wound. It is serious, but someone did a good job cauterizing the internal damage. I'm sorry, Princess, but this is all I can manage at the moment."

"It's wonderful, thank you so much." She wanted to hug the priestess, but held back for the sake of both their dignities. Instead, she settled for squeezing Amane's shoulder.

A few yards away, Daktari had resumed his usual expression. She walked over and asked, "Bad news?"

"I'm not certain. Bane says all the monsters besieging the temple have withdrawn. The monks think this means we've won."

"But we know better."

"That we do. Since we haven't won, I can't help wondering where they've gone. Ultimately it doesn't matter.

We need to get you to the pit and the sooner the better. Are you up to it?"

"Does it matter?"

He smiled. It might have been the first expression of genuine amusement she'd seen on his face. "For all practical purposes, no, but if you feel strong and ready, it gives you a better chance of success, so I ask."

A powerful ripple ran through the ether, vibrating Shara to her core. "Did you feel that?"

"Yes." He looked to the sky. "We are out of time. The battle has begun."

K weeg hid in the shadows of the jungle, sword poised, ready to cut down the humans that wanted to steal his reward. The collapsed temple sat only a few yards away, so it seemed impossible that he might miss them when they emerged.

A deep breath settled Kweeg's racing heart. Soon he would meet his master in the flesh or scales or whatever a demon was made of. Balthis would praise Kweeg for his hard work and no doubt offer more and better meat and females.

His mouth watered just thinking about it.

Distracted by his fantasies, Kweeg nearly missed it when a dark bubble burst out of the ruins and raced away toward the water.

"No!" Kweeg started to swing the sword but quickly understood that they were already too far away. No one told him so much as he felt it.

The jaguar appeared at his command and he took off after the humans. As soon as Kweeg cleared the treetops he looked around, but the humans were gone.

Never mind for now. Return to the pit. It's up to you to defend it until Balthis arrives.

Kweeg frowned. Wasn't he talking to his master? If not, then who spoke through the sword?

I am The Void and your master serves me. Now go!

Kweeg didn't even have time to think it before the cat started flying back across the water far faster than it had ever moved before.

"Those humans already killed all the pirates. How can Kweeg stop them all by himself?"

You won't be by yourself. My army will be waiting for you. The voidlings are strong, but they need a general to lead them.

Kweeg's jaw dropped. A general? Kweeg?

He puffed out his thin chest with pride. Yes! General Kweeg would protect his master's master.

In less time than he would have dreamed possible, Kweeg spotted land followed quickly by the jungle. He pet the cat's head. It had done a good job flying him here so quickly.

As they came in to land, Kweeg gaped in surprise at the gathering that filled the clearing. He couldn't even begin to count the monsters, some of them three times as tall as Kweeg with blue-tinted skin and others that looked like animals standing on two legs like goblins.

They reached the ground and the cat vanished, leaving Kweeg alone, surrounded by monsters that towered over him. He swallowed and tried to look confident.

Kweeg, no General Kweeg, cleared his throat. "Kweeg is here to lead you to victory over the nasty humans, so please don't eat him. Okay?"

The monsters just stared into space. Six more animal men emerged from the pit. They shuffled out of the way and joined in staring at nothing.

"How is Kweeg supposed to lead these stupid things?"

They've been slaved to your will through the sword. They will do whatever you tell them too.

Kweeg's stomach rumbled. Well, time to test. He stared at one of the biggest creatures. "You, blue monster, put your arm down beside Kweeg."

It leaned over and presented a forearm bigger around than Kweeg's whole body. He bit a chunk of meat out, drawing no reaction.

Kweeg immediately spit the meat out. "Blech."

He'd never tasted meat so rancid that he didn't want to eat it. Maybe one of the animal men would taste better.

A lightning bolt to the brain made him twitch. Right. Eating his new army was probably a bad idea. Time to focus and think like a proper general. Other than shouting orders, what, exactly did a general do?

I don't care what you do as long as you keep the girl from entering the pit.

That should be easy enough. Kweeg pointed at four of the biggest monsters. "Stand around the pit and stop anyone from entering. By killing them."

He added that last bit just to be sure. Just in case they were actually as stupid as he thought, better if Kweeg didn't take any chances.

The monsters lumbered into place, forming a wall of flesh so tight he doubted a rat could slip through. Kweeg licked his lips. Roasted rat would be nice right now.

He winced, expecting a lightning bolt that didn't come.

What did come was a group of humans. They emerged from a patch of jungle and had the screechy girl with them.

Kweeg didn't need to see anything else. "Kill them!"

· ─✧

After the first explosive clash between Balthis and the dragon, Daktari fully understood that he needed to accelerate his plan. While he'd hoped to give everyone, especially the princess, a chance to rest and recover, that simply wouldn't work now. Even from here the dragon's almost unimaginable might made the ether tremble. Unfortunately, he also sensed Balthis's and they were pretty much an even match. That meant it would come down to luck. And he hated relying on luck.

"What do we do?" Shara asked. She seemed torn between wanting to stay with her slowly recovering father and what she knew she had to do.

"We fight."

Robert and Blade headed towards them. Even with his limited ability, Robert must have enough of a connection to the ether to have sensed that first clash. To his surprise, one of the black-clad men watching the jungle also came to join them.

He flipped his hood back and Daktari nodded a greeting. "Nadir. A bit bright out for you and your followers, isn't it?"

The assassin smiled at the dig. "The Reaper has spoken to me. I have orders to do whatever is necessary to see the princess safely to the void pit."

"We're certainly in no position to refuse your help. Robert, Blade, Shara, allow me to introduce the Reaper's Guild Master Nadir Graves. I have no idea what might be waiting for us, but if it needs to die, Nadir is a good man to have on your side. Given how twisted the ether is around pit, we'll have to walk, and the faster the better."

Nadir whistled and pointed into the jungle. The other assassins leapt into the trees and vanished among the shadows. "They will scout ahead and deal with any threats that stand between us and the pit."

"Unless they have powerful magic or mithril weapons, I fear they may be in for a rough time should they encounter any of The Void's monsters."

"They have black iron and while it might not kill a horror like the former prince, I'm confident that anything less will fall."

Daktari shrugged. He didn't especially care what happened to the assassins. "Blade, if you would be so kind as to take point, your sword should protect us from any unforeseen dangers."

She turned without comment and started down a path that led to the pit. Robert followed a step behind, then Nadir, and finally Shara and him. As they walked through the oddly silent jungle, he wished he'd had time to collect a slab of stone from the Black Ice Mountains. It would have made a fine shield against any void energy blasts.

"I'm not sure I can do this," Shara said.

"You've already done it once. If anything, you should be confident of victory."

She looked at him with a wan smile. "There's a little more on the line this time."

"No, there isn't. Both pits need to be sealed. If you'd failed at the first one, we'd be in just as much trouble as we will be if you fail at this one." He met her worried gaze without hesitation. "You can do this. I've seen your power firsthand. You need only do exactly what you did last time, and you will save the world."

"It sounds so much bigger when you say it out loud."

He refused to downplay the situation. She'd earned that much respect. "Let's just focus on getting there. Then we move on to the next step."

The vibrations running through the ether grew more frequent as Balthis and the dragon's battle intensified. Once in a while the earth itself rattled. They'd be lucky if the titanic clash didn't do The Void's work for it.

"Oh shit." Robert's crude exclamation brought Daktari's full focus back to the material world.

In the clearing where the void pit waited, scores of ogres and beastmen milled around. Well, now he knew where the besieging army ended up. But how did they get here with the second pit sealed?

He dismissed the thought as irrelevant. They were here now and they had to deal with them.

"Kill them!" a shrill voice from behind the army shouted.

As one, the voidlings turned and moved toward their small group.

Robert waved Heat's Bane and the front row stopped, their feet encased in ice. Daktari had to give the man credit, he'd proven every bit as adept with the sword's magic as Nord and after much less instruction.

Blade and Nadir charged in next. The assassin's black-iron sword seemed to appear out of nowhere, slashing and stabbing into the mob. And while it proved adept at slicing them open, the void energy inside closed the wounds nearly as fast as he made them.

Blade's sword, on the other hand, proved much more useful. The dragon's enchantment allowed her to absorb the void energy and prevent the monsters from healing.

A beastman that looked like a wolf or dog darted around the front row and charged Daktari.

Blueish flames roared out, reducing the monster to ash. A black blob dropped to the ground and immediately shot into one of the frozen ogres. His offensive magic seemed to be working perfectly which surprised him given how close they were to the pit. All the void energy must be going to maintain the monsters. Still, he wouldn't want to attempt any complex sorcery.

Outside of the mountains, this was going to be much more difficult.

The advance group of assassins came rushing out of the trees and attacked the voidlings' flank. Much like their master, they were unable to score a decisive hit.

The ground shook and he risked a glance at the sky. At the very limit of his vision, he spotted the gigantic forms of Soom and Balthis. They were getting closer all the time. Soom probably had to hold back lest he permanently damage the planet, but Balthis wouldn't care. The elder demon reveled in destruction, must like Daktari himself used to when he lived under the demon's influence.

"What are we going to do?" Shara asked. "The ether is so agitated I'm afraid I won't be able to work it properly."

"It's not affecting my magic, so you should be fine. Unfortunately, the closer those two get, the worse the disturbance will grow. We don't have time to kill all these voidlings." Daktari incinerated another monster, a cat-looking thing this time, that dared get too close. Once again, the leftover void energy leapt from the ground into the nearest functional monster. "I'll try and fly us over them. Hold on."

She grabbed his arm and he conjured the bubble. The ethereal construct immediately fissured and started to fall apart. He focused harder, demanding the ether take the shape he required. The cracks sealed, but he knew without a doubt that the slightest distraction would send it flying apart like a window hit with a rock.

He rose slowly straight up. Levitation seemed to work better than forming the bubble. If the end of the world wasn't in sight, he would have happily spent days trying to figure out why.

A chunk of rock came flying right at them only to shatter against his bubble and fall to earth. The source of the attack appeared to be a quartet of ogres standing well behind the main force. He spotted the goblin a moment later. It still carried the void sword and was pointing at them while gibbering at one of the ogres.

The ogre finished absorbing its verbal abuse, picked up another piece of the ruins and hurled it at Daktari. The stone crashed to earth with equally little results.

He understood then. Not only did The Void not have enough extra power to fully warp the ether, it must not have enough to allow the goblin to send black fire at them. It appeared the goblin, or more precisely the sword, controlled the voidlings. If they killed the little beast, that should weaken and maybe even disable the voidlings.

A spear of shadow magic lanced out at the goblin only to be instantly blown apart by a burst of void energy. So it still had strength enough to protect its servant from his spells. Pity, but hardly surprising.

Daktari started a spell to connect his mind to Nadir's and winced. Dividing his focus sent a jagged bolt of pain through his brain but he powered through. *There's a goblin controlling the voidlings. If you can kill it, that should weaken them.*

Nadir sent a thought acknowledging the information and Daktari ended the spell. The pain vanished at once and he dearly hoped he wouldn't have to do that again.

Below them, Nadir disengaged from the ogre he'd been hacking fruitlessly at and sprinted for the edge of the voidling formation. A beastman sprang at him but the assassin simply leapt, made a full flip, and resumed running.

"Wow," Shara said.

Daktari couldn't disagree with her assessment. Nadir hadn't gotten to be master of the Reaper's Guild by chance.

A few feet from the goblin, it sent a blade of black flames at Nadir.

As soon as it did, one of the voidlings staggered, confirming Daktari's theory. The Void had reached the single pit's limit. He found it reassuring to know that it at least had a limit in the mortal world.

"Shouldn't we help him?" Shara asked.

"My magic is useless against that thing. Don't worry. If anyone can kill that goblin, Nadir can."

Another tremor sent a nearby tree crashing down.

And if he failed, they weren't apt to live long enough to complain.

· —✦

K weeg felt his army falling apart. Literally one by one the humans cut them to pieces. He tried to think of a good order, but nothing came to mind. He'd already told them what they needed to do, so that should be enough. A general shouldn't have to oversee every little detail.

You are doing well, little goblin. It matters not how many of the voidlings die as long as the pit remains secure. Soon Balthis will arrive and then the pests will be wiped away in an instant.

Yes! Kweeg's master would show the nasty humans how weak they were.

Another voidling died and he looked up at the sky. Despite the brightness, Kweeg could just see two figures locked in battle. Hurry, Master, Kweeg can't last forever.

As if drawn by the thought, a human in black appeared and sprinted at Kweeg.

He screeched and swung his sword, sending a black arc of flames at the human. The magic caused a voidling to collapse, but better a monster than Kweeg.

The human dove under the spell and rolled to his feet, hardly slowing. "Die, goblin!"

An inky black scythe flew at Kweeg.

Another swing of his sword hacked it to pieces.

The human closed to within a few steps.

Kweeg scrambled back, mind racing for a way to stop the speedy man. A wall of black flames sprang up between them and he felt two more voidlings die.

Be careful or you'll run out of servants.

Kweeg didn't care about the stupid voidlings that failed to even kill a few humans. You couldn't enjoy a reward if you died.

He barely had time to draw a breath before the man in black appeared from the far side of the fire wall.

More dead voidlings allowed Kweeg to surround himself with flames.

The stubborn human came from above, ready to drive his sword into Kweeg's face.

"I quit!" Kweeg dropped the sword and ran through the dying flames toward the jungle. He'd find a tribe somewhere and take over. The females and meat were nice, but not nice enough to die for.

Hopefully he could find a less demanding master to serve.

⸎

Nadir couldn't believe what just happened. The goblin had escaped him. His thrown dagger still quivered in the trunk of the tree it darted behind at the last second. Not only that, it had cut apart the most lethal spell he knew like it was nothing. That spell drew directly on the Reaper's power and the void sword had shattered it like so much glass.

Well, dead or gone, at least it no longer commanded the

monsters. Even better, it had dropped the sword when it fled. Maybe if he claimed it for the Reaper he'd salvage something of his reputation from this debacle.

He bent and reached for the hilt.

A spark of darkness shot out, barely missing his fingers. More darkness gathered around the weapon. He stared as it rose from the ground.

Only decades of training saved him from the claws of a catlike beastman. He sprang back from her slash with an inch to spare. The beastwoman had black fur and only a loincloth offered a smattering of modesty.

She picked up the sword and darkness flooded into her. Not just from the sword, but the remaining voidlings as well. Only the four massive ogres guarding the pit remained standing. The beastwoman now appeared made of void flames.

His magic wouldn't work and he had serious doubts about his black-iron sword. Whatever she'd become, his instincts screamed for him to escape. His pride argued that as one of the Reaper's most favored servants, fleeing would be an insult to his master.

His instincts won an instant before a wave of black flames as powerful as anything Nord unleashed at them came roaring for his life.

Nadir vanished and reappeared from the shadows of a tree about fifty feet away. Twice now that spell had saved his life.

He turned to watch the catwoman cut one of his followers in half with almost contemptuous ease. Assuming any of them survived, he'd need to work on training their danger sense.

Speaking of danger, the swordswoman with the dark blade separated herself from her companion and stalked straight at the catwoman.

A torrent of flames shot out at her only to be absorbed by her sword.

Nadir couldn't help smiling. Assuming they still had a world tomorrow, he would have to try and recruit her for the guild. She might not know it, but that woman was born to serve the Reaper.

—✴—

B lade hacked and slashed, severing the arms that reached for her, removing heads from bodies, and generally laying waste to everything that came within reach. Anyone that had ever met her knew she loved to fight, but this wasn't a fight. Not really. Much like the Tao arena, this was something else. The monsters had no skill, only brute strength in the ogres' case and speed in the beastmen's.

Her dragon-sword, as she'd come to think of it, destroyed them both with equal ease. It parted flesh and bone as easily as it did air. Only their numbers concerned her, but with Bobby beside her using the sultan's enchanted weapon to block, slow, and generally impede anything that tried to sneak around her guard, that threat amounted to little.

They made a perfect, merciless team and yet despite that she feared they had no hope of winning. She'd lost track of how many of the creatures she'd killed, but more kept coming at her. If the sorcerer told the truth, and she had no reason to suspect he hadn't, they had a limited amount of time for Shara to do what she had to.

"How are you holding up, darling?" Bobby asked.

"I could do this all day." Blade hacked off the reaching arm of an ogre and sliced open its chest on the backswing, sucking out the void energy.

"You might have to. Our friends in black seem less than effective against these things."

She grunted, not daring to look away from the mass of enemies in front of her. "How's the kid holding up?"

"Oh, she's fine. Daktari has her in a bubble way out of reach above us. I thought he planned to fly her into the pit, but something must be blocking the path besides these things."

She cut a beastman in half with a single overhead swing. "Why doesn't he just blast them all? I thought he was supposed to be so powerful."

"The ether's too messy up here. I wouldn't even know where to begin casting the simple spells I know. I can't imagine how he managed what he did."

"That's the problem with relying on magic, you never know when it might stop working."

"Speaking of that, I have some unfortunate news. The sword's magic reserve is running down. I'm going to be reduced to swinging this thing in about five minutes."

"Don't use it unless you absolutely have to." She stepped back, cut an ogre down at the knee, and stabbed it through the chest.

"That's precisely what I've been doing up until now. I—"

As one the monsters threw back their heads and opened their mouths.

Darkness shot out and entered a beastman that looked like a black, humanoid cat. All the others fell flat on their faces and didn't move. The catperson held out its hand and the sword lying abandoned on the ground nearby flew into it.

"Is this good for us or bad for us?" Bobby asked.

One of the assassins rushed forward, eager to end things.

She managed to close half the distance between her and the surviving monster before it shot forward like a crossbow bolt and sliced her in half at the waist with a single swing.

"I'm going to say bad," Bobby said.

"No." Blade adjusted her grip on the dragon-sword. "This is

better. I can fight a single opponent more easily than an army. Don't interfere, Bobby, this one's all mine."

⋅—✴

Daktari couldn't have been more surprised when the voidlings all collapsed. It made considerably more sense when the sole standing creature took up the sword and sliced an assassin half. It seemed The Void had decided to go with quality over quantity. Pity it left the four ogres intact as they guarded the pit. Until he dealt with those, they had no hope of getting inside.

"I can't believe the goblin escaped. That thing must have more lives than a cat." Shara chewed her lip and frowned. "Shouldn't we get going?"

"Not yet. If we move too quickly, The Void's new champion will burn us out of the sky. With all the void energy concentrated in one place, I don't know what it might be capable of."

She pointed. "Looks like Blade means to find out."

He looked just in time to watch the woman's enchanted sword absorb a blast of void flames that would have blown away an entire company of soldiers.

"This is perfect. As soon as they're fully committed to combat, we'll make our move. Either we make it through without issue, or the distraction allows Blade to defeat the monster."

"What if she needs help?" Shara asked.

He checked the sky. The figures of the dragon and demon were fully distinguishable now. "That help will have to come from others. Our time is running out, quickly."

The swords clashed and he willed his bubble forward. As soon as he reached the pit, his flames roared out. Unlike the earlier voidlings, the ogre guardians resisted them.

He grimaced and put every bit of power at his command into the spell.

The flames turned from blue to white and the monsters' flesh finally yielded. When the flames died out he flew them down the shaft into the pit.

The deeper they went the more twisted the ether became. He needed every bit of his focus to maintain the bubble.

"I can see it," Shara said.

He didn't even look. Daktari cared only about reaching the floor in one piece.

Some angel must have been looking out for them because he landed and dissolved the bubble before they crashed.

He dropped to his knees and gasped. No magic had ever exhausted him like this, not even as a first-year apprentice.

Shara put a hand on his shoulder. "Are you okay?"

"Fine, just tired." Daktari scrubbed a hand across his face. "Don't worry about me. Get to work."

She walked over beside the shiny pool of darkness and ether exploded out from the key. Its power seemed undiminished by The Void's presence.

Sensing that, for the first time, he thought they had a real chance of winning.

CHAPTER 19

When Blade absorbed the black flames, her sword actually felt heavier for a second. That had never happened before and it told her just how powerful an opponent she faced. Blade knew she shouldn't be grinning from ear to ear, but couldn't help herself. After so long, maybe she'd finally found a challenge.

The catwoman lunged, covering the twenty paces separating them in a blink.

Blade barely got her sword up in time to turn aside the thrust.

She had no time to think as the blows rained down.

Instinct took over, keeping her alive by the narrowest of margins.

Each blow sent a vibration down the sword and into her arm. Too many of those and her hand would go numb.

If she lost the dragon-sword that would be the end.

She caught a cross slash and twisted her wrist, locking the swords together.

Bad idea.

Blade had hoped for a breather. Instead, she ended up flying across the clearing to crash into the ground ten feet away.

Rolling to her feet, she met the next charge.

The catwoman swung even harder than Shale despite being half his size. Even worse, she hadn't slowed down even a fraction despite the furious assault.

She kicked herself. This wasn't a living, breathing opponent, but rather some sort of magical vessel.

The next blow nearly smashed the dragon-sword from her grasp.

A follow-up side kick sent her flying a second time.

What did Bobby always tell her, be careful what you wished for lest you get it? She wished for a challenge and by heaven she'd gotten one. Her brutal flight ended with her slamming into one of the remaining standing stones hard enough to knock the air out of her lungs.

Before she had a chance to suck in a breath, the catwoman stood above her, sword poised to strike.

Ice wrapped the catwoman from knees to neck.

"Get out of there!" Bobby shouted.

Good advice. She scrambled away trying to catch her breath.

Cracks formed in the ice. Another few moments and the battle would be on again.

Strength and vitality rushed into her, washing away the pain. She looked at Bobby who pointed across the clearing.

Nadir had both hands raised, dark energy crackling around them. He caught her eye and nodded.

So much for winning this fight on her own.

The ice shattered and her opponent immediately rushed at her.

It must have been the magic, but it seemed the catwoman moved a little slower.

Blade turned aside several blows, not easily, but with growing confidence. With Nadir's magic fortifying her, she could fight this thing on even terms.

Spinning away from a thrust, she countered with a cross slash. A fraction too slow, but she did shave a few hairs off the monster's back.

Grinning like a madwoman, she pressed the attack.

The catwoman didn't need to block. She just flexed out of the way like she had a spine made of rubber.

Time for something a little more advanced.

Blade's next strike dove at her opponent's left hip.

The moment she twisted to avoid the strike, Blade flicked her wrists, sending the dragon-sword back up and to the right, cutting a shallow line across the catwoman's chest.

Just as she thought. The voidling might have the advantage in speed and raw strength, but it had no real fighting skill. Now that Blade matched its power, the creature had no chance.

Perhaps The Void realized it as well. The catwoman bared her fangs and charged harder than ever.

Blade leapt back, planted her heel, and thrust.

The catwoman impaled herself on the dragon-sword and the void energy sustaining her drained into the weapon.

Blade let the corpse fall and blew out a long breath. She hadn't come that close to dying in a long time and contrary to what she liked to say, she hadn't especially enjoyed it.

Bobby hurried over. "You okay?"

She shot him a mock glare. "I thought I told you to stay out of it."

Bobby just grinned. "Yeah, but I figured when I stopped that thing from running you through, you wouldn't complain too much. It's your lucky day too, the sword's all out of magic."

Blade wrapped her arm around his neck and kissed him hard on the lips. "Thanks."

Soft applause from behind them prompted Blade to turn. Nadir approached, a thin smile on his humorless face. "A masterful display, young lady."

"Lady?" Robert said.

Blade swatted him on the shoulder then returned her attention to Nadir. "I couldn't have done it without your magic fortifying me."

"Not mine, the Reaper's. Had he disapproved of you, nothing would have happened and you would likely be dead right now. That the magic worked and worked well, means you have a strong affinity for him. I suspected as much the moment I saw you wield a sword. When this matter is resolved, assuming we still have a world, I'd like to invite you to join the Reaper's Guild."

An assassin, her? Blade didn't especially like the idea of murdering people. Though as a bandit, she'd certainly killed her share of innocents.

"Say, where did Daktari and the kid get to anyway?" Bobby asked, saving her from having to answer.

"As soon as your battle began, they forced their way past the ogres and entered the pit." Nadir never took his eyes off her. "No need to answer right now. Just think about my offer and let your heart guide you. I think you'll find the right answer lies with us."

He wandered off to rejoin his black-clad minions.

"That is one creepy guy," Bobby said. "How are you holding up?"

She slumped against Bobby's chest and he caught her. "I need a rest. And I see that look on your face. Don't worry, I have no intention of running off to join the Reaper's Guild. Think we should try and get down there to help the kid?"

Bobby helped her over to the shade of a palm tree and they sat down side by side. "That's a relief. I'm sure I could figure a way to make money at it, but I'd just as soon stick to trading. As for Shara, if Daktari can't help her, we certainly can't. Besides, neither of us is exactly in top shape."

No denying that. Blade leaned her head against his shoulder and closed her eyes. Whatever happened in the pit, Blade was glad she'd be with him when it all ended, for good or ill.

⋅—✩

Shara looked back over her shoulder for what seemed like the hundredth time but was probably only the third or fourth. Daktari sat slumped, eyes closed, on the cold stone floor. So little light reached the pit, that she could barely make him out. If just getting them here took that much out of a sorcerer of his experience, what hope did she have of completing her task?

You have no hope.

The deep, dark voice seemed to come from everywhere, but somehow, she knew it really originated from the disk of absolute black that filled the center of the cavern. In the end this was the thing she fought. Everything else, the voidlings, her uncle, the demon, all of them were mere extensions of this creature.

Thing? Creature? I am The Void, you ignorant speck of nothing. I existed before this universe came into being and I will exist long after it vanishes. Your world will die today. Just like all other worlds will die. And at last, when my servants have ripped the fabric of Creation to shreds, all reality will die. Then only my perfect darkness will remain, unblemished by you screeching mortals, the lights and madness of the ether, and anything else that might disturb my eternal peace.

Shara put her shoulders back and raised her chin in defiance. She wouldn't let this monster destroy everything she knew and cared about.

A single, deep breath calmed her racing heart. Steady now, she drew on the ether.

It came easily, eagerly, through the key and into her hands. She smushed it down into a tight ball, collected more, and repeated the process. Bit by bit she gathered the energy she'd need to form the seal.

It's pointless. You mortals struggle and struggle. For what? All that awaits you is a future as a speck of heaven or hell. Surrender this pointless resistance and you can have a place in my eternal darkness. Dream an endless dream free from grief and struggle.

She thought about Robert, Blade, Sarafin, and her father. They'd all supported her, fighting so hard to get her here and they all depended on her to do what she had to in order to save the world. No matter what, she refused to let them down. So Shara ignored the voice and its easy promises and kept building her seal.

Even if you succeed, it doesn't matter. Some other mortal will seek out my secrets and make a new pit and then the war will begin anew. Anything you accomplish is temporary. I am eternal.

"You also don't know when to shut up." She clenched her teeth and expanded the seal. Halfway there. Soon enough she'd silence the monster forever.

· —✧·

Daktari hadn't suffered the effects of true magical backlash in over a century. Nevertheless, he clearly remembered the pain and mental fatigue. That day years ago couldn't hold a candle to what he felt right now. Every nerve in his body burned and he had to fight to open his eyes. He felt weak and he hated it.

But it didn't matter. He'd gotten Shara here and even now her began power build. He had no doubt that the girl would do what she had to. He'd trained her after all.

He forced his eyes open and smiled at the ether glowing around her. He'd seen the ether wielded by many wizards, but none of them conjured as pure a light as her. No doubt being a direct conduit made all the difference. She didn't try to change it into anything the way a wizard did, she merely forged the pure substance into the shape she needed. Even after seeing it many times he still marveled at the process.

You don't have to be weak. With my power at your fingertips, you could be the most powerful wizard that ever lived.

He choked on a laugh and coughed. "Your power comes at too high a price even for me. All the power in the world means nothing if I'm not alive to wield it. Truly I have no idea how you convince anyone to serve you. What's the point if there's no universe left?"

Once the universe is gone, for those that serve, there will still be the eternal dream. Endless peace, no pain, no striving for power and status. You'd be surprised how many people long for such a fate.

Daktari shifted in search of a more comfortable position. "Cowards too weak to succeed on their own merit. I'll thank you not to lump me in with them."

If not power, then knowledge. Stop the Key Bearer and I will help you learn all the secrets of the universe. And once you know them all, we end it, so no one else ever knows as much as you. Think about that.

He did think about it. He thought long and hard. No other offer held the allure this one did. Even as he considered the offer, he rejected it. The value of a secret came not from the knowledge itself, but from the effort of learning it. Having knowledge given to him by a cosmic entity rendered it valueless. At least in his eyes.

That's madness. Knowledge is no different regardless of the source. No one else can give you access to all I know. Secrets beyond your limited, mortal imagination are there for the taking. Just kill the girl and I'll tell you anything you want to know.

"You're sounding pretty pathetic and desperate for the help of a limited mortal like me. What's wrong, none of your other servants survive?"

The air seemed to crackle with The Void's frustration. The feeling pleased Daktari a great deal.

You...Don...How?

He forced his eyes open in time to watch Shara slam the seal into place. A moment later she collapsed in a heap.

He smiled to himself. Some pair of conquering heroes they were.

But at least The Void had been sealed away, hopefully for a very long time.

⋅—✦

The instant the demon appeared above the world that Soom was bound to protect, he attacked. Shadow flames slammed into it, driving the horned monstrosity back.

But only a few feet. That blast would have reduced a city to charred stone and Balthis shrugged it off like it was nothing.

His connection to The Void must have rendered him resistant to normal magic, even magic as powerful as Soom's.

"I expected more from this world's one true dragon." If evil had a sound, Balthis's sibilant voice was it. "You can't stop me."

"We shall see."

If magic wouldn't do the job, claws and fangs would. A single beat of his powerful wings sent Soom hurtling into his opponent.

They slammed together hard enough to rattle the planet.

Talons so strong they could tear down mountains scrabbled against onyx scales without gaining purchase. Soom spun and lashed his tail against Balthis's chest. A deafening crack was followed by a chuckle.

Shock turned to pain when Balthis backhanded him across the sky.

Soom caught himself immediately and moved to block the demon's advance. But now they were closer.

And so it went. Blow after futile blow landed against Balthis's impenetrable hide followed by a mighty wallop that forced the battle ever closer to the ground.

Only Balthis's equal inability to seriously harm him allowed Soom to stay in the fight. Against any lesser foe, Balthis would have won already.

"This fight is pointless," the demon said after anther exchange that once again saw them a hundred yards closer to the ground. "You must know you can't beat me."

"It doesn't matter." Soom panted for breath. "The humans will seal the final pit and then we'll see who laughs last."

Balthis laughed. "Humans. You're a fool to rely on them. They'll betray you and leave your world in pieces. Dealing with humans has led me to nothing but bitter regret."

"Then they've done at least one good thing." If the demon

wanted to talk, Soom wouldn't complain. Every second gave the humans more time to get the Key Bearer to the pit.

"Eouaugh!" A tremor ran through Balthis as he howled in agony, his scales turning from onyx to gray.

Soom felt an immediate drop in the demon's power.

He swung his tail again. This time the force of the impact sent Balthis flying back, scales broken and body bleeding.

A shot of shadowfire blasted Balthis toward the ocean like a burning comet.

Soom dove after him.

The demon hit, sending a gout of water fifty feet into the air.

Soom hovered above the ocean's surface and would have frowned had his dragon form permitted. He felt something down there, something corrupt and powerful, but not Balthis. He waited half a minute, but nothing moved and the other power source grew ever stronger. The source also grew clearer and he felt a moment of pity for Balthis.

But only a moment.

Snapping his wings, Soom soared toward land. He needed to make sure the pit had fully sealed and that no one would ever try and reopen it.

He landed in a jungle clearing littered with inhuman corpses and that reeked of void poisoning. All but two of the humans he'd sensed earlier were gone. Now only his champion and her companion remained. The two humans got up from their places under a palm tree and staggered over. Soom sensed their exhaustion, but refrained from using his magic to eliminate it. Sometimes letting nature and time work did less harm than magic.

"Where is the Key Bearer?" Soom asked.

The man grunted and nodded toward the pit. "Daktari and the kid are still down there. Can't say what happened, but it must have taken a toll on them. I wanted to check on them, but right now, standing is about my limit."

The woman held up the sword he'd enchanted. "Are you going to want this back? I think it might be full."

Soom passed a hand over the sword and shook his head. "Not quite full, but it will need to be drained. As for the weapon, we'll discuss that later."

He left the humans looking at each other and flew down the shaft. Despite housing a void pit for centuries, the ether had already begun restoring itself. Of all The Creator's works, he believed the ether was the most brilliant. It kept everything moving and made all possible. Invisible and indestructible, it held all the potential in the universe, for good or ill.

Lights appeared at his mental command. He didn't conjure them for himself, his eyes saw perfectly fine in the dark, but rather for the survivors. He spotted them a moment later along with the sealed pit.

A glance told him everything he needed to know. She'd done it and done it right. Nothing less than another Key Bearer would have any hope of opening the pit and no void energy leaked out. He'd seen many remarkable feats of magic since the world formed and this one sat right up near the top.

Satisfied with his inspection, Soom turned to the survivors. The Key Bearer lay unconscious on the stone floor, her head resting on the man's lap. He looked up, his eyes shadowed with exhaustion.

"You would be Soom, the shadow dragon?" he asked.

"Indeed. And you would be the current Shadow Man, Daktari. I must admit, you certainly faced a graver challenge than your predecessor. Congratulations on surviving it. And on training her. The seal is impeccable."

"I can't take much credit. Shara controls the ether in a way different than any I've encountered. She can't see it, only feel it."

"Really? That's a first for me as well. But we can discuss the details later. What say we get you out of this hole and into the fresh air?"

"That sounds like an excellent idea."

Quick as thought the trio flew up and out of the pit. Soom deposited the humans on the dirt near the other two and turned his focus back to the shaft. He channeled ether into the void poisoned earth and yanked. Dirt and stone collapsed and soon enough the entrance had been filled to the top. Next he switched to fire and heated the rubble until it turned molten and fused into a single plug of stone.

"So it's over?" his champion asked.

Soom offered a humorless smile. "It's never over, but for now our world is safe."

"What about Balthis?" Daktari asked.

"The demon is no longer a threat."

"That's all great," the man said. "How about a ride back to my ship? The crew's got to be getting antsy."

"Don't forget the priests and assassins," she added.

"I'll send the other humans back," Soom said. "We need to have a long discussion about the future and your ship will be an acceptable place to have it."

The humans all traded nervous looks. Perfectly reasonable given what he was. When a dragon said he needed to talk, all sensible creatures felt their insides tighten.

Soom ignored them and with a thought sent those lingering near the purified temple back to the High Kingdom just outside the main gates of Sultan's Oasis.

At last, he conjured a sphere around the remaining four and took to the air.

B althis sank through the water, his entire body screaming from the dragon's fiery blast. He'd never felt pain like this. And weakness. His connection to The Void had been nearly severed. Only the tiniest fragment allowed him to maintain his physical form. That had to mean all the pits had been sealed. His hope for absolute power now lay in ruins. The nearest planet with a functioning pit was so far away he had no hope of reaching it in his current state.

The light grew dimmer as he sank. He would have to hide in the deepest trenches and wait for a new pit to open. He had all the time in the world after all. That was the greatest advantage of immortality. There would always be another chance as long as you survived. Balthis would heal and marshal his strength and when the time came, he would avenge himself on all those who cast him low.

He'd sunk another hundred yards when he felt the familiar tingle of power. It came from directly below. He turned to see a pair of glowing eyes approaching.

Hellfire blossomed to life, revealing the form of a tiny, pathetic human.

Balthis shivered. "Chosen."

"No, though I wear his flesh."

That voice, like the scream of a dying animal being torn apart by sharks. "Master."

"You dare call me that after your betrayal? My greatest creation turning to serve the bane of all reality. The other nine laughed at me. THEY LAUGHED!"

Dagon's shout sent Balthis tumbling backward. He thought to flee but immediately dismissed the idea. Here, in the heart of Dagon's realm, he had no hope of escape. Only forgiveness would save him and demon lords weren't known for their generous nature.

"Please, Master. Let me return to your side. The only reason I betrayed you was the promise of greater power. I did only what was in the nature you gave me."

"You seek to blame me for your betrayal? I'll give you credit for gall if nothing else." Balthis screamed, sending out a flood of bubbles, as watery tentacles ripped every scale at once from his flesh. "I'm going to tear you apart an inch at a time until I figure out how The Void got its hooks into you. Once I've flensed the void energy from your body, I'm going to bring whatever remains back to my hell and impale it on the walls of the Coral Palace as a lesson for any of my other servants that might think to give in to their greedy natures."

Balthis's screams would have deafened a city, but down here, nothing could hear him give vent to the pain as Dagon ripped his very essence apart.

CHAPTER 20

Their flight back to the *Journey* took only minutes. Soom flew so fast everything below them appeared as a blur, first green then blue. Robert dearly wanted a long nap, but until Soom had his say, he doubted that wish would be granted. Beside him, Blade looked like he felt. She'd done all the hard stuff after all. Not that the kid looked fantastic. Shara hadn't so much as flinched since they collected her and took off. He would have been more worried, but both Soom and Daktari assured him that she'd simply worn herself out and would be fine once she woke up.

Speaking of the sorcerer, Daktari looked as...mortal as Robert had ever seen him. Slumped over, fine black and purple robe plastered to his back with sweat that dripped off his bald head. He could have been an ordinary man coming back after a long day in the fields. Not that Robert had guts enough to make that comparison.

Only Soom appeared untroubled by the day's events. The human-looking dragon held his expression impassive, giving away no hints as to the thoughts swirling in his immortal head.

The ocean looked like blue glass below them. He'd never seen it so calm. It almost felt like the entire world had breathed a sigh of relief that they survived.

"There she is." Robert pointed at his ship bobbing peacefully and smiled. Talk about a sight for sore eyes. A two-masted caravel had never looked so good.

Soom took them down and they landed gently on deck. The crew all stopped what they were doing and stared. Probably surprised to see them back alive.

Thompson creeped closer, seeming afraid to look anyone in the eye. "Is all well, sir?"

Robert grinned. "Yes. For the first time in a while, I believe it is. Any trouble here?"

"No, sir. We've seen no sign of pirates or the serpent or anything else that might threaten the ship. We did hit one huge wave. Damndest thing I've ever seen. Perfectly clear day and it came out of nowhere. The boys ended up a little waterlogged, but nothing worse. Shall we set sail?"

Robert glanced at Soom who shook his head. "Not just yet."

"We'll be belowdecks having a conference. As soon as we have a bearing, I'll let you know."

"Aye, sir." Thompson returned to his post at the helm without further questions, heaven bless him.

Robert led the way downstairs and Shara brought up the rear, floating silently in an ethereal bubble. Soom manipulated the ether with such skill Robert hadn't even noticed him casting. Even Daktari didn't have that sort of control. Of course, the sorcerer wasn't an immortal true dragon either, so the comparison wasn't exactly fair.

The cabin he shared with Blade didn't have enough room for all of them, so Robert made his way to the hold. They had little beyond food and other basic supplies. Food, water, and miscellaneous junk had all been sorted in perfect order. No doubt Sean, their new quartermaster, had seen to that.

Without waiting for permission, Robert sat on an unopened water barrel. "So, what's left to discuss? The Void is sealed away by Shara's magic. We won, right?"

Soom's smile looked bitter, like he'd bit into a lemon, or maybe a rotten egg. "I have *won* against The Void many times. But winning isn't permanent. The Void doesn't say 'Good job, I'll leave your world alone now.' No, winning is an ongoing process. Your successes have weakened its efforts on our world by a vast amount, but there are still void artifacts out there. No doubt the secret to opening a new pit is drifting around through the hands of collectors of the exotic as well."

"So what, we have to keeping fighting this thing forever?" Robert asked.

Soom shrugged. "Someone does. Better we fight the little battles now, than let matters come to a head again in a few thousand years. Next time, we might not have a Key Bearer to seal any new pits that form. Next time, the world may die. Of course, it's your choice. I will soon return to my rest. Acting openly drains a great deal of my strength. If I'm to be of any use in the most extreme circumstances, a few centuries of rest will be vital."

Robert tried and failed to comprehend the scale Soom worked at. In a hundred years everyone he knew and cared about would certainly be dead. Did he really need to spend whatever time he had left hunting void relics and fighting for his life?

"What do you propose?" Daktari asked.

"I can give you the means to find any remaining void arti-facts and teach you how to extract the void essence from them. If the artifacts can be rounded up along with any written mate-rials, The Void will be reduced to speaking to potential disciples through their dreams and only a few people have the sort of psychic damage to be open to that contact. While there are no guarantees, if you can accomplish this task, our world will be as secure as we can make it."

"I'm willing to learn the extraction techniques if you'll teach me more advanced shadow magic as well," Daktari said.

"Always looking to make a deal, human?" Soom didn't sound angry, just amused. "I've been considering taking an apprentice off and on for a millennia, but now it seems like an especially prudent move. My psychic form can train you while my physical form sleeps. But we still need agents to hunt down the artifacts and bring them to the temple for extraction and storage."

Soom and Daktari both looked at him and Blade.

He wanted to scream no at the top of his lungs, but one look at Blade's broad smile killed the word in his throat. "You really want to do this? After Thompson and the men get the gems I promised them, there's no way they'll stick with us."

"We can hire a new crew. How hard could it be?" Blade asked. Having seen his father struggle to find reliable men for a simple trading journey, he suspected hiring sailors willing to hunt void artifacts would be considerably more difficult. "This is something I need to do. I can finally use my skills for something good. We might have been pawns of higher powers, but we still made a difference. I liked how that felt."

"Hunting down lethal artifacts wielded by no doubt madmen, piece of cake. But if you want to do it, you know I'm with you."

She kissed him. "Never doubted it."

"What about the kid?" Robert asked.

All eyes turned to Shara.

"I have no idea what channeling that much ether might do to an ordinary human," Soom said. "Though it might be difficult, she's free to return to her normal life. The key will likely remain with her until her death, but it does her no harm and might even come in handy. Ultimately, the decision is hers. Now, give me the compass you used to locate my lair as well as the sword I enchanted."

Robert brought the compass out of his satchel and passed it over. Blade did the same with her sword.

Soom's eyes glowed dark purple and soon the compass did as well. The ether swirled, but Robert couldn't begin to understand what the dragon had done. Daktari stared with a rapt expression, like a father seeing his child for the first time.

Next a drop of liquid darkness emerged from Blade's sword. That tiny piece of void energy merged with the compass before the ether calmed and Soom handed the compass back.

"I've have altered the enchantment so now the compass will seek out void energy instead of mine. The sword is nearly full and will need to be drained before you begin your hunt. Daktari and I will handle that at the temple before I return to sleep. You will need time to prepare and find a proper crew. There is no rush to begin your mission. Take the girl home and get ready. I will return your sword before you set out."

Blade grimaced. She probably felt worse than naked without a sword.

Robert unbuckled Heat's Bane and handed it to her. "You can hold on to it, at least until we get the kid home. Her old man will probably want it back."

She buckled the sword and looked instantly at ease. "Thanks."

Soom moved closer to Daktari. "Safe journey to you."

The pair vanished into the ether.

"Guess I'd better give Thompson a heading."

"This is the right thing, you know that, don't you?" she asked.

Robert nodded. As far as he was concerned, as long as he and Blade were together, it would always be the right thing.

Shara woke in a strange, hard bed with a strange ceiling over her head. A moment later her stomach rebelled and if she'd had anything in it, she would have hurled it in the nearby bucket. That confirmed she was on a ship. How did she end up here anyway? The last thing she remembered, she'd just finished sealing the void pit before darkness swallowed her.

"Hey, kid."

She turned her head a fraction to see Robert sitting in a folding chair beside her. "How did I get here? What happened?"

"A dragon brought us to my ship. As to what happened, you saved the world."

Her heart leapt. The magic had worked. "So, it's over?"

"More or less. The big part of the job is done. Soom basically hired Blade and me to hunt down any remaining void artifacts. Daktari's made himself the dragon's apprentice." Robert shook his head. "Never figured he'd be the sort to make himself second to anyone."

"If the dragon knows things he doesn't," Shara said. "He'd do whatever he had to in order to pry those secrets loose. How's my father?"

"Sorry, kid, no idea. The dragon sent them all back to Sultan's Oasis. Considering how many priests are there, he should be fine. I've tried to reach the palace, via the crystal ball, but nothing so far. Of course, it's only been three days since the battle. I expect when he's feeling better, your father will order one of his wizards to reach out."

Shara nodded, but until she saw her father safe and sound, she wouldn't really believe it. She put a hand on her stomach.

"Yeah, it's still there. The key is yours until you die. Hopefully now that the pits are sealed, no one will bother you. If anyone's earned a normal life, you have."

Her laugh sounded bitter in her ears. "I'm not certain I know what normal is anymore."

"I hear you. But Blade will tell you what it is, is overrated. She's crazy excited about this new job. Hopefully being basically a bounty hunter will work out better than her last career as a gladiator."

Shara rolled over on her side to fully face him. "What about you?"

Robert grinned his familiar grin. "As long as I'm with Blade and she's happy, nothing else matters to me. Though I do hope that anyone with a void artifact keeps it in a gold-filled vault."

Shara laughed and felt perhaps a hint of that normalcy he mentioned. "How long until we get home?"

"Weeks, I'm afraid. You going to be okay?"

She took a deep breath and found her insides had calmed a bit. "Yes, I think I will be."

⁕

Kweeg thought the nasty humans would never leave. He'd been watching the clearing for hours just to be safe. But now he felt safe enough to take a look for anything valuable. He stepped out from the edge of the jungle and looked up at a tree trunk to his left. The dagger stuck there had nearly hit his head. He shivered when he remembered the scary human in black.

Well, scary or not, Kweeg wouldn't leave a perfectly good dagger behind. He gripped it with both hands and pulled with all his might, staggering when it suddenly came loose. Kweeg barely touched the edge of the black blade and it cut his finger.

"Stupid knife." He stuck his finger in his mouth and moved closer to the hole that led to his females and meat.

A low wail of despair escaped him. A plug of solid rock filled the hole. He'd never be able to get back to the meat now. Just as the master had warned, the humans had stolen his reward. He wanted to complain, but no voice answered his prayers now. Once again Kweeg was on his own, no master, no tribe, no meat, no nothing.

Well, technically he did have meat. Dozens and dozens of dead monsters littered the lifeless earth. But Kweeg knew better than to try and eat them. They'd tasted bad enough live, he couldn't imagine how nasty they were now.

He picked his way through the bodies. None of them carried anything of value. He kicked a dead ogre and winced, hopping around on one foot. After a particularly high hop he stopped. Kweeg saw something a little way away.

Hurrying over he stared. His sword, bigger again, but undamaged, lay on the ground beside a dead beast thing.

He picked it up and shook it. "Cat? Are you in there? Come out and help Kweeg."

No reply and no reaction. If the cat was in there, it refused to come out.

Kweeg glowered at the sword. "At least get smaller so Kweeg can use you properly."

No reaction again.

He screamed and squeezed the hilt like he wanted to strangle it. "Smaller! Smaller!"

Darkness engulfed the blade and it shrank to the correct size.

Kweeg stared in delight. "Good sword."

Little...Goblin.

Kweeg screeched and ducked, expecting a lightning bolt to the brain. "Master?"

No, that was the other voice.

"Master's master? Kweeg is sorry he ran away, but he didn't want to die." Kweeg waited a moment then added. "How do I get back to the females and meat?"

Tonight...Dream.

Kweeg didn't want to dream about females and meat, he wanted the real things. Well, dreaming about it wouldn't be so bad.

"Do you have any more magic for Kweeg? He'll need help to take over a new tribe."

Black flames, weak but familiar, ran along the sword's edge.

Yes, that would do nicely.

—☆—

Daktari blinked against the bright sunlight and found himself standing in the sand surrounded by the bodies of dead pirates. Soom had brought them to Serpent Island instead of the temple.

"Why are we here?"

Soom took a few steps, crouched, and picked up the pirate's void sword. All around his hand a purple aura of shadow magic crackled. "We can't very well leave one of these lying around. I glimpsed its fate in your mind and made a side trip to pick it up. This, along with the second sword waiting in the jungle, will make excellent practice pieces for your training."

"If you were so worried, why not collect the other sword before we left?"

"I wanted to get the Key Bearer somewhere secure as

quickly as possible. A couple of hours doesn't really matter for such minor items."

Soom moved back beside him and the world shifted again.

Now they stood surrounded by dead monsters in the jungle. Soom let out a little growl, just enough to send a shiver up Daktari's spine. At this point in his life, little could affect him so, but the shadow dragon's displeasure did the job easily.

"What's wrong?" Daktari asked.

"The sword's gone. I wasn't quick enough."

Another shift and they stood in the center of the temple surrounded by a large open space. Soom had teleported them straight through the wards as if they didn't exist. Doubtless given that he created them, he had a way around them.

As with most of the rooms, this one had little in the way of decorations beyond doors leading to other areas of the temple.

Seconds after their arrival, those doors opened and monks came streaming in. Since they carried no weapons Daktari wondered what they intended to do about intruders, ask them politely to leave?

Bane came soaring through one of the doors, landed on his shoulder, and rubbed his head against Daktari's cheek. "Welcome back, Master."

Daktari rubbed between Bane's wings until he trilled.

"Fine work," Soom said, nodding toward the homunculus.

"Thank you. Bane is one of my proudest achievements."

Abbot came trundling in last, his great stomach wobbling as he hurried along. "Shadow Man! How did you get through our wards and who have you brought?"

"Abbot, let me introduce you to Soom, the shadow dragon, and creator of your temple. And he brought me not the other way around."

Abbot dropped to his knees and touched his head to the floor. The other monks quickly followed suit.

"Lord Soom, welcome home," Abbot said. "We believed you long dead. How is it you survived and why does our current Shadow Man call you a dragon?"

"He calls me that because I am a dragon and immortal, which answers your first question. I will be sleeping in the cavern beneath your temple for the foreseeable future. We will also be using your temple as a base for our current mission, retrieving the void artifacts scattered around the world." Soom turned his glowing gaze on Abbot. "I trust you have no objections?"

"Of course not, Lord Soom. This temple is yours, we are only humble caretakers. However you wish to use it, we will aid you in any way we can."

"A good answer." Soom set out and Daktari fell in behind him.

They traveled down halls and through doors before finally reaching the room that granted access to the tunnel leading to the void pit. A wheezing Abbot had somehow managed to keep up, though Daktari feared he might collapse on the spot.

"Wait in here, Abbot," Soom said. "My apprentice and I will go the rest of the way on our own."

Abbot, seeming incapable of speech for the moment, waved a hand in acknowledgment.

Soom brushed away the powerful wards without breaking stride. Even watching closely, Daktari barely saw how he manipulated the ether. Compared to the shadow dragon, he felt like a rank amateur.

They marched down the tunnel in a silence broken only by the thud of their boots. When they reached the void pit Soom looked around the cavern and nodded. "This will serve my needs perfectly."

Soom's body grew and shifted until the man had vanished and a dragon with purplish-black scales appeared and nearly filled the cavern. Soom turned a circle like a cat before lying down and closing his eyes. A moment later a ghostly figure of the man he'd been appeared.

Now, let us begin your training.

Soom's voice sounded exactly the same in his mind as it did in his ears. Daktari offered a satisfied smile. He could hardly wait.

EPILOGUE

Robert and Blade stood in the prow of the *Journey* and watched as Port Haydrien grew ever larger in the distance, the low tan homes mingled with sprawling warehouses. From here at least the damage didn't look too bad. Hopefully the bulk of the rubble had been cleaned up and repairs made.

He'd gotten in touch with Abin a few weeks ago. Apparently, the wizard had finally been released from his sickbed and immediately went to work searching for Shara on her father's orders. Both sides had been delighted to find the other relatively healthy and safe.

"Where do you think we'll go first?" Blade asked.

Robert had been too nervous to check the compass and so had no idea. "Beats me. Besides, it's going to take some time to find a crew willing to follow us on this particular journey. Not to mention Soom hasn't returned your sword yet. I don't know about you, but I have no desire to take on anything void related without it."

"Me either. Getting reduced to ash by black flames wouldn't be much of a fight."

A clatter of footsteps heralded Shara's arrival. Sean had given her some herbal concoction that kept her stomach calm. For a moment Robert had thought the princess might kiss his new quartermaster and from the look on Archibald's face he'd had the same concern.

"Not much further," Robert said. "Are you eager to get home?"

Her face crinkled and she didn't answer right away. That came as a surprise. Considering all the danger she'd faced, he figured the thought of returning to the palace with its servants and luxury would be right at the front of her mind.

"I'm not sure," she said at last. "I know my responsibilities, but marrying and becoming sultana doesn't really appeal to me anymore. I was having doubts before all this and now, after nearly dying a few times, I'm not sure I want to spend the rest of my life doing something that will make me miserable."

"Then don't," Blade said. "You only get one life. Live it the way you want."

Shara offered a wan smile. "I wish it were that simple. Abandoning my duties won't sit well with Father. I suggested he remarry and produce a new heir, but he didn't seem enthusiastic."

"Your old man loves you, kid. Take some time, talk to him, and make sure *you* really know what you want. After that, everything else will take care of itself."

They reached the docks an hour or so later. The crew worked to tie them up. At the end of the dock, Vilos, Abin, and Kent stood waiting with an honor guard of soldiers a polite distance behind.

As soon as the gangplank hit the dock, Shara sprinted to

her father and received a hug and spin in return. Robert smiled. He'd give them a few minutes of privacy.

"Thompson, gather the men!"

When his first mate had the crew assembled on deck, Robert pulled out the pouch of gems and said, "Somehow we survived. As promised, each of you will receive an emerald valuable enough to set you up for life. As for Blade and I, we're continuing the mission, hunting down anyone that might be looking to use that dark magic to threaten the world again. You've all proven your loyalty and worth. Should you wish to stay on the crew, you'll be welcome. Now fall in."

The men formed a line and Robert handed a knuckle-sized emerald to the first one, a dusky-skinned man that had the look of a High Kingdom native. "Sorry, sir. I've got family in Port Haydrien. This is going to make a lot of peoples' lives better. You'll be in our prayers to the archangels every night."

Robert shook his hand and moved on to the next man. He went through ten before finding one, a grizzled sailor missing his left eye, who took the gem and said, "I'll stay on, sir. I got nothing waiting for me on land and this sounds like an adventure I don't want to miss."

Robert clapped him on the shoulder. "Glad to have you. We'll need time to get set so feel free to enjoy some shore leave. Check back in a week and I should have more information."

The sailor nodded and took his gem.

In the end they kept five men, all single and eager for adventure, as well as Thompson, Archibald, and Sean. Eight was more than Robert expected, but not nearly enough to run the ship. Still, they'd make a strong core.

"Not bad," Blade said. "I suppose we should go give the sultan his sword back?"

"I suppose we should."

Blade led the way down the ramp and over to the gathered royals. She held out Heat's Bane. "We took good care of it for you. The magic saved my life."

"I'm pleased to hear it." Vilos took the sword and belted it on. "Shara told me about your plans. Sounds dangerous, but I'm pleased that the two of you are taking it on. Having those artifacts out in the world is too dangerous. The High Kingdom will always be a safe port for you. My brother has offered to keep you well stocked with supplies."

Kent offered a shallow bow of acknowledgement but didn't speak.

"We're most grateful, Majesty," Robert said. "As soon as Blade gets her sword back and we can put a crew together, we'll be heading out."

"Of course," Vilos said. "The sooner the better."

"But you can spare a few nights right?" Shara asked. "You could stay at the palace and get your strength back."

Robert glanced at Blade who nodded. "I suppose we could at that. Any chance of getting the same room as last time?"

Vilos laughed. "I guarantee it. Let's go."

Shara was staring at the *Journey*. "When did you change her name?"

"I didn't." Robert followed Shara's gaze. The nameplate beside their figurehead now read *Voidhunter*. "Soom must have done it when we agreed to help. Appropriate I guess."

They fell in together. Behind them, a squad of soldiers remained behind to watch the ship. Robert hadn't left much of any great value behind, but he appreciated having someone keep an eye on it all the same.

Robert took a deep breath of dry desert air, glad to be back. The High Kingdom felt more like home than anywhere he'd ever lived. Robert planned to enjoy it for as long as possible.

He grinned. Probably until Blade dragged him out of the

palace by the ear so she could get to hunting. Well, as long as they were together, nothing else mattered.

AUTHOR NOTE

And so we've come to the end. Shara is safe and secure. The Void is once more sealed away. and Balthis is off to Dagon's hell to endure a much deserved eternity of pain.

If you'd like to keep up with my work and be the first to hear about new releases, you can sign up for my newsletter at www. jamesewisher.com You'll also get a free copy of Lizzy's First Bearer, a novella set in my Soul Force Saga universe.

Until next time, thanks for reading,

James

ABOUT THE AUTHOR

James E. Wisher is a writer of science fiction and fantasy novels. He's been writing since high school and reading everything he could get his hands on for as long as he can remember.

To learn more:
www.jamesewisher.com
james@jamesewisher.com

Soul Force Saga

Disciples of the Horned One Trilogy:

Darkness Rising

Raging Sea and Trembling Earth

Harvest of Souls

Disciples of the Horned One Omnibus

Chains of the Fallen Arc:

Dreaming in the Dark

On Blackened Wings

Chains of the Fallen Omnibus

The Complete Soul Force Saga Omnibus

The Aegis of Merlin:

The Impossible Wizard

The Awakening

The Chimera Jar

The Raven's Shadow

Escape From the Dragon Czar

Wrath of the Dragon Czar

The Four Nations Tournament

Death Incarnate

Atlantis Rising

Rise of the Demon Lords

Aegis of Merlin Omnibus Vol 1.

Aegis of Merlin Omnibus Vol 2.

The Complete Aegis of Merlin Omnibus

Other Fantasy Novels:

The Squire

Death and Honor Omnibus

The Rogue Star Series:

Children of Darkness

Children of the Void

Children of Junk

Rogue Star Omnibus Vol. 1

Children of the Black Ship